JN011828

大修館
シェイクスピア双書
第2集

THE

TAISHUKAN

SHAKESPEARE

2nd Series

大修館書店

ウィリアム・ハント画
「クローディオとイザベラ」（1850年）

ウィリアム・シェイクスピア

尺には尺を

William Shakespeare

MEASURE FOR MEASURE

佐々木和貴

編注

大修館シェイクスピア双書 第2集（全8巻）について

　大修館シェイクスピア双書 第1集（全12巻）の刊行が始まったのは1987年4月。その頃はシェイクスピア講読の授業を行う大学もまだ多く、双書はその充実した解説と注釈において（手頃な値段という点においても）、原典に親しむ学生の心強い味方となり、教員の研究・教育に欠かせないツールとなった。

　そうした時代に比べれば、シェイクスピアよりも実用英語という経済性偏重の風潮もあって、シェイクスピア講読の科目を有する大学は数えるほどになったが、双書が役割を終えたわけでは全くなかった。そのことは発行部数からもよくわかる。2010年代になっても双書のほとんどは継続的に増刷を続けており、例えば『ロミオとジュリエット』の総発行部数は15,000に届く勢いだ。英文学古典の注釈書としてはかなりの部数と言える。

　これは大学の教員や学生のみならず、多くの一般読者にも双書が届いているからに他ならない。実際、周囲を見回せば、通信教育、生涯学習講座、地域のカルチャー・センター、読書会や勉強会でシェイクスピアの原典を繙く人は少なくない。そういう読者に双書が選ばれているのだとすれば、その主な理由は第1集編集委員会の目指した理念が好意的に受け取られているからだろう。

　原文のシェイクスピアをできるだけ多くの人に親しみやすいものにすること。とは言え、入門的に平易に書き直したりダイジェスト版にしたりするのではなく、最新の研究成果に基づいた解説や注釈により、原文を余すところなく読み解けるようにすること。そのために対注形式を取り、見開き2ページで原文と注釈を収めて読みやすさを重視すること。後注や参考文献により学問的な質を高く保ちつつ、シェイクスピアの台詞や研究の面白さを深く理

解できるようにすること。こうした第 1 集の構想が、第 2 集においてもしっかりと受け継がれていることは言うまでもない。また、表記の仕方などを除いて、厳密な統一事項や決まりなどは設けず、編集者の個性を十分に発揮していただく点も第 1 集と同様である。

　一方、重要な刷新もある。第 1 集では Alexander 版（1951）のテクストを基本的にそのまま用いたが、当時と比べれば近年の本文研究は大きな進展をみせ、現在 Alexander 版は必ずしも使いやすいテクストではない。むしろ編者が初期版本の性質を見極めた上で、そこからテクストを立ち上げ、様々な本文の読みを吟味しつつ編集作業を行う方が（負担は増すものの）、意義ある取り組みになるのではないか。そうした考え方に基づいて第 2 集では大きく舵を切り、各編者がテクストすべてを組み上げた。そのため作品によっては本文編集に関する注釈を煩雑に感じる読者もおられようが、注釈に目を通していただくと、問題になっている部分が実は作品の読みを左右する要なのだとご納得いただけると思う。

　第 2 集の企画を大修館編集部の北村和香子さんにご検討いただいたのは 2017 年秋。無謀とも思える提案に終始にこやかかつ冷静沈着に耳を傾け、企画全体を辛抱強く推し進めて下さった。第 2 集 8 巻の作品選定は大いに悩んだが、第 1 集『ハムレット』で編者を務めた河合祥一郎氏からのご提言もいただき、喜劇・悲劇・歴史劇・ローマ劇・ロマンス劇からバランスよく作品を選ぶことができた。ご両名にこの場を借りて心から御礼を申し上げる。「さらに第 2 期、第 3 期と刊行をつづけ、やがてはシェイクスピアの全作品を網羅できれば」という初代の思いが次に繋がることを願いつつ、あとは読者諸氏のご支援とご叱正を乞う次第である。

　　大修館シェイクスピア双書　第 2 集　編集者代表　　井出　新

まえがき

　『尺には尺を』は「問題劇」というカテゴリーで論じられることが多い。それは、風刺と笑劇が混在し、寓意的かと思えば時事的でもあり、しかも悲劇的展開が最後でロマンティック・コメディに切り替わるなど、通常のシェイクスピア喜劇の枠組みに収めることが難しいからだろう。本書は、このユニークな芝居に興味を持ち、原語で読んでその魅力にふれてみたいという読者のために編まれたものである。

　まず「テクスト」については、現存する初期版本はシェイクスピアの最初の全集（The First Folio, 1623）に収められたものだけであり、本書もこれを底本に採用した。ただし編者自身の判断で、いくつか過去の版本の校訂を採用した箇所もある。

　また「注釈」については、現代の主要な版本や *The Oxford English Dictionary* に当たりながら、テキストの言葉について、字義と文法を明らかにすることを一番に目指した。読者の鑑賞の妨げにならないように、語句の説明はできるだけ簡潔にすること、そしてあまりに専門的な議論には立ち入らないことにも留意した。

　さらに「解説」については、紙幅の関係上、この作品を理解するために最低限必要と思われる情報を最初に提供し、その上で、編者自身がこの「問題劇」の特質をどのように捉えたかを、コンパクトなかたちで示すにとどめた。したがって、読者諸氏には「参考文献解題」を活用して、作品の理解をいっそう深めていただければ幸いである。

　なお本書の注作成の際に最もお世話になったのは、研究社版『尺には尺を』であった。市河三喜・峰卓二両先生という「巨人の肩の上に立つ」ことで何度も難所を乗り越えられたことを、感謝と

共にここに記しておきたい。

　最後に、遅々とした仕事の進捗に対して、終始丁寧に対応していただいた大修館書店編集部の北村和香子さんにもこの場を借りて感謝したい。この仕事は編者の退職と重なったため、研究環境が激変した上に腰痛まで発症し、思わぬ時間を取られてしまった。なんとか出版まで漕ぎつけることができたのは、彼女の協力と適切な助言に負うところ大である。

2023年　初夏

佐々木 和貴

目次

挿絵リスト

凡例・略語表

1. 本文・注釈・引用

(1) 本文

　本書のテクストはファースト・フォリオ（The First Folio, 1623）を底本とする。ただし、綴りは現代風に直している。また行数の表示については、本書の版組みにしたがった。

(2) 注釈

　語義、文意の理解に関する注釈は、本文の対向ページに示した。説明がスペースを取る場合や聖書からの長めの引用を含むものは、原則として「後注」とし、巻末に置いた。訳語・訳文は「　」の中に入れている。

　なお本書では、幕と場および行数の表示にはアラビア数字を用いるため、たとえば「2 幕 2 場 13 行目」は「2. 2. 13」と表記する。またト書き（SD）の場合は、行数に SD と注釈の対象部分を加え、たとえば「20. SD. *Exit Queen*」のように表記する。

(3) 引用

　シェイクスピア作品からの引用は *The Arden Shakespeare Third Series Complete Works*（The Arden Shakespeare, 2021）、日本語訳は原則として、松岡和子氏の『シェイクスピア全集』（ちくま文庫）による。また聖書からの引用は *The Geneva Bible: a facsimile of the 1560 edition*（U of Wisconsin Press, 1969）を、日本語訳は『文語訳 新約聖書』（岩波文庫、2014 年）を用いた。

2. 略語表

Arden 2	*Measure for Measure.* Edited by L.W. Lever, Methuen, 1965 (The Arden Shakespeare Second Series)
Arden 3	*Measure for Measure.* Edited by A. R. Braunmuller and Robert N. Watson, Bloomsbury, 2020 (The Arden Shakespeare Third Series)
Folger	*Measure for Measure.* Edited by Barbara A. Mowat and Paul Werstine, Simon & Schuster Paperbacks, 1997 (The Folger Shakespeare Library)
Folio	*Measure, for Measure. Mr. William Shakespeares Comedies, histories, & tragedies*, 1623 (The First Folio)
New Cambridge	*Measure for Measure.* Edited by Brian Gibbons, Cambridge UP, 1991 (The New Cambridge Shakespeare)
OED	*The Oxford English Dictionary: Second Edition on CD-ROM*

Oxford   *Measure for Measure*. Edited by N.W. Bawcutt, Oxford UP, 1991（The Oxford Shakespeare）

研究社   *Measure for Measure*. Edited by Sanki Ichikawa and Takuji Mine, Kenkyusha, 1965（The Kenkyusha Shakespeare）

大修館シェイクスピア双書　第2集

尺には尺を

MEASURE FOR MEASURE

解　説

1. テキスト

　シェイクスピア作品のテクストを校訂する場合、通常は現存する複数の版本を照合することが必要になる。また例えば『リア王』のように、ほとんど別の版と考えざるをえないほど多くの異同を含んだテクストが、並存することさえある。だが『尺には尺を』の場合、初期版本は最初の一冊本全集であるファースト・フォリオ（The First Folio, 1623）に収められたものだけだ。（ちなみにフォリオとは当時の本の規格で、標準となる紙を一度折って2葉4ページとする大型本を指す。）したがって、後代の諸版はすべ

図1　ファースト・フォリオのタイトル・ページ

図2　ファースト・フォリオの『尺には尺を』本文冒頭ページ

てこれを底本にしている。なお 18 世紀以降の編者たちは、難解な、あるいは不自然な箇所が多いこの作品のテクストについて、筆写の際の恣意的な修正や印刷工の不注意なミス、さらには行の欠落など、さまざまな要因を推測して校訂を試みている。だが照合できる他の版本が存在しない以上、本書ではフォリオ版の表記をできるだけ尊重することを原則とした。

2．初演と制作年代

　『尺には尺を』に関する最初の上演記録は、1604-05 年の宮廷祝宴局（The Revels Office）の台帳にある、'By his Maiesties Plaiers. On St. Stiuens night in the Hall A Play Caled Mesur for Mesur. Shaxberd' という記載である。したがって 1604 年 12 月 26 日（聖ステファノの日）に、ホワイト・ホールの饗宴の間で上演されたことは確かだ。だがこのときジェイムズ一世の御前で初めて演じられたのか、それともすでにグローブ座で上演されていたのかは、定かではない。また、いつごろ書かれたのかも他に情報がないため確定できないが、以下に手がかりになりそうな傍証をいくつか挙げておこう。

（1）1. 2. 77-79 行目でミストレス・オーヴァーダンは不穏な世相と商売の不振を嘆いている。またそれに続く 87-91 行目で、今度はポンペイが郊外の娼家取り壊しの布告について言及している。詳しくは注に譲るが、これらの時事的なネタは 1603 年の秋から冬にかけての出来事と関係があるようだ。つまりシェイクスピアは、すでにこのころから『尺には尺を』の下準備を始めていたのかもしれない。

（2）1603 年 3 月 19 日から 1604 年 4 月 9 日までは、エリザベス女王の崩御とそれに続くペストの感染拡大のため、劇場はすべて閉められている。とすれば、シェイクスピアが『尺には尺を』を

実際に書き始めたのは、早くとも劇場再開のめどがたった春頃からと考えるのが自然だろう。

（3）ジェイムズ一世夫妻が1604年3月中旬に王立取引所をお忍びで訪れた時、事前に情報が漏れて群衆が殺到したため、王が強い不快感を示したという記録が残っている。これはアンジェロの「あるいは／一般庶民が敬愛する国王を迎えるときもそうだ、／みな一斉に持ち場を離れ、愚かな敬意の表し方だが／御前に密集して、思わぬ非礼を／働くようなものだ。」（even so / The general subject to a well-wished king / Quit their own part, and in obsequious fondness / Crowd to his presence, where their untaught love / Must needs appear offence.）（2. 4. 26-30）という台詞そのままの事件である。シェイクスピアがこのエピソードを取り入れたとすれば、制作時期は1604年の春から夏頃と推定できるだろう。

（4）ルーチオと紳士たちとの会話で、いささか唐突に「海賊」が登場する場面（1. 2. 7-16）がある。これは1604年8月18日にスペインとの間で調印された和平条約と関係があるかもしれない。というのも、この条約締結後は、それまでスペイン商船を餌食にしていたイギリスの私掠船（戦争状態にある政府から、敵国の船を攻撃しその船や積み荷、荷物を奪う許可を得た個人の船）は、「海賊」とみなされることになったからだ。新王ジェイムズがこれまでの外交方針を大転換したこの条約の話題で、この頃、おそらくロンドン中が持ちきりだっただろう。シェイクスピアがこの時事ネタを取り入れたとすれば、制作時期は1604年の夏頃ということになる。

　以上、傍証から推して、シェイクスピアが『尺には尺を』を実際に制作した時期は、1604年の春から夏にかけてというのが、おそらく妥当なところだろう。

3.　材源

　『尺には尺を』の主筋は、他の多くのシェイクスピア作品と同様に彼のオリジナルではなく、当時すでに流布していた物語に依拠している。　シェイクスピア材源研究の第一人者ジェフリー・ブロー（Geoffrey Bullough）によれば、この喜劇の主な材源は、イタリア人ジェラルディ・チンティオ（Geraldi Cinthio）の『百話集』（*Hecatommithi*, 1565）第 85 話と、それをジョージ・ウェットストーン（George Whetstone）が翻案した戯曲『プロモスとカッサンドラ』（*Promos and Cassandra*, 1578）である。

　まずチンティオの『百話集』だが、これは『尺には尺を』とほぼ同時期に書かれた『オセロー』（*Othello*, 1604）の主たる材源としても有名である。当時まだ英訳はないので、シェイクスピアはこの物語集を直接イタリア語で、あるいは 1584 年に出版されたフランス語版で読んでいたものと思われる。以下は第 85 話のあらすじである。

　「ローマ皇帝マクシミアヌスは、代理人としてジュリストにインスブルックを統治させる。レイプの罪で死刑判決を受けたヴィコの妹エピシァは、ジュリストに兄の助命を乞うが、彼はエピシァが自分に身を任せることをその条件にする。ところがジュリストと一夜を過ごした翌朝ヴィコが処刑されたため、憤激したエピシァは皇帝に直訴し、皇帝はジュリストを彼女と結婚させた上で、処刑しようとする。ところが彼女は今は夫となった彼の助命を乞い、皇帝もそれを許して、二人はその後、幸福な生涯を送る。」

　一方『プロモスとカッサンドラ』のあらすじは、以下の通りだ。

　「ジュリオという町ではプロモスが支配者となるや、眠っていた厳しい法律を容赦なく適用したため、アンドルッジオは密通の罪で死刑宣告を受ける。兄の助命を嘆願する貞淑な妹カッサンドラに対し、プロモスは彼女が身を任せれば釈放すると提案する。

一旦は拒絶したカッサンドラだが、兄の必死の懇願に説き伏せられ、兄の釈放と自分との結婚を条件にプロモスと一夜を過ごす。ところがプロモスは違約して、アンドルッジオを処刑する命令を下す。この無法な行為に憤った獄吏は、別の首を届けて彼を逃すが、それを知らない彼女は、自殺しようとする。その後、思い直してハンガリー王に直訴したところ、王はプロモスを彼女と結婚させた上で、処刑するように命じる。カッサンドラは夫となったプロモスに愛情を感じて、王に助命を乞うが許されない。そこへ妹の悲嘆を見かねたアンドルッジオが変装を捨てて登場したため、王はプロモスもアンドルッジオも許す。」

　両者を比較してみると、細部の類似からして、シェイクスピアが主に依拠したのは、おそらくウェットストーンだと思われる。ただもちろん、シェイクスピアは例によって材源に大きく手を加えている。『尺には尺を』の場合、以下の3点が重要な変更と言えるだろう。

(1) 材源では支配者たる皇帝や王が実際に役割を果たすのは、ヒロインの訴えを裁定する最後の場面だけだが、『尺には尺を』では、公爵が変装して劇の展開に最初から最後まで関わっている。この「変装した支配者」というのは、当時少年劇団で流行していた意匠だが（詳しくは次節を参照）、シェイクスピアはそれを目ざとく取り入れて、公爵をこの劇の主役兼狂言回しに仕立てているのだ。

(2) マリアナという登場人物を創造し、イザベラの身代わりとしてアンジェロと一夜を共にさせている。この「ベッド・トリック」も先行する材源には存在しないが、『尺には尺を』ではこれがプロットの要となっている。ちなみに、セックスの相手をすり替えるといういささかショッキングなこの仕掛けは、当時の芝居ではさほど珍しいものではなく、シェイクスピア自身『終わりよけれ

ばすべてよし』でも使っている。

(3) ルーチオ、ポンペイ、エルボー、ミストレス・オーヴァーダンら、風刺や笑いの源となりこの劇を賑やかに彩っている個性的な脇役たちは、シェイクスピアのオリジナルである。彼らはまさに同時代ロンドンの住人たちであり、陰鬱な主筋に彼らが活躍する脇筋を交錯させながら、多様なジャンルが錯綜する芝居に仕上げている点も、シェイクスピア独自の工夫と言えるだろう。

4. 少年劇団と「変装した公爵」

　少年劇団とは、元々は教会付属聖歌隊の少年たちを母体にしたアマチュア劇団だったが、1600 年前後からはベン・ジョンソン（Ben Jonson）、ジョン・マーストン（John Marston）らの洗練された風刺喜劇を上演するようになっていた。そして例えば『ハムレット』（Hamlet, 1600）に登場する旅役者たちが少年劇団のために都落ちしてきたという設定（2.2）にも窺えるように、当時その人気は成人劇団にとって侮りがたいものだったようだ。したがってペストによる劇場閉鎖がようやく解除された 1604 年の春から夏にかけて、新作（すなわち『尺には尺を』）を準備していたシェイクスピアは、当然、ライヴァルである少年劇団の演目を気にしていたはずである。なかでも彼の念頭にあったのは、チャペル・ロイアル少年劇団で初演されたジョン・マーストンの『不満の士』（The Malcontent, 1602-04）に始まり、当時少年劇団で流行していた「変装した支配者」という趣向だったのではないだろうか。例えば、同時期のセント・ポール少年劇団によるトマス・ミドルトン（Thomas Middleton）作『フィーニックス』（The Phoenix, 1604）にも、さらに翌年のチャペル・ロイアル少年劇団による同じマーストン作『食客あるいは太鼓持ち』（Parasitaster, or the Fawn, 1605）にも、同様のキャラクターが登場し

ている。シェイクスピアが材源には存在しない「変装した公爵」を『尺には尺を』に登場させたのも、おそらくこうした流行を意識してのことと考えて、まず間違いないだろう。

ただ少年劇団の演目の場合、支配者が変装するのはもっぱら「悪事を暴き正す」ためである。例えば同じ「変装した公爵」アルトフロントが主役の『不満の士』は、腐敗したジェノアの宮廷や世相への辛辣な風刺に満ちており、しかも暗い人間関係が絡んだある種の復讐劇に仕立てられている。一方『尺には尺を』でも舞台は「悪徳がぐつぐつ煮えたぎり鍋から吹きこぼれそうな」(corruption boil and bubble / Till it o'errun the stew) (5. 1. 316-17) ウィーンだが、「変装した公爵」ヴィンセンショーの役割はいつのまにか、当初の「悪徳の懲罰者」からこれまでの「変装」物でおなじみの「求婚者」にすり替わっている。つまりシェイクスピアは『尺には尺を』で「変装した支配者」という趣向は借用しながら、少年劇団で演じられていた風刺喜劇／復讐劇を自分の十八番であるロマンティック・コメディに、書き換えてみせたといってもよいだろう。

5. 上演史

1604年の宮廷上演のあと1642年の劇場閉鎖までの期間に、『尺には尺を』が国王一座のレパートリーとして定着していたかは不明である。ただ王政復古直後に演劇が再開された際に、二大勅許劇団のひとつ「公爵一座」(The Duke's Company) を率いていたウィリアム・ダヴェナント (William Davenant) がこの喜劇の筋をほぼなぞりながら、そこに『空騒ぎ』の有名なカップルであるビアトリスとベネディックを入れ込んだ翻案劇『恋人たちに辛い法律』(*The Law against Lovers*, 1662) を上演している。これはダヴェナントによるシェイクスピア翻案物の第1弾であり、

おそらく『尺には尺を』が当時それなりの知名度を保っていた間接的な証拠にはなるだろう。ちなみに同時代の海軍省の役人で演劇愛好家サミュエル・ピープス(Samuel Pepys)は、その有名な日記の中で「良い芝居で上手に演じられていた」('a good play and well performed') と、この翻案について好意的にコメントしている。

図3　公爵を演じるジョン・フィリップ・ケンブル

　また18世紀に入ると、この頃からほぼ完全に残っているロンドンでの上演記録のおかげで、この喜劇が定期的に舞台に掛けられていたことがわかっている。特に18世紀末に名優ジョン・フィリップ・ケンブル（John Philip Kemble）が公爵を演じ、姉のこれまた名女優サラ・シドンズ（Sarah Siddons）がイザベラを演じた上演は名高い。

　だが19世紀に入ると、そのあからさまにセクシュアリティと関わる内容がヴィクトリア朝のモラルに抵触したためか、この喜劇の人気は徐々に衰える。そしてこうした風潮は20世紀

図4　悲劇のミューズとしてのシドンズ夫人

前半も続き、この喜劇は上演されることが稀になった。したがって『尺には尺を』を「再発見」したのは、ピーター・ブルック（Peter Brook）が演出し、サー・ジョン・ギールグッド（Sir John Gielgud）がアンジェロを演じた1950年のシェイクスピア記念劇場での上演ということになるだろう。ウィーンの宮廷社会と下層民との対比を強調したブルックの鮮烈な演出と、名優ギールグッドの緻密な演技力は、この喜劇の新しい魅力を引き出したものとして、高い評価を得た。その後、この喜劇はシェイクスピア作品のレパートリーとして復活し、海外ではかなりの頻度で上演されている。また我が国でも2016年に蜷川幸雄による彩の国さいたま芸術劇場での上演が評判を呼んだのは、まだ記憶に新しいところだ。

図5　ギールグッドのアンジェロ

6. 作品分析

　以下においては、第4節で指摘した風刺喜劇からロマンティック・コメディへの書き換えに着目し、シェイクスピアがそのために施した仕掛けを主要登場人物ごとに分析する。これはまた「変換／交換」という視点から、『尺には尺を』という喜劇の特色を明らかにする試みともなるだろう。

　まずアンジェロとマリアナである。アンジェロは「相手があばずれの淫売なら、生まれつきの美しさと手練手管で迫ってきても眉ひとつ動かさない俺だ」（Never could the strumpet / With all her double vigour, art and nature, / Once stir my temper）（2. 2. 187-89）と性的誘惑に対する自制心を自負し、ルーチオからは「自動人形」（a motion generative）（3. 2. 99）と揶揄されるほどの堅物だ。だがそれにも関わらず（あるいはだからこそ）、イザベラに突如として激しい欲望を抱き、新たに得た権力を悪用して、兄クローディオの助命嘆願にきた彼女にそれと引き換えに身を任せるように迫る。ところがここまでは材源に忠実だったシェイクスピアは、ここで突然マリアナという新しいキャラクターを登場させ、その後の展開を大きく変えてしまうのだ。材源ではイザベラの貞操を奪うはずのアンジェロは、公爵の仕組んだ「ベッド・トリック」によって、捨てられても彼を待ち続けていた婚約者マリアナをイザベラと信じこんで床入りし、結果的に「かねてからの結婚の契約」（a pre-contract）（4. 1. 71）を履行することになるのである。それゆえ私たちは、アンジェロの行いを多少は容赦し、マリアナの「ほとんどの人は少し悪いことをした分だけ善良になるとか、私の夫もそう。」（for the most become much more the better / For being a little bad. So may my husband.）（5. 1. 437-38）という弁護にも耳を傾ける気になるだろう。また公爵が

11

最後に彼を許して、「彼女［マリアナ］を愛してやれ、アンジェロ」（Love her [Mariana], Angelo）（5. 1. 524）と声をかけたとき、大団円の「結婚の輪」に迎え入れることができるのである。つまりシェイクスピアは、「ベッド・トリック」という女性の「交換」装置を使って、風刺喜劇／復讐劇の住人のはずのアンジェロを、まるで手品のように、ロマンティック・コメディの世界に移動させたということになるだろう。

　一方、アンジェロに一方的に婚約を破棄されたマリアナは、公爵の「ならば何でもないのだな、娘でも人妻でも未亡人でもないのなら？」（Why, you are nothing then: neither maid, widow, nor wife?）（5. 1. 177）という台詞に明らかなように、当時の一般的な女性のカテゴリーのどれにも属することができない。ルーチオに「娼婦」（punk）（5. 1. 178）ではないのかと揶揄されても、むしろ仕方がない立ち位置にいるのだ。そしてシェイクスピアが「ベッド・トリック」という女性の「交換」装置でマリアナから実質的に拭い去ったのは、まさにこの不安定性（＝娼婦性）だったのではないだろうか。結果として、婚約者にようやく「妻として抱かれた」（He knew me as a wife）（5. 1. 229）マリアナは、結婚という安定したシステムに回収されることになる。そして公爵から「おめでとう、マリアナ」（Joy to you, Mariana.）（5. 1. 524）と祝福のことばをかけられ、アンジェロとともに「結婚の輪」（＝ロマンティック・コメディの世界）に加わることになるだろう。

　続いては、クローディオである。彼は劇中では不合理な法の犠牲者という同情される役回りだ。だがたとえ合意の上とはいえ、婚前交渉で恋人を妊娠させてしまう彼のような若者を放置しておけば、「放恣放埒が正義の鼻面を引き回し、赤ん坊は乳母をなぐり、秩序も礼節もひっくり返ってしまう。」（liberty plucks justice by the nose, / The baby beats the nurse, and quite athwart / Goes all decorum.)（1. 3. 30-32）と懸念しているのは、実は公爵自身である。さらにこうした正式な結婚の手続きを軽視して性交渉をする若者たちは、当時機能を強化しつつあった教会裁判所から見れば、教会法に抵触する懲罰の対象でもあったろう。つまりクローディオは、風刺喜劇でお馴染みの、放埒な欲望が矯正されるべきキャラクターでもあるのだ。そして彼をロマンティック・コメディの世界に迎え入れるために、シェイクスピアは、ここでは「首のすげ替え」という仕掛けを持ち出してくる。ちなみに材源の『プロモスとカッサンドラ』でも、獄吏がプロモス（＝アンジェロ）の無法な行為に憤って別の首を届け、アンドルッジオ（＝クローディオ）を逃す場面はある。だがこの「首のすげ替え」は舞台裏で行われており、詳しい説明は一切ない。これに対して『尺には尺を』では、まず公爵が監獄長に、クローディオのかわりに「自堕落な囚人」（a dissolute prisoner）バーナディンを処刑して首を差し出すよう依頼し（4.2）、次の場では逆に監獄長が公爵に提案して、ちょうど熱病で亡くなった「年恰好もクローディオと同じくらい、髭も髪も同じ色」（A man of Claudio's years, his beard and head / Just of his colour）（4. 3. 65-66）の海賊ラゴジンの首を、クローディオのものとしてアンジェロに差し出すことになる。これら２人の囚人はモラル面で、あるいは容貌において、まさにクローディオの「分身」たちと読めるだろう。そしてクローディオの代わりに「分身」の首を切り落とすとは、象徴的な意味で彼を去勢し、その放埒の罪を罰することに他ならない。したがって、最後に登場する「クローディオそっくり」（As like almost to Claudio as himself）（5. 1. 488）の覆面の男とは、罪を償ったクローディオであり、だからこそ公爵は「クローディオ、お前が傷付けた女性の名誉は回復してやれ。」（She, Claudio, that you wronged, look you restore.）（5. 1. 523）と死の淵から蘇った彼に声をかけて、ジュリエッタとの「結婚」を認知することができるのである。言い換えれば、シェイクスピアは首の「すげ換え」というトリックを使って、若者の無軌道な欲望の処罰という風刺喜劇のトピックを、若者の仮死を経た再生と大人の社会への参入というロマンティック・コメディにふさわしいトピックに、「書き替え」たと言えるだろう。

　さらにルーチオの場合を考えてみよう。彼は謹厳実直な公爵のことすら「あっちの方は、もうダメなのによ。それでも、いいかよく聞け…まだ乞食女にだってキスするんだ、黒パンとニンニクの匂いがぷんぷんしているのに。」（He's now past it, yet ― and I say to thee ― he would mouth with a beggar though she smelt brown bread and garlic.）（3. 2. 159-61）と、その手当たりしだいの好色さを吹聴して笑い物にする。彼にかかっては、誰もが風刺の対象になってしまうのだ。したがって、大団円においてアンジェロさえも罪を許してロマンティック・モードへ導き入れる公爵が、この根っからの風刺喜劇の住人ルーチオだけは「ここに一人、どうしても許せない男がいる」（here's one in place I cannot pardon）（5. 1. 498）と恩赦を拒否するのも、むしろ当然だろう。そして公爵がこの馴致不可能な男に最終的に下す罰とは、彼が子供まで作ったケイトという馴染みの娼婦とかつて交わしていた結婚の約束の履行なのである。つまりシェイクスピアはここでも、まるでアンジェロとマリアナの場合のパロディのように、いわばある種の「ベッド・トリック」を用いて、「娼婦ケイト」を正式な「妻ケイト」と「交換」しているのだ。そして懲罰が同時に結婚の祝福となるこの巧妙な仕掛けによって、「淫売との結婚は、閣下、死の石責めだ、鞭打ちの刑だ、絞首刑だ。」（Marrying a punk, my Lord, is pressing to death, whipping, and hanging.)（5. 1. 520-21）という抗議もむなしく、ルーチオもまた、ロマンティック・コメディの世界に組み込まれることになるだろう。

　最後は公爵とイザベラである。まず公爵だが、彼もまたその変装にあわせて役割が「変換」されている。当初修道士に変装する際、公爵はそれが「欲望に身を焦がす若者には思いも及ばぬ謹厳で老成した目的」（a purpose / More grave and wrinkled than the aims and ends / Of burning youth）（1. 3. 4-6）があってのことだと述べている。しかも「仮に権力が人を変えるとすれば、権力を持った偽善者がどうなるか、見ようというのだ。」（Hence shall we see / If power change purpose, what our seemers be.）（1. 3. 54-55）と、その目的が「悪徳の矯正」にあることも暗示している。つまり公爵は変装することによって、少年劇団風の風刺喜劇／復讐劇の世界に身を投じたといってよいだろう。ところが、第5幕で変装を解いて支配者にもどった公爵は、悪を罰するよりも、ほかの仕事に忙しい。まず本当の身分を明かしたとき、公爵はイザベラに「身なりは変えても心は変わらない。いつでもあなたの力になるつもりだ」（Not changing heart with habit, I am still / Attorneyed at your service）（5. 1. 380-81）と、早速特別な好意を示す。さらにクローディオが生きていたことが明らかになった折には、「その手を、そして私の妻になると言ってくれれば、この男は私の兄になる。だがその話はもっとふさわしい折に。」（Give me your hand, and say you will be mine, / He is my brother too ― but fitter time for that.）（5. 1. 491-92）と彼女に求婚しかけて、思いとどまる。そして最後の台詞では「愛しいイザベラ、私はあなたの幸福につながる申し込みをしたい。喜んで

耳を傾けてくれるなら、私のものは、あなたのもの、あなたのものは私のものだ。」(Dear Isabel, / I have a motion much imports your good, / Whereto if you'll a willing ear incline, / What's mine is yours, and what is yours is mine.) (5. 1. 532-35) と、ついに正式に求婚するのだ。つまり変装を解いたあとの公爵の「役割」は、「懲罰者」から自らが救い出した美しい清らかな乙女に対する「求婚者」に「変換」されているのである。もちろんこうした公爵の突然の変貌は、今の私たちのリアリズムの物差しで測れば、いささか不自然に見えるかもしれない。しかし風刺喜劇／復讐劇をロマンティック・コメディで上書きすることが、シェイクスピアにとってこの喜劇の骨格をなす戦略だとすれば、公爵の「恋」がその完成のための最も重要なパーツであることは、言うまでもないだろう。また、ロマンティックな「変装」物を見慣れていた当時の公衆劇場の観客も、むしろこの「恋する」公爵の姿を見て、違和感よりは、ある種の既視感あるいは安心感すら覚えたのではないだろうか。

　一方、イザベラもまたその属性が劇中で「変換」される。彼女は最初クララ会修道女見習いとして登場する。つまり恋や結婚の可能性は、あらかじめ排除されているキャラクターなのだ。またクローディオの懇願に対しても、アンジェロに体を汚されるくらいならば、兄が婚前交渉の罪のために「さっさと死んだ方がいい。」('Tis best that thou diest quickly.) (3. 1. 151) とまで言い放つような、性に対して過度に潔癖で、情味に欠ける性格に設定されている。さらにクローディオが処刑されたと聞き、「あの男のところへ行って両目を抉り出してやります！」(O, I will to him, and pluck out his eyes!) (4. 3. 113) とアンジェロへの復讐を叫ぶ彼女の台詞には、旧約聖書の「目には目を、歯には歯を」(eie for eie, toothe for toothe) (レビ記 24: 21) という教えがこだまして

いることは明らかだろう。つまり第４幕までのイザベラはロマンティック・コメディとは無縁の、むしろ風刺喜劇／復讐劇に似つかわしい住人なのだ。ところが公爵がイザベラの望みを叶えるべく「クローディオにはアンジェロを、死には死を…類には類を、尺には尺をもって報いるのだ。」(An Angelo for Claudio, death for death; ... Like doth quit like, and measure still for measure.)（5. 1. 405-07）とアンジェロの処刑を命じたとき、シェイクスピアは彼女の心境に変化を生じさせる。まるで「天より地上にふりそそぐ慈悲の雨」(the gentle rain from heaven / Upon the place beneath)（*The Merchant of Venice*, 4. 1. 181-82）が彼女の憎しみに満ちた硬い心を溶かしたかのように、イザベラはマリアナの懇願に応じて一緒に跪(ひざまず)くのである。そして「この人は私に目を留めるまでは職務を忠実に果たしていたと思いたい。ですから死刑はおやめください。」(I partly think / A due sincerity governed his deeds, / Till he did look on me; since it is so, / Let him not die.)（5. 1. 442-45）と、アンジェロを憐れんで復讐を放棄し、その助命を請うのだ。もちろんこの彼女の性格の「書き換え」も、公爵の場合と同様、私たちの感覚からすれば、多少唐突に感じられることは否めないだろう。しかしこれも、イザベラを風刺喜劇／復讐劇の世界から一旦切り離し、公爵と一緒にロマンティック・コメディの世界に参入させるためのシェイクスピアの仕掛けと考えれば、納得がいくのではないだろうか。また当時の公衆劇場の観客も、公爵の役割が第５幕で明らかに「求婚者」に変わった以上、イザベラの属性がそれに合わせて大きく「変換」されたとしても、それで困惑するよりは、むしろ「変装」物のお約束として喜んで受け入れたように思われる。

　そして、こうしたさまざまな下準備をしたうえで、公爵が結び

の台詞でイザベラに求婚し、『尺には尺を』は幕を閉じる。それはまた、4つの「結婚の輪」が同時に完成し、この喜劇がロマンティック・コメディに変貌した瞬間ということになるだろう。だがシェイクスピアは、最後にここにもうひとつの「変換／交換」を仕組んでいるようだ。つまり、懲罰者から求婚者に変身した公爵がすべての登場人物たちを許したのちに、復讐者から慈悲の乙女に生まれ変わったイザベラと結婚することで、実はこの喜劇の題の意味するところも変容するのである。*Measure for Measure*とは、このとき、旧約聖書の「目には目を」という同害報復の教えであることをやめ、「なんじら人を審（さば）くな、審かれざらん為なり。…己がはかる量（measure）にて己も量らる（measure）べし」というイエスの山上の垂訓、すなわち新約聖書の寛容と慈悲の教えに「変換／交換」されるのだ。

　こうして、ジャンルの書き換えというシェイクスピアのユニークな試みと、そのためのさまざまな「変換／交換」の仕掛けによって、結果的に『尺には尺を』は、苦くて（＝風刺喜劇）甘い（＝ロマンティック・コメディ）、深刻なのに（＝復讐劇）笑える（＝笑劇）芝居に仕上がった。だが1つの枠に収めるのが難しいその特質ゆえに、この喜劇は同時期に書かれた『トロイラスとクレシダ』（*Troilus and Cressida*, 1601-02）や『終わりよければすべてよし』（*All's Well That Ends Well*, 1603-04）と一緒に、20世紀以降、「問題劇」（problem plays）というカテゴリーで論じられることになる。命名者のフレデリック・ボアズ（Frederick Boas）が「私たちは興奮し、魅了され、そして困惑する…テーマと特質があまりに風変わりなので、厳密な意味では喜劇とも悲劇とも呼ぶことができない」（*Shakespeare and his Predecessors*, p. 345）と指摘するように、結局のところ、この劇のジャンルの

交雑・混淆[こんこう]が、いわば「問題」視されてきたのである。しかし本節では、むしろこうした『尺には尺を』の特質を、「変換／交換」というシェイクスピアの戦略的な仕掛けが生み出したものと捉え、そのハイブリディティ（＝混種性）を肯定的に「読み替え」る可能性を探ってみた。結果として、読者諸氏にこの喜劇の新たな魅力を多少なりとも示せていれば、幸いである。

参考文献解題

　以下では、編者が参照できた限られた範囲の文献の中から、作品の理解にとって有益あるいは重要と判断したものを挙げた。したがって、より網羅的な最新の参考文献リストを確認したい読者は、例えば 1.(2)巻末の References などに当たられたい。

　なお、近年の『尺には尺を』批評は、現代の私たちにつながるような視点からさまざまな議論が積み重ねられている。したがって、そこにアクチュアルな「問題」が読み取れるという意味では、今こそ『尺には尺を』は「問題劇」と呼ぶにふさわしい芝居かもしれない。

1. 注釈・材源
　現代の校注版としては、次の 2 冊を推す。
⑴　Shakespeare, William. *Measure for Measure.* Edited by N. W. Bawcutt, Oxford UP, 1991.（The Oxford Shakespeare）
　字句の説明が丁寧で解釈も妥当。
⑵　——. *Measure for Measure.* Edited by A. R. Braunmuller and Robert N. Watson, Bloomsbury, 2020.（The Arden Shakespeare Third Series）　参考文献リストが最新で充実している。

　材源に関しては以下が標準的文献である。
⑶　*Narrative and Dramatic Sources of Shakespeare, Vol. II: The Comedies, 1597-1603.* Edited by Geoffrey Bullough, Routledge and Kegan Paul, 1963.　解説と主な材源の英訳を含む。

2. 上演史
⑷　Leiter, Samuel. *Shakespeare Around the Globe: A Guide to Notable*

Postwar Production. Greenwood Press, 1986.

　1946年から85年までの主な上演についての詳細な情報が得られる。

⑸　Shakespeare, William. *Measure for Measure.* Edited by Brian Gibbons, Cambridge UP, 1991.（The New Cambridge Shakespeare）

　イントロダクションを読めば、17世紀から現代までの上演史を俯瞰できる。

3．時代背景

⑹　Cressy, David. *Birth, Marriage, And Death: Ritual, Religion, and the Life-Cycle in Tudor and Stuart England.* Oxford UP, 1997.

　当時のライフ・サイクルや結婚に関する歴史学の基本文献。

⑺　Ingram, Martin. *Church Courts, Sex and Marriage in England, 1570-1640.* Cambridge UP, 1987.

　当時の教会裁判所についての理解が得られる。

⑻　*Measure for Measure: Texts and Contexts.* Edited by Ivo Kamps and Karen Raber, Bedford/St. Martins, 2004.

　第2部 Cultural Context の解説と資料の抜粋が有益。

⑼　*The Mental World of the Jacobean Court.* Edited by Linda Levy Peck, Cambridge UP, 1991.

　ジェイムズ一世の宮廷に関する歴史学と文学との優れた共同研究。

⑽　Salgado, Gamini. *The Elizabethan Underworld.* J. M. Dent, 1977.

　エリザベス朝の裏社会についての基本図書。

⑾　Shapiro, Michael. *Children of the Revels: The Boy Companies of Shakespeare's Time and their Plays.* Columbia UP, 1977.

　少年劇団に関して包括的な情報を与えてくれる。

⑿　安達まみ『イギリス演劇における修道女像：宗教改革からシェイクスピアまで』岩波書店、2017。

　修道女というトピックを通史的に追った力作。

4．批評・研究

⒀　Adelman, Janet. 'Bed Tricks: On Marriage as the End of Comedy in *All's Well That Ends Well* and *Measure for Measure*.' *Shakespeare's Personality*, edited by Norman Holland, Sidney Homan, and Bernard Paris, U of California Press, 1989, pp.151-74.　フェミニズムの視点からの「ベッド・トリック」論。

⒁　Boas, Frederick S. *Shakespeare and his Predecessors*. Charles Scribner's Sons, 1900.　「問題劇」と初めて命名した批評書。

⒂　Desens, Marliss C. *The Bed-trick in English Renaissance Drama: Explorations in Gender, Sexuality, and Power*. U of Delaware Press. 1994.　「ベッド・トリック」物の包括的研究。

⒃　Dollimore, Jonathan. 'Transgression and Surveillance in *Measure for Measure*.' *Political Shakespeare: New Essays in Cultural Materialism*, edited by Jonathan Dollimore and Alan Sinfield, Cornell UP, 1985, pp.72-87.
　　「性」を介した権力の監視と支配についての考察。

⒄　Everett, Barbara. 'A Dreame of Passion: Shakespeare's Most Peculiar Play.' *London Review of Books* 25. 1, 2 January 2003, https://www.lrb.co.uk/the-paper/v25/n01/barbara-everett/a-dreame-of-passion　碩学の簡にして要を得た作品論。

⒅　Freeburg, Victor Oscar. *Disguise Plots in Elizabethan Drama: A Study in Stage Tradition*. Columbia UP, 1915.　「変装」物研究の古典。

⒆　Grav, Peter F. 'The Exchange Economy of *Measure for Measure*: "You will needs buy and sell men and women like beasts".' *Shakespeare and the Economic Imperative: "What's aught but as 'tis valued?"*. Routledge, 2008, pp.108-30.
　　「市場取引」から作品を読み込む新経済批評。

⒇　Greenblatt, Stephen. *Shakespearean Negotiations*. U of California Press, 1988.

公爵と『テンペスト』のプロスペローの同質性・連続性を論じた章を含む。

⑵1) Gurr, Andrew. 'Measure for Measure*'s Hoods and Masks: the Duke, Isabella, and Liberty.' English Literary Renaissance* 27.1 (1997) : 89-105. 頭巾とマスクの役割からオリジナル上演を推定。

(22) Knight, G. Wilson. *The Wheel of Fire: Interpretations of Shakespearian Tragedy with Three New Essays*. Methuen, 1949.
福音書との関係を詳細に論じた章を含む。

(23) Lever, J. W. 'The Date of *Measure for Measure.' Shakespeare Quarterly* 10 (1959): 381-88.
Arden 2の編者による制作年代についての精緻な議論。

(24) Mowat, Barbara A. 'Shakespearean Tragicomedy.' *Renaissance Tragicomedy: Explorations in Genre and Politics*, edited by Nancy Klein Maguire, AMS Press, 1987, pp.80-96.
シェイクスピア流の実験的悲喜劇として論じる。

(25) Quarmby, Kevin A. *The Disguised Ruler in Shakespeare and His Contemporaries*. Routledge, 2012.
「変装した支配者」物を詳細に論じた最新の研究書。

(26) Shuger, Debora K. *Political Theologies in Shakespeare's England: The Sacred and the State in* Measure for Measure. Palgrave, 2001.
宗教改革後のイングランドの政治思想を読みこむ。

(27) Tennenhouse, Leonard. *Power on Display: The Politics of Shakespeare's Genres*. Methuen, 1986.
「変装した支配者」物を論じた章を含む新歴史主義批評。

(28) 五十嵐 博久「『尺には尺を』における権力とエクイティ」『シェイクスピアとの往還』研究社、2021、61-82頁。
ジェイムズ一世の権限をめぐる法学論争を視野に入れた読解。

(29) 勝山 貴之「『尺には尺を』と貨幣」*Shakespeare Journal* 8 (2022): 23-33. 当時の私鋳貨幣とその取り締まりの問題を読み込む。

5. 批評集

⑶0 Critical Essays on Shakespeare's *Measure for Measure.* Edited by Richard P. Wheeler, G. K. Hall, 1999.

　1980〜90年代の主要な論文が読める。

⑶1 *Measure for Measure.* Edited by Nigel Wood and contributed by Peter Corbin et al., Open UP, 1996.

　上演／歴史／女性／権力を切り口とした理論的な4つの作品読解。

⑶2 William Shakespeare's *Measure for Measure.* Edited by Harold Bloom. Chelsea House Publishers, 1987.

　1940〜80年代の主要な論文を収めている。

MEASURE FOR
MEASURE

The names of all the Actors [1]

VINCENTIO, *the Duke.*
ANGELO, *the Deputy.*
ESCALUS, *an ancient lord.*
CLAUDIO, *a young gentleman.*
LUCIO, *a fantastic.*
Two Other Like Gentlemen.
PROVOST.
THOMAS. ⎫
PETER. ⎬ *2 Friars.*
ELBOW, *a simple constable.*
FROTH, *a foolish gentleman.*
CLOWN [POMPEY, *a tapster and pimp*]. [2]
ABHORSON, *an executioner.*
BARNADINE, *a dissolute prisoner.*
[VARRIUS, a friend to the Duke]
ISABELLA, *a sister to Claudio.*
MARIANA, *betrothed to Angelo.*
JULIETTA, *beloved of Claudio.*
FRANCISCA, *a Nun.*
MISTRESS OVERDONE, *a Bawd.*
[Attendant Lords, Officers, Servants, Citizens, a Boy.]

SCENE: *Vienna*

---

(1) 本書の「登場人物」は、Folio 版劇本文のあとに付けられたものを利用した。
(2) 近代の版にならって、Folio 版にはない名前や役柄を [　] で補足した。

登場人物

ヴィンセンショー	公爵
アンジェロ	公爵代理
エスカラス	年配の貴族
クローディオ	若い紳士
ルーチオ	放恣な男
他の二人の紳士	
監獄長	
トマス 〕	
ピーター 〕	二人の修道士
エルボー	間抜けな巡査
フロス	愚かな紳士
道化〔ポンペイ	番頭兼ポン引き〕
アブホーソン	死刑執行人
バーナディン	自堕落な囚人
〔ヴァリアス	公爵の友人〕
イザベラ	クローディオの妹
マリアナ	アンジェロの婚約者
ジュリエッタ	クローディオの恋人
フランチェスカ	修道女
ミストレス・オーヴァーダン	売春宿の女将
〔お付きの貴族たち、役人たち、召使たち、市民たち、少年〕	

場面：ウィーン

[ACT I, SCENE I]

Enter Duke, Escalus, Lords

DUKE   Escalus.

ESCALUS   My Lord.

DUKE   Of government the properties to unfold,
    Would seem in me to affect speech and discourse,
    Since I am put to know that your own science   5
    Exceeds in that the lists of all advice
    My strength can give you. Then no more remains
    But that to your sufficiency, as your worth is able,
    And let them work. The nature of our people,
    Our city's institutions, and the terms   10
    For common justice, you're as pregnant in
    As art and practice hath enrichèd any
    That we remember. There is our commission,
    From which we would not have you warp. Call hither,
    I say, bid come before us Angelo.   *[Exit a Lord]*   15
    What figure of us think you he will bear?
    For you must know, we have with special soul
    Elected him our absence to supply,
    Lent him our terror, dressed him with our love,
    And given his deputation all the organs   20
    Of our own power. What think you of it?

ESCALUS   If any in Vienna be of worth
    To undergo such ample grace and honour,
    It is Lord Angelo.

Enter Angelo

DUKE   Look where he comes.

ANGELO   Always obedient to your grace's will,   25
    I come to know your pleasure.

DUKE   Angelo,

〔**1.1**〕**あらすじ**……………………………………………………………

　旅に出ようとしている公爵は、徳高いと評判のアンジェロと老練な臣下エスカラスに後事を託す。とりわけアンジェロには自らの代理として強大な権限を与える。アンジェロは重責を辞退しようとするが、公爵はそれを許さず、急ぎ出立する。

……………………………………………………………………………………

3. Of government the properties to unfold 「統治の本質を明らかにすること」以下の文の主部となる。

4. affect 「好む、楽しむ」　**discourse** 「(華やかな) 演説、説教」

5. put to know 「認めざるを得ない」　**science** 「(特定の領域の) 知識」

6. in that = in the properties of government　**lists** 「限界、域」

7-9. Then no more remains ... And let them work 意味が不明瞭なため脱落があるとされる箇所。⇒詳しくは後注参照。

7-8. no more ... But = no more ... than

8. sufficiency 「権威、能力」　**worth** 「高潔さ、道徳的な値打ち」

10. terms 「(司法の) 手続き」

11. pregnant 「熟知している」この劇の主題と関わる「妊娠した」という意味をも連想させる。

12. art and practice 「理論と実践」よくペアで使われる言葉。

enrichèd = endowed with mental wealth

13. we 「余」王侯が自らを指す「尊厳の複数 (royal plural)」である。

commission 「辞令、任命書」

14. warp 「逸れる、外れる」

15. SD. [*Exit a Lord*] このように [　] で示されている箇所は、フォリオ版にはないことを表す (以下同)。

16. figure ... bear 「代理を担う、似姿を持つ」この劇にたびたび現れる「貨幣 (coin)」や「証印 (seal)」に「(王侯の) 打ち型をうつ (stamp)」ことと関わる表現の最初のもの。

17. with special soul 「誠心誠意、特別の思いで」

19. terror 「(処罰によって) 臣民に与える恐怖」　**love** 「臣民に対する愛」

20. deputation = office of deputy　**organs** 「機能」

22-23. be of worth / To undergo 「受けるに値する」

23. grace = favour

26. pleasure 「思し召し、意向」

There is a kind of character in thy life,
That to the observer doth thy history
Fully unfold. Thyself and thy belongings
Are not thine own so proper as to waste   30
Thyself upon thy virtues, they on thee.
Heaven doth with us as we with torches do,
Not light them for themselves; for if our virtues
Did not go forth of us, 'twere all alike
As if we had them not. Spirits are not finely touched   35
But to fine issues, nor nature never lends
The smallest scruple of her excellence
But, like a thrifty goddess, she determines
Herself the glory of a creditor,
Both thanks and use. But I do bend my speech   40
To one that can my part in him advertise.
Hold therefore, Angelo:
In our remove, be thou at full ourself.
Mortality and mercy in Vienna
Live in thy tongue and heart. Old Escalus   45
Though first in question, is thy secondary.
Take thy commission.

ANGELO   Now, good my Lord
Let there be some more test made of my mettle,
Before so noble and so great a figure
Be stamped upon it.

DUKE   No more evasion.   50
We have with a leavened, and preparèd choice
Proceeded to you, therefore take your honours.
Our haste from hence is of so quick condition
That it prefers itself, and leaves unquestioned
Matters of needful value. We shall write to you,   55
As time and our concernings shall importune,
How it goes with us, and do look to know

27. character ＝ （1）obvious sign for all to see　（2）cipher for secret communication

28. history　「来歴」

29. belongings　「（付与された）資質」

30. proper ＝ exclusively

30-31. waste / Thyself upon thy virtues, they on thee　「自らをおのれの徳を高めるために、またその徳をおのれのために浪費する」

32-35. Heaven doth with us ... As if we had them not　聖書と関わる表現である。　⇒後注

32. Heaven doth with us as we with torches do　「天は我々人間を、我々が松明を扱うように扱う」

34. go forth of　「外にあらわれる」

35. Spirits ＝ minds, souls　　**finely touched** ＝ skillfully handled

36. to fine issues　「見事な結果のために」
　nor ... never　「必ずや…する、…せずにはいない」二重否定の用法。

37. scruple　「少し、微量」

38-40. she determines ... thanks and use　「彼女（自然の女神）は自らが債権者に対する特権、つまり感謝と利子を定める」

39. glory ＝ privileges

41. my part in him　「彼に付与した私の権力」　　**advertise** ＝ instruct, inform

42. Hold ＝ take（this commission）

43. at full ourself　「あらゆる面で余の代理」

44. Mortality and mercy　「生殺与奪、生かすも殺すも」

46. first in question　「（年長なので）最初に考慮したが」

48. test　「（貴金属の含有量を）試す」　　**mettle**「地金」

49. figure　「（王侯の）顔の像」

50. stamped　「刻印される」ll. 48-50 は貨幣鋳造に関わる縁語の連続。Cf. l.16 解説

51. leavened　「熟慮した」原義は「パン種を入れて、発酵させる」。

52. you　これまで公爵はアンジェロに thou と呼びかけていたが、ここでより丁寧な you に切り替える。アンジェロが公爵代理という身分に変わったためか。

53. quick condition ＝ urgent nature

54. prefers itself　「優先する」　　**unquestioned** ＝ undiscussed, unexamined

56. importune ＝ urge

57. look　「期待する」

What doth befall you here. So fare you well.
To the hopeful execution do I leave you
Of your commissions.

ANGELO   Yet give leave, my lord,   60
That we may bring you something on the way.

DUKE   My haste may not admit it.
Nor need you, on mine honour, have to do
With any scruple. Your scope is as mine own,
So to enforce or qualify the laws   65
As to your soul seems good. Give me your hand,
I'll privily away. I love the people,
But do not like to stage me to their eyes.
Though it do well, I do not relish well
Their loud applause and aves vehement,   70
Nor do I think the man of safe discretion
That does affect it. Once more fare you well.

ANGELO   The heavens give safety to your purposes!

ESCALUS   Lead forth and bring you back in happiness!

DUKE   I thank you, fare you well.   *Exit*   75

ESCALUS   I shall desire you, sir, to give me leave
To have free speech with you, and it concerns me
To look into the bottom of my place.
A power I have, but of what strength and nature
I am not yet instructed.   80

ANGELO   'Tis so with me. Let us withdraw together,
And we may soon our satisfaction have
Touching that point.

ESCALUS   I'll wait upon your honour.   *Exeunt*

[ACT I, SCENE II]

Enter Lucio, and two other Gentlemen

LUCIO   If the Duke, with the other dukes, come not to

59. hopeful = successful

61. bring you something on the way 「途中まで少しお見送りする」

63-64. have to do / With any scruple = entertain any feeling of doubt or hesitation

64. scope 「権限、行為の自由」

65. enforce or qualify 「強要するなり、手心を加えるなり」

67-72. I'll privily away ... That does affect it. 群集に対する公爵のこうした態度は、ジェイムズ一世のそれと類似しているという説もある。とすれば、この箇所は宮廷上演（1604）の際の新王へのお世辞（flattery）かもしれない。

68. stage me 「（舞台上の役者のように）公に身を晒す」

69. do well = be convenient

70. aves 「歓呼の声、万歳」（ラテン語の ave = hail より）

71. safe 「まともな、しっかりした」

72. That = who　前行の the man を受ける。

74. [The heavens] **Lead forth ... in happiness!**

77. concerns me = is important to me

78. look into the bottom = carefully examine the nature or extent

83. wait upon = attend

〔1. 2〕あらすじ……………………………………………………………………………

　ルーチオが2人の紳士と下品な会話をしているところへ、売春宿の女主人オーヴァーダンが登場し、アンジェロが姦淫についての厳しい法律を適用して、婚約者のジュリエッタを婚前交渉で妊娠させたクローディオを逮捕し、速やかに処刑すると伝える。護送途中にちょうど通りかかったクローディオは、知人のルーチオを見つけ、見習い修道女の妹イザベラに、アンジェロへの助命嘆願をするよう伝えてくれと依頼する。

………………………………………………………………………………………………

composition with the King of Hungary, why then all the
dukes fall upon the King.

FIRST GENTLEMAN   Heaven grant us its peace, but not the King
of Hungary's!   5

SECOND GENTLEMAN   Amen.

LUCIO   Thou conclud'st like the sanctimonious pirate, that
went to sea with the ten commandments but scraped one out
of the table.

SECOND GENTLEMAN   'Thou shalt not steal'?   10

LUCIO   Ay, that he razed.

FIRST GENTLEMAN   Why, 'twas a commandment to command
the captain and all the rest from their functions: they put
forth to steal. There's not a soldier of us all that, in the
thanksgiving before meat, do relish the petition well that   15
prays for peace.

SECOND GENTLEMAN   I never heard any soldier dislike it.

LUCIO   I believe thee, for I think thou never wast where grace
was said.

SECOND GENTLEMAN   No? A dozen times at least.   20

FIRST GENTLEMAN   What, in meter?

LUCIO   In any proportion, or in any language.

FIRST GENTLEMAN   I think, or in any religion.

LUCIO   Ay, why not? Grace is grace, despite of all controversy;
as, for example, thou thyself art a wicked villain, despite of 25
all grace.

FIRST GENTLEMAN   Well, there went but a pair of shears
between us.

LUCIO   I grant, as there may between the lists and the velvet.
Thou art the list.   30

FIRST GENTLEMAN   And thou the velvet. Thou art good velvet;
thou'rt a three-piled piece, I warrant thee. I had as lief be a
list of an English kersey, as be piled as thou art piled for a
French velvet. Do I speak feelingly now?

2. composition = agreement

the King of Hungary 隣国ハンガリーへの言及は、この劇の舞台がウィーンであることを観客に想起させる。

3. fall upon = attack

7-9. Thou conclud'st like ... of the table 「せっかく peace を祈っても、最後でハンガリー王を除外するのでは、モーゼの十戒を刻んだ板からひとつだけ（「汝盗むなかれ」という）戒律を削って海に出る、信心深いふりをした海賊のようなものだ」 海賊関連の ll. 7-16 については解説 4 ページ参照。

7. sanctimonious = pretending piety

13. from their functions = to give up their trade or occupation

15. thanksgiving before meat 「食前の感謝の祈り」当時は、食前の祈りは平和への祈願で終えるのが通例。

relish 「好む」

18. grace 「食前の祈り」

21. What, in meter? 「何と、韻を踏んでいるのか?」諸説あるが、紳士 2 の前行（A dozen times at least）が、弱強格（iambic）になっていることをからかっているという Arden 3 版の説明が一番腑に落ちる。

22. In any proportion 「どんな形式でも」

24. Grace is grace ルーチオは grace の意味を「食前の祈り」から「神の恩寵」にずらしている。

controversy 当時のカトリックとプロテスタント間の恩寵と救済をめぐる論争を指す。

25-26. despite of all grace (1) いくら食前に祈っても (2) あらゆる恩寵にもかかわらず

27-28. there went but a pair of shears between us 「我々の間には（同じ布を裁断した）ハサミしかない、俺たちは似たりよったりだ」当時の一般的なことわざ的表現。

29. the lists 「（布の）端っこ」

32. a three-piled 「毛足（pile）が三重の、最上質の」の意。

piece 「反物」

had as lief 「…のほうがましだ」

33. an English kersey 「イギリス製のカージー織」サフォーク州カージー産の粗い素朴な毛織物。

33-34. piled for a French velvet 「フランス産のビロードのように毛羽立てられる」に「フランス産の梅毒でハゲる（pilled）」をかけた言葉遊び。

34. feelingly = appropriately, to the purpose

35

LUCIO   I think thou dost, and indeed with most painful feeling   35
of thy speech. I will, out of thine own confession, learn to
begin thy health, but whilst I live forget to drink after thee.

FIRST GENTLEMAN   I think I have done myself wrong, have I
not?

SECOND GENTLEMAN   Yes, that thou hast, whether thou art   40
tainted or free.

Enter [Mistress Overdone, a] Bawd

LUCIO   Behold, behold, where Madam Mitigation comes. I
have purchased as many diseases under her roof, as come
to —

SECOND GENTLEMAN   To what, I pray?   45

LUCIO   Judge.

SECOND GENTLEMAN   To three thousand dolours a year.

FIRST GENTLEMAN   Ay, and more.

LUCIO   A French crown more.

FIRST GENTLEMAN   Thou art always figuring diseases in me,   50
but thou art full of error; I am sound.

LUCIO   Nay, not as one would say, healthy, but so sound as
things that are hollow. Thy bones are hollow; impiety has
made a feast of thee.

FIRST GENTLEMAN   How now, which of your hips has the most   55
profound sciatica?

MISTRESS OVERDONE   Well, well. There's one yonder arrested
and carried to prison was worth five thousand of you all.

SECOND GENTLEMAN   Who's that, I pray thee?

MISTRESS OVERDONE   Marry, sir, that's Claudio, Signior   60
Claudio.

FIRST GENTLEMAN   Claudio to prison? 'Tis not so.

MISTRESS OVERDONE   Nay, but I know 'tis so. I saw him
arrested, saw him carried away; and which is more, within
these three days his head to be chopped off.   65

35-36. with most painful feeling of thy speech ルーチオは前行の feelingly を painfully の意味にずらして、「お前は（梅毒で口がただれているので）話すとひどく痛いだろう」とからかう。

36. out of thine own confession 「君が（梅毒だと）認めるのだから」

learn = remember

37. begin thy health = propose a toast to you

[I will] **forget to drink after thee**「お前のあとで（同じカップでは）飲まない」

38. I have done myself wrong 「墓穴を掘る、自分で自分の首を絞める」

41. tainted = infected with disease

free = sound

42. Madam Mitigation 彼女が売春宿のおかみとして「客の性的な欲望を和らげる / 静める（mitigate）」仕事をしているため。ちなみに、こうした命名法からも、この喜劇のアレゴリカルな性質が窺える。

43-44. come to = amount to

47. dolours 「嘆き、悲しみ」と「ターレル銀貨」（thaler）の言葉遊び。当時、この大型銀貨が同音異義語の dollar(s) と呼ばれていたことによる。

49. A French crown 「フランスで鋳造された金貨 / フランス病（＝梅毒）によるハゲ頭」の言葉遊び。シェイクスピアお気に入りの bawdy joke。

50. figuring = imagining

52-53. so sound as things that are hollow. Thy bones are hollow ルーチオは sound を「健康な」から「音がする」に意味をずらし、紳士 1 の骨が梅毒の末期症状で hollow「すかすか」になっているとからかう。

53-54. impiety has made a feast of thee 「不信心がお前をごちそうにしている、食らい尽くしている」

55. How now = Hello 当時の出会い頭の挨拶のひとつ。

56. profound = deep-seated

sciatica 「坐骨神経痛」当時は梅毒の兆候と考えられていた。

60. Marry = Indeed 'By the Virgin Mary'という誓言が省略された形。

LUCIO   But after all this fooling, I would not have it so. Art thou sure of this?

MISTRESS OVERDONE   I am too sure of it, and it is for getting Madam Julietta with child.

LUCIO   Believe me, this may be. He promised to meet me two   70
hours since, and he was ever precise in promise-keeping.

SECOND GENTLEMAN   Besides, you know, it draws something near to the speech we had to such a purpose.

FIRST GENTLEMAN   But most of all, agreeing with the proclamation.   75

LUCIO   Away, let's go learn the truth of it.

Exeunt Lucio [and two Gentlemen]

MISTRESS OVERDONE   Thus, what with the war, what with the sweat, what with the gallows, and what with poverty, I am custom-shrunk.

Enter [Pompey]

How now? what's the news with you.   80

POMPEY   Yonder man is carried to prison.

MISTRESS OVERDONE   Well, what has he done?

POMPEY   A woman.

MISTRESS OVERDONE   But what's his offence?

POMPEY   Groping for trouts in a peculiar river.   85

MISTRESS OVERDONE   What, is there a maid with child by him?

POMPEY   No, but there's a woman with maid by him. You have not heard of the proclamation, have you?

MISTRESS OVERDONE   What proclamation, man?

POMPEY   All houses in the suburbs of Vienna must be plucked   90
down.

MISTRESS OVERDONE   And what shall become of those in the city?

POMPEY   They shall stand for seed. They had gone down too, but that a wise burgher put in for them.   95

66. all this fooling ルーチオと紳士たちの性的放埒をネタにしたここまでの冗談を指す。

70. Believe me = Indeed

73. to such a purpose = with regard to this subject　ルーチオと紳士たちは、新たに布告された厳しい法令について、すでに話題にしている様子である。

74. agreeing with = in accord with

77-79. Thus, what with the war ... I am custom-shrunk スペインとの長引く戦争、サー・ウォルター・ローリーと関わる内乱罪の裁判と処刑、貿易の不振などといった、当時の時事問題への言及とする版（Arden 2）もある。解説 p. 3 も参照。

78. sweat 当時、梅毒治療として行われていた「発汗療法」（sweat treatment）への言及。

79. custom-shrunk 「閑古鳥が鳴いている、商売上がったりだ」

82. done オーヴァーダンは「しでかした」の意味で使っているが、ポンペイは「寝た」という俗語的な意味に取っている。

85. Groping for trouts 「鱒のエラをくすぐって手づかみで捕える漁法（tickling trout）」を指すが、もちろん、性的な含意がある。

peculiar = private

87. No, but there's a woman with maid by him オーヴァーダンが前行で「彼によって子供を身ごもった処女（maid）がいるのか」と聞いたのに対して、ポンペイがもうジュリエッタは処女ではないから、「彼によって処女 / 童貞（maid）を身ごもった女がいる」と訂正したものか？　OED によれば maid には幼魚の意味もあるので、86 行目の鱒取りとつながる比喩かもしれない。

88. proclamation 1603 年 9 月 16 日に出された布告を指すと思われる。当時蔓延していたペストへの予防措置として、売春宿などが立ち並ぶ郊外の家屋を取り壊すよう指示が出された。解説 3 ページも参照。

90. houses = bawdy houses「売春宿」

suburbs「郊外」ロンドン市当局の管轄外、すなわち城壁の外の地区を指す。

94. stand for seed 「種籽として残す」

had = would have

95. but that = unless

burgher = citizen (from the wealthy middle class)

put in「仲介する、嘆願する」

MISTRESS OVERDONE   But shall all our houses of resort in the
  suburbs be pulled down?

POMPEY   To the ground, mistress.

MISTRESS OVERDONE   Why, here's a change indeed in the
  commonwealth! What shall become of me?   100

POMPEY   Come, fear not you; good counsellors lack no clients.
  Though you change your place, you need not change your
  trade. I'll be your tapster still. Courage, there will be pity
  taken on you, you that have worn your eyes almost out in the
  service, you will be considered.   105

Enter Provost, Claudio, Juliet, Officers, Lucio, and two Gentlemen

MISTRESS OVERDONE   What's to do here, Thomas tapster?
  Let's withdraw.

POMPEY   Here comes Signior Claudio, led by the Provost to
  prison, and there's Madam Juliet.

          Exeunt Mistress [Overdone and Pompey]

CLAUDIO   Fellow, why dost thou show me thus to the world?   110
  Bear me to prison, where I am committed.

PROVOST   I do it not in evil disposition,
  But from Lord Angelo by special charge.

CLAUDIO   Thus can the demy-god, authority,
  Make us pay down for our offence by weight.   115
  The words of heaven: on whom it will, it will,
  On whom it will not, so; yet still 'tis just.

LUCIO   Why, how now, Claudio? Whence comes this restraint?

CLAUDIO   From too much liberty, my Lucio, liberty.
  As surfeit is the father of much fast,   120
  So every scope by the immoderate use
  Turns to restraint. Our natures do pursue
  Like rats that raven down their proper bane,
  A thirsty evil, and when we drink, we die.

LUCIO   If I could speak so wisely under an arrest, I would send   125

96. our houses of resort　売春宿のこと。

98. To the ground = thoroughly

100. commonwealth = state

101. counsellors = counselling lawyers　「顧問弁護士」

103. still = always

104-05. have worn your eyes almost out in the service　「このご奉公でほとんど目が見えなくなった」売春をご奉公（service）と呼ぶところが滑稽。

106. What's to do = what is to be done

Thomas　tapster の一般的な呼称。

110-13. Fellow, why dost thou ... by special charge　クローディオは自分が見世物にされることに憤っているが、典獄はそれがアンジェロの特別な命令（special charge）であると弁解している。つまりアンジェロは、クローディオの件を最初から特例扱いしていることになる。

115. pay down　「（その場で）支払う」

by weight　「重さで量って、きっちり」当時、貨幣の価値を確認するため、枚数だけでなく重さも量ったことによる。

116-17. The words of heaven ... yet still 'tis just　聖書の表現を踏まえている。⇒後注

118. restraint　「拘留、拘束」

liberty　(1) freedom　(2) licentiousness の両義。

120. surfeit　「飽食、過食」

fast　「断食、節制」

121. scope = license　「自由、放縦」

123. raven down　「貪り食らう」

their proper bane　「（ネズミ）専用の毒」猫いらず（ratsbane）のこと。

124. A thirsty evil = an evil that causes thirst

125-26. send for certain of my creditors　「（債務監獄に入るために）借金取りを若干名（= some）迎えにやる」

for certain of my creditors. And yet, to say the truth, I had as lief have the foppery of freedom as the mortality of imprisonment. What's thy offence, Claudio?

CLAUDIO   What but to speak of would offend again.

LUCIO   What, is't murder?   130

CLAUDIO   No.

LUCIO   Lechery?

CLAUDIO   Call it so.

PROVOST   Away, sir, you must go.

CLAUDIO   One word, good friend. Lucio, a word with you.   135

LUCIO   A hundred, if they'll do you any good. Is lechery so looked after?

CLAUDIO   Thus stands it with me: upon a true contract
I got possession of Julietta's bed.
You know the lady, she is fast my wife,   140
Save that we do the denunciation lack
Of outward order. This we came not to,
Only for propagation of a dower
Remaining in the coffer of her friends,
From whom we thought it meet to hide our love   145
Till time had made them for us. But it chances
The stealth of our most mutual entertainment
With character too gross is writ on Juliet.

LUCIO   With child, perhaps?

CLAUDIO   Unhappily, even so.
And the new deputy, now for the Duke —   150
Whether it be the fault and glimpse of newness,
Or whether that the body public be
A horse whereon the governor doth ride,
Who, newly in the seat, that it may know
He can command, lets it straight feel the spur;   155
Whether the tyranny be in his place,
Or in his eminence that fills it up,

127. foppery = foolishness, folly

　mortality = deadliness　morality という校訂を採用している版も多いが、ここは Folio 版の原綴りに従う。

129. What = That which

　but = only

137. looked after = closely watched

138. Thus stands it with me = I am in such circumstances

138-39. upon a true contract ... Julietta's bed.　クローディオとジュリエッタの関係は、教会からすれば秘密結婚なので、アンジェロが復活させた法律でそれが姦淫の罪に問われたことにも理はある。

138. contract = marriage contract

140. fast = securely, firmly

141. denunciation = official, formal or public announcement

142. order　「通常の手続き」

143. propagation of a dower = increase of dowry

144. her friends　「彼女の身内の者」

146. for us　「私たちの味方」

　it chances = it happens

148. character = letter　ここではジュリエッタの妊娠を指す。

　gross = evident

149. even so　「まさにそうなんだ（= just so）」

151. fault and glimpse of newness　「慣れない地位についたため、目がくらんでの過ち」

152. the body public　「国家、国民」

154-55. it ... it　horse と the body public の両方を受けている。

155. straight = immediately

156-57. the tyranny be in his place, / Or in his eminence that fills it up　「圧政は統治者という地位につきものなのか、あるいはアンジェロが占めた地位の高さによるものなのか」

I stagger in — but this new governor
Awakes me all the enrollèd penalties
Which have, like unscoured armour, hung by the wall   160
So long that nineteen zodiacs have gone round,
And none of them been worn; and for a name
Now puts the drowsy and neglected act
Freshly on me. 'Tis surely for a name.

LUCIO   I warrant it is; and thy head stands so tickle on thy   165
shoulders, that a milkmaid, if she be in love, may sigh it off.
Send after the Duke, and appeal to him.

CLAUDIO   I have done so, but he's not to be found.
I prithee, Lucio, do me this kind service:
This day, my sister should the cloister enter,   170
And there receive her approbation.
Acquaint her with the danger of my state,
Implore her, in my voice, that she make friends
To the strict deputy; bid herself assay him.
I have great hope in that, for in her youth   175
There is a prone and speechless dialect
Such as move men; beside, she hath prosperous art
When she will play with reason and discourse,
And well she can persuade.

LUCIO   I pray she may, as well for the encouragement of the   180
like, which else would stand under grievous imposition, as for
the enjoying of thy life, who I would be sorry should be thus
foolishly lost at a game of tick-tack. I'll to her.

CLAUDIO   I thank you, good friend Lucio.

LUCIO   Within two hours.   185

CLAUDIO   Come, officer, away.   *Exeunt*

158. I stagger in = I'm unable to decide

159. Awakes me = makes active　me は当事者の興味、関心を示す「心的与格（ethical dative）」という歴史的用法。「私に対して」という程度の意味。

　enrollèd = recorded in the laws

160. unscoured　「サビだらけの、サビが擦り取られていない」

161. zodiacs　「黄道 12 宮」だが、ここでは「1 年間のめぐり」の意。

162. them = penalties

　worn　「身につける＝運用される」160 行目の鎧（armour）を受けた比喩。

　for a name　「名声をえるために」

163-64. puts ... on　「当てはめる、適用する」

165. tickle = unstable

166. a milkmaid, if she be in love, may sigh it off　「乳搾りの娘が、そっと恋のため息をついたら落ちるだろう」

169. I prithee　「お願いだから（＝ I pray thee）」

170. should = is supposed to

171. approbation　「修道女見習い（の承認）」

173. in my voice = in my name

174. assay　「難事を試みる」　原義の「試金する（to test a metal）」の意味も効いている。

176. prone = eager

　speechless dialect「声なき言葉」すなわち、身振りや表情のこと。

177. move　主語が単数なのに動詞が複数形なのは、先行する形容詞が 2 つあるため。

　prosperous art = successful skill

180-81. the like　「（クローディオと）同様の法令違反者」

181. stand under grievous imposition = be severely accused

183. a game of tick-tack　古い形のバックギャモン（西洋すごろく）のこと。駒（peg）を穴（hole）にさしたことから、婉曲に性交を意味する。

[ACT I, SCENE III]

Enter Duke and Friar Thomas

DUKE   No, holy father, throw away that thought,
Believe not that the dribbling dart of love
Can pierce a complete bosom. Why I desire thee
To give me secret harbor hath a purpose
More grave and wrinkled than the aims and ends   5
Of burning youth.

FRIAR   May your grace speak of it?

DUKE   My holy sir, none better knows than you
How I have ever loved the life removed,
And held in idle price to haunt assemblies   10
Where youth and cost witless bravery keeps.
I have delivered to Lord Angelo,
A man of stricture and firm abstinence,
My absolute power and place here in Vienna;
And he supposes me travelled to Poland,   15
For so I have strewed it in the common ear
And so it is received. Now, pious sir,
You will demand of me why I do this.

FRIAR   Gladly, my lord.

DUKE   We have strict statutes and most biting laws,   20
The needful bits and curbs to headstrong weeds,
Which for this fourteen years we have let slip,
Even like an o'ergrown lion in a cave
That goes not out to prey. Now, as fond fathers,
Having bound up the threatening twigs of birch,   25
Only to stick it in their children's sight
For terror, not to use, in time the rod
More mocked than feared; so our decrees,
Dead to infliction, to themselves are dead,
And liberty plucks justice by the nose,   30

　公爵は修道士トマスに対し、国内に留まって密かにアンジェロの統治ぶりを観察したいという意図を明かし、変装用に修道士の衣服を手に入れる。

……………………………………………………………………………………………

2. dribbling dart 「流れ矢」キューピッドの恋の矢のこと。

3. complete 「（恋に対して）完全無欠の」

4. harbor ＝ shelter, lodging

5. grave and wrinkled 「真面目で老熟した」

6. burning ＝ inflamed with passion

9. life removed 「隠遁生活、隠棲」

10. held in idle price ＝ consider [it] of little worth

　　assemblies ＝ social gatherings

11. youth and cost witless bravery keeps 「若さと浪費と愚かな見せびらかしが横行する」youth ... bravery をまとめて単数動詞でうけている。

13. stricture ＝ strictness

16. strewed ＝ spread, scattered

18. demand of ＝ ask from

20. biting ＝ keen, pungent

21. bits and curbs 「（馬の）はみと轡」

　　weeds ＝ lawless and uncontrolled impulses　比喩を一貫させるため、長らく「馬（steeds）」という校訂がなされてきたが、近年は Folio 版の原綴り（weeds）を残す版が多くなった。

22. let slip ＝ let pass unnoticed

23. o'ergrown ＝ that has grown too large

25. twigs of birch 「樺の小枝（を束ねた鞭）」

29. Dead to infliction ＝ never used as punishment

　　to themselves are dead 「空文化している」

30-32. And liberty plucks justice ... Goes all decorum Oxford 版はこうした「あべこべな世界」の滑稽なイメージが、シェイクスピアのオリジナルではなく、たとえばブロードシート（安価な 1 枚の紙の片面に、多くの場合、バラッド、韻文、ニュースおよび時に木版画のイラストレーションを印刷したもの）などを通じて、当時一般に流通していたと指摘している。

30. plucks ... by the nose 「鼻面を引き回す」

The baby beats the nurse, and quite athwart
Goes all decorum.

FRIAR   It rested in your grace
To unloose this tied-up justice, when you pleased;
And it in you more dreadful would have seemed
Than in Lord Angelo.

DUKE   I do fear, too dreadful.   35
Sith 'twas my fault, to give the people scope,
'Twould be my tyranny to strike and gall them
For what I bid them do, for we bid this be done,
When evil deeds have their permissive pass
And not the punishment. Therefore, indeed, my father,   40
I have on Angelo imposed the office,
Who may, in the ambush of my name, strike home,
And yet my nature never in the fight
To do in slander. And to behold his sway
I will, as 'twere a brother of your order,   45
Visit both prince and people. Therefore, I prithee,
Supply me with the habit and instruct me
How I may formally in person bear
Like a true friar. Mo reasons for this action
At our more leisure shall I render you;   50
Only, this one: Lord Angelo is precise,
Stands at a guard with envy, scarce confesses
That his blood flows, or that his appetite
Is more to bread than stone. Hence shall we see
If power change purpose, what our seemers be.   *Exeunt* 55

[ACT I, SCENE IV]

Enter Isabell [a] and Francisca, a Nun

ISABELLA   And have you nuns no farther privileges?
NUN   Are not these large enough?

31. athwart = in opposition to the proper course

34. dreadful = awe-inspiring

36. Sith since の古形。   **scope** = freedom

37. gall = wound 原義は「(馬の) 皮膚を擦りむく」。

39. When = considering ...   **permissive pass** = permission to act

42. in the ambush of my name 「私の名前に隠れて」

home = effectively, directly

43. my nature 「私自身」前行の my name との対比。

in the fight 「最中に、渦中にあって」

44. To do in slander 「誹謗中傷を受けるような行動をする」

45. a brother of your order 「あなたの修道会の (同僚の) 僧」

46. prince 「王侯宰相」暗にアンジェロを指す。

47. habit = dress

48. in person「外見的に」   **bear** = behave

49. Mo More の古形。

51. precise 「規則通りの、几帳面な」Arden 3 版は、当時 precisian といえ
ば、ピューリタンの異名だったことから、アンジェロに清教徒のイメージが投
影されているとするが、Oxford 版はこうした深読みに否定的である。

52. at a guard with = on his defense against

confesses 「事実だと認める」

53. blood flows 「血が流れている」と「性欲がある」の両義。

54. more to bread than stone これも聖書的な表現である。   ⇒後注

54-55. Hence shall we see ... what our seemers be 「権力と人間」はこの劇の
中心的なテーマのひとつ。なお、see と be が韻を踏んでいるのは、イザベラ
と尼僧に出番を知らせる合図 (cue) でもある。

55. purpose 「性癖」   **seemers** 「うわべを繕っている連中」

〔1. 4〕あらすじ……………………………………………………………………
　　ルーチオは尼僧院に赴き、イザベラにクローディオの陥っている危機的な状況
を説明する。イザベラは助命嘆願のため、ただちにアンジェロのもとに赴くこと
を決意する。
……………………………………………………………………………………

2. large = generous

ISABELLA   Yes, truly. I speak not as desiring more,
   But rather wishing a more strict restraint
   Upon the sisterhood, the votarists of Saint Clare.   5
LUCIO   [*Within*]   Ho? Peace be in this place!
ISABELLA   Who's that which calls?
NUN   It is a man's voice. Gentle Isabella,
   Turn you the key and know his business of him.
   You may, I may not; you are yet unsworn.
   When you have vowed, you must not speak with men   10
   But in the presence of the prioress;
   Then if you speak, you must not show your face,
   Or if you show your face, you must not speak.
   He calls again. I pray you answer him.
ISABELLA   Peace and prosperity! Who is't that calls?   15

[Enter Lucio]

LUCIO   Hail virgin, if you be — as those cheek-roses
   Proclaim you are no less. Can you so stead me
   As bring me to the sight of Isabella,
   A novice of this place and the fair sister
   To her unhappy brother Claudio?   20
ISABELLA   Why 'her unhappy brother'? Let me ask,
   The rather for I now must make you know
   I am that Isabella and his sister.
LUCIO   Gentle and fair, your brother kindly greets you.
   Not to be weary with you, he's in prison.   25
ISABELLA   Woe me! For what?
LUCIO   For that which, if myself might be his judge,
   He should receive his punishment in thanks:
   He hath got his friend with child.
ISABELLA   Sir, make me not your story.
LUCIO   'Tis true.   30
   I would not, though 'tis my familiar sin

5. **votarist** 「修道尼」

   Saint Clare 「聖クララ会」聖クララ（1194-1253）。目や眼病の守護聖人。アッシジの聖フランチェスコに最初に帰依した女性のひとりで、1212年にフランチェスコ会の女子修道会クララ会（キアラ会とも）を創始した。クララ会は清貧ときびしい禁欲生活を通じ、神との交わりを目指す観想生活を特色とする。修道女たちは囲い地の中に白い衣を着て暮らし、厳格な規則のもと、孤独と沈黙のなかで、祈りと労働を日課としていた。

6. **Ho?** 人を呼ぶときの言葉。「おーい、誰か」

   Peace be in this place! 挨拶によく用いられる聖書的表現。

9. **unsworn** 「（尼になる）誓いを立てていない」イザベラはまだ見習い中。

11. **prioress** 「女子修道院の院長」

15. **Peace and prosperity!** 「平安と反映のあらんことを！」6行目のルーチオの呼び掛けへの返答。同様に聖書的響きあり。

16. **if you be** 「もし処女であればですが」ルーチオは誰に対しても bawdy joke を言う性癖がある。

17. **stead** 「役立つ（＝ available to）」

19. **novice** 「修練女」まだ「誓願を立てていない（unsworn）」修練中の人。

22. **The rather for** ＝ The more because

25. **Not to be weary with you** 「（退屈させないため）単刀直入に言えば」

26. **Woe me!** 「なんてこと！（＝ Woe is to me）」

28. **He should receive his punishment in thanks.** 「彼が受ける罰は感謝の言葉だったでしょうに」 should ＝ would have

29. **friend** 「恋人、愛人」

30. **make me not your story** 「私をからかわないで」 story ＝ a theme of mirth（*OED*）

31. **familiar** ＝ habitual

With maids to seem the lapwing and to jest
Tongue far from heart, play with all virgins so.
I hold you as a thing enskied and sainted,
By your renouncement an immortal spirit,   35
And to be talked with in sincerity
As with a saint.

ISABELLA   You do blaspheme the good in mocking me.

LUCIO   Do not believe it. Fewness and truth, 'tis thus:
Your brother and his lover have embraced.   40
As those that feed grow full, as blossoming time
That from the seedness the bare fallow brings
To teeming foison, even so her plenteous womb
Expresseth his full tilth and husbandry.

ISABELLA   Someone with child by him? My cousin Juliet?   45

LUCIO   Is she your cousin?

ISABELLA   Adoptedly, as school-maids change their names
By vain though apt affection.

LUCIO   She it is.

ISABELLA   O, let him marry her.

LUCIO   This is the point.
The Duke is very strangely gone from hence;   50
Bore many gentlemen, myself being one,
In hand and hope of action. But we do learn,
By those that know the very nerves of state,
His givings-out were of an infinite distance
From his true meant design. Upon his place,   55
And with full line of his authority,
Governs Lord Angelo, a man whose blood
Is very snow-broth; one who never feels
The wanton stings, and motions of the sense,
But doth rebate and blunt his natural edge   60
With profits of the mind, study and fast.
He, to give fear to use and liberty,

32. seem the lapwing 「見せかけで惑わす」タゲリ（lapwing）は巣から離れたところで鳴き、捕食者を騙して雛を守る習性があると言われているところから。

33. Tongue [being] **far from heart** 「心にないことを言って」

34. enskied 「天に昇って」

35. By your renouncement 「（俗世を）捨てることで」

38. the good 「善き人たち、聖者たち」

39. Do not believe it 「とんでもない」

Fewness and truth ＝ In few words and truly

41. feed ＝ eat   **full** ＝ fat

42. seedness 「種まき」   **fallow** 「休耕地」

43. teeming foison 「豊かな稔り」   **plenteous** ＝ fertile

44. Expresseth 「（外に）あらわす」   **tilth and husbandry** ともに「耕作」の意。なお husbandry は husband との言葉遊びにもなっている。

45. cousin 当時この呼称は、いとこの他に親戚一般あるいは親しい友人にも使われていた。

47. Adoptedly ＝ As though by adoption（*OED*）

change ＝ exchange 「交換」はこの劇の最も重要なモチーフのひとつ。これから様々な箇所にあらわれる。

48. vain ＝ foolish   **apt** ＝ natural

51-52. Bore ... In hand and hope   (a) bore in hand ＝ deluded, deceived
  (b) bore in hope ＝ kept in hope   したがって「欺かれて、期待して待つ」

52. action 「軍事行動」

53. nerves ＝ those things, parts, or elements, which constitute the main strength or vigour of something（*OED*）

54. givings-out 「公言、宣言」

56. full line ＝ complete scope

58. very ＝ nothing but   **snow-broth** 「（冷たい）雪解け水」

59. stings ＝ urges to desire   **motions of the sense** ＝ sexual impulses

60. rebate and blunt ともに「鈍らせる、鈍麻させる」

61. fast 「断食」飲食は欲望を掻き立てるとされていたため。

62. use and liberty 「常習的な放縦さ」and によって結合された2語で1つの複雑な概念を表す「二詞一意（hendiadys）」という修辞的な技法の例。シェイクスピア作品ではよく見かける。

Which have for long run by the hideous law
As mice by lions, hath picked out an act
Under whose heavy sense your brother's life   65
Falls into forfeit. He arrests him on it,
And follows close the rigor of the statute
To make him an example. All hope is gone,
Unless you have the grace by your fair prayer
To soften Angelo. And that's my pith of business   70
'Twixt you and your poor brother.

ISABELLA   Doth he so,
Seek his life?

LUCIO   Has censured him already,
And as I hear the Provost hath a warrant
For's execution.

ISABELLA   Alas! What poor ability's in me
to do him good?

LUCIO   Assay the power you have.   75

ISABELLA   My power? Alas, I doubt.

LUCIO   Our doubts are traitors,
And makes us loose the good we oft might win
By fearing to attempt. Go to Lord Angelo
And let him learn to know, when maidens sue
Men give like gods; but when they weep and kneel   80
All their petitions are as freely theirs
As they themselves would owe them.

ISABELLA   I'll see what I can do.

LUCIO   But speedily!

ISABELLA   I will about it straight,
No longer staying but to give the mother   85
Notice of my affaire. I humbly thank you.
Commend me to my brother; soon at night
I'll send him certain word of my success.

LUCIO   I take my leave of you.

63. run by = disregarded

　hideous = dreadful

64. mice by lions　イソップの有名な寓話「ライオンと鼠」は、「眠っているライオンの体の上を乗り越えた鼠が捕まるが、恩返しを約束して放してもらう。鼠は、後日、猟師に捕らえられたライオンの紐を噛み切って、約束を果たす」という話。だが Oxford 版によれば、15世紀スコットランドの詩人ロバート・ヘンリーソン作 *The Morall Fabillis of Esope the Phrygian* では、眠っているライオンは「義務を怠った王」に、鼠は「支配者が怠慢だと不品行な行いをする庶民」にたとえられているそうである。シェイクスピアはこちらも知っていたのかもしれない。

65. heavy sense = severe import

66. Falls into forfeit = comes to be lost

68. example　「見せしめ、戒め」

69. grace = good fortune

70. pith = essential part, essence

72. censured = sentenced

75. Assay　Cf. 1. 2. 174

76. doubts = self-doubts, lack of confidence

79. learn to know = come to realize

　sue = plead

81. are ... freely theirs = are freely granted them

82. As = as if

　owe = own, possess

84. will about it = will set about doing it

85. the mother　「尼僧院長」

86. Notice of my affaire = information of my business

87. soon at night = tonight

88. certain = certainly

　word「知らせ、便り」この意味では通例無冠詞。

　success「首尾、結果」

89. take my leave of = bid farewell

ISABELLA   Good sir, adieu.   *Exeunt*

[Act II, Scene I]

Enter Angelo, Escalus, and Servants,[and a] Justice

ANGELO   We must not make a scarecrow of the law,
   Setting it up to fear the birds of prey,
   And let it keep one shape till custom make it
   Their perch and not their terror.
ESCALUS   Ay, but yet
   Let us be keen, and rather cut a little   5
   Than fall and bruise to death. Alas, this gentleman
   Whom I would save had a most noble father.
   Let but your honour know,
   Whom I believe to be most strait in virtue,
   That in the working of your own affections,   10
   Had time cohered with place, or place with wishing,
   Or that the resolute acting of our blood
   Could have attained the effect of your own purpose,
   Whether you had not sometime in your life
   Erred in this point, which now you censure him,   15
   And pulled the law upon you.
ANGELO   'Tis one thing to be tempted, Escalus,
   Another thing to fall. I not deny
   The jury passing on the prisoner's life
   May in the sworn twelve have a thief or two   20
   Guiltier than him they try. What's open made to justice,
   That justice seizes. What knows the laws
   That thieves do pass on thieves? 'Tis very pregnant,
   The jewel that we find, we stoop and take't,
   Because we see it; but what we do not see   25
   We tread upon and never think of it.
   You may not so extenuate his offence
   For I have had such faults, but rather tell me,
   When I that censure him do so offend,

　エスカラスはアンジェロにクローディオの減刑を提案するが、アンジェロはそれを聞き入れず、明朝処刑するよう命じる。そこへ巡査のエルボーが、ポン引きのポンペイと客のフロスを連れて登場。風俗紊乱のかどで逮捕したのだが、エルボーの言葉の誤用のため審理は紛糾し、あきれたアンジェロは途中退席する。そのあとでエスカラスは、フロスには酒場への出入りを禁じ、ポンペイには次に逮捕されたら鞭打ちに処すると告げ、エルボーには、後日、自分の館を訪れるよう指示する。

2. fear ＝ scare, frighten

3. till ... 以下の節は till が導く仮定法。

　　custom ＝ their familiarity with it

5-6. Let us be keen ... bruise to death　ガーデニング（植木の剪定）の比喩だが、外科手術の喩えにも読める。

5. keen ＝ sharp-edged

8. know ＝ understand, acknowledge

9. strait ＝ strict

10. affections ＝ passions, desires

11. Had time cohered with ＝ if time had agreed with

12. Or that ＝ or if

　　resolute ＝ determined

14. Whether　l. 8 の know に続く。

15. which ＝ for which

　　censure ＝ condemn, sentence

16. pulled ... upon ＝ bring ... upon

19. passing on　「判決をくだす」

20. the sworn twelve　当時イングランドでは、陪審員（jury）12 名による刑事裁判が行われていた。事前に神に宣誓するため sworn という形容詞がつく。

21. What's open made to justice ＝ what is made obvious to justice

22. seizes　「逮捕する」

　　What knows the laws ＝ the laws don't care ...　強調のための修辞疑問文。

23. pregnant ＝ evident, clear

28. For ＝ because

Let mine own judgement pattern out my death,   30
And nothing come in partial. Sir, he must die.

Enter Provost

ESCALUS   Be it as your wisdom will.
ANGELO   Where is the Provost?
PROVOST   Here if it like your honour.
ANGELO   See that Claudio
Be executed by nine tomorrow morning.
Bring him his confessor, let him be prepared,   35
For that's the utmost of his pilgrimage.   [*Exit Provost*]
ESCALUS   Well, heaven forgive him, and forgive us all.
Some rise by sin, and some by virtue fall.
Some run from breaks of ice and answer none,
And some condemnèd for a fault alone.   40

Enter Elbow, Froth, Pompey and Officers

ELBOW   Come, bring them away. If these be good people in a
commonweal, that do nothing but use their abuses in
common houses, I know no law. Bring them away.
ANGELO   How now, sir, what's your name? And what's the
matter?   45
ELBOW   If it please your honour, I am the poor Duke's
constable, and my name is Elbow. I do lean upon justice, sir,
and do bring in here before your good honour two notorious
benefactors.
ANGELO   Benefactors? Well, what benefactors are they? Are   50
they not malefactors?
ELBOW   If it please your honour, I know not well what they
are; but precise villains they are, that I am sure of, and void
of all profanation in the world that good Christians ought to
have.   55
ESCALUS   This comes off well; here's a wise officer.

30. pattern out = be a pattern for, give an example for

31. nothing come in partial = no partiality intervene

33. See [to it] **that** 「…となるように取り計らう」

36. utmost = furthest point

　pilgrimage　人生を巡礼の旅に喩えるのは、当時の一般的発想。

37-40. heaven forgive him ... for a fault alone　この芝居に多用される対句を用いた格言風の表現。

39. breaks of ice　「氷を何度も割って」Folio 版の brakes では意味が不明なため、さまざまな校訂が提案されてきた難解な箇所。ここでは現行の大半の版に従って breaks を採った。

　answer none = pay no penalty

42. commonweal = commonwealth　「国家」

42-43. use their abuses in common houses　「売春宿でいかがわしい行為をする」commonweal と common house の言葉遊びにもなっている。

46. poor Duke's　もちろん、Duke's poor と言うべきところ。エルボーの滑稽な言い間違いの連発は、この場を笑劇に変えてしまう。

47. lean upon = depend upon for support（*OED*）　エルボーは自分の名前の入った「片肘をつく（lean on one's elbow）」という表現を踏まえて、しゃれているつもり。

49. benefactors　「恩人、篤志家」もちろん、ここも malefactor と言うべきところ。リチャード・シェリダンの『恋がたき』(1775) に登場するマラプロップ夫人にちなみ、今日ではこうした滑稽な誤用癖をマラプロピズムと呼ぶ。

53. precise = exact, perfect

54. profanation　「冒瀆」こちらも「信仰告白（profession）」の言い間違いか？

56. comes off well = is well said　続く a wise office とあわせて、エスカラスはエルボーをからかっている。

ANGELO   Go to. What quality are they of? Elbow is your
name? Why dost thou not speak, Elbow?

POMPEY   He cannot, sir, he's out at elbow.

ANGELO   What are you, sir?   60

ELBOW   He, sir? A tapster, sir, parcel bawd, one that serves a
bad woman, whose house, sir, was, as they say, plucked down
in the suburbs; and now she professes a hot-house, which I
think is a very ill house too.

ESCALUS   How know you that?   65

ELBOW   My wife, sir, whom I detest before heaven and your
honour —

ESCALUS   How, thy wife?

ELBOW   Ay, sir, whom I thank heaven is an honest woman —

ESCALUS   Dost thou detest her therefore?   70

ELBOW   I say, sir, I will detest myself also, as well as she, that
this house, if it be not a bawd's house, it is pity of her life, for
it is a naughty house.

ESCALUS   How dost thou know that, constable?

ELBOW   Marry, sir, by my wife, who, if she had been a woman   75
cardinally given might have been accused in fornication,
adultery, and all uncleanliness there.

ESCALUS   By the woman's means?

ELBOW   Ay, sir, by Mistress Overdone's means; but as she spit
in his face, so she defied him.   80

POMPEY   Sir, if it please your honour, this is not so.

ELBOW   Prove it before these varlets here, thou honourable
man, prove it.

ESCALUS   [To Angelo]   Do you hear how he misplaces?

POMPEY   Sir, she came in great with child, and longing, saving   85
your honour's reverence, for stewed prunes. Sir, we had but
two in the house, which at that very distant time stood, as it
were, in a fruit dish, a dish of some three pence; your honours
have seen such dishes, they are not china dishes, but very

57. Go to 「もういい」アンジェロはエスカラスとは対象的に、エルボーに苛^{いら}立っている。

quality = rank or occupation

59. out at elbow 「肘が出た服を着ている、貧乏だ」に「（知恵が）品切れ（out）」をかけた冗談。

61. parcel = part-time, partly

63. professes = claims to be running

a hot-house 「浴場」当時 brothel とほぼ同義だった。

66. detest 「嫌悪する」これも「証言する（attest）」あるいは「誓う（protest）」の言い間違い。

69. honest = chaste

72. pity of her life = a very sad thing for her

73. naughty = wicked

75. by my wife エルボー夫人がどのような目にあったのかは語られないが、おそらく女将オーヴァーダンに売春婦になるよう誘われたのだろう。

76. cardinally 「基本的に」これも「好色な（carnally）」の言い間違い。

given「好む、しがちで」

76-77. accused in fornication, adultery, and all uncleanliness この表現も聖書からの影響だろう。　⇒後注

78. By the woman's means? = through your wife?

79. by Mistress Overdone's means エルボーは前行の 'the woman' を間違えて、オーヴァーダンと取っている。

79-80. she ... she エルボーの妻を指す。

80. his ... him ポンペイ（あるいはフロス）を指す。

82. varlets 「下僕」アンジェロとエスカラスを指す。

82-83. honourable man 「立派な方」ポンペイを指す。

84. misplaces 「（呼びかけを）取り違える」

85-86. saving your honour's reverence 「閣下に申しあげるのは失礼ながら」

86. stewed prunes 干しプラムを煮たもの。当時、梅毒予防や治療の効能があるとされ、娼家で出す定番の食べ物だった。転じて「娼婦」自体も含意するため、ポンペイは「失礼ながら」と断った。

87. at that very distant time 「ちょうどその時（at that very instant time）」と言うべきところ。ポンペイはわざとエルボーのマネをして言い間違っている。

89. china dishes 当時、中国製陶器は非常に高価だった。売春宿ではもちろん見かけない。

good dishes — 90

ESCALUS   Go to, go to, no matter for the dish, sir.

POMPEY   No indeed, sir, not of a pin, you are therein in the
right; but to the point. As I say, this Mistress Elbow, being, as
I say, with child, and being great-bellied, and longing, as I
said, for prunes; and having but two in the dish, as I said, 95
Master Froth here, this very man, having eaten the rest, as I
said, and, as I say, paying for them very honestly — for, as
you know, Master Froth, I could not give you three pence
again —

FROTH   No, indeed. 100

POMPEY   Very well! You being then, if you be remembered,
cracking the stones of the foresaid prunes —

FROTH   Ay, so I did indeed.

POMPEY   Why, very well. I telling you then, if you be
remembered, that such a one and such a one were past cure 105
of the thing you wot of, unless they kept very good diet, as I
told you —

FROTH   All this is true.

POMPEY   Why, very well then —

ESCALUS   Come, you are a tedious fool, to the purpose: what 110
was done to Elbow's wife, that he hath cause to complain of?
Come me to what was done to her.

POMPEY   Sir, your honour cannot come to that yet.

ESCALUS   No, sir, nor I mean it not.

POMPEY   Sir, but you shall come to it, by your honour's leave. 115
And I beseech you, look into Master Froth here, sir, a man of
four-score pound a year, whose father died at Hallowmas —
was't not at Hallowmas, Master Froth?

FROTH   All-hallond Eve.

POMPEY   Why very well; I hope here be truths. He, sir, sitting, 120
as I say, in a lower chair, sir — 'twas in the Bunch of Grapes,
where indeed you have a delight to sit, have you not?

92. not of a pin 「意味がない」「価値がない（not worth a pin）」という慣用
表現を踏まえたもの。

98-99. give ... again ＝ give ... back（in change）「お釣りを返す」

102. stones 「（ウメ・モモなどの果実の）核、種」

105. past cure ＝ incurable

106. the thing you wot of 「あなたがご存知のもの」暗に梅毒を指す。

　diet 「食養生、食事療法」

112. Come me to what was done to her 「彼女は何をされたのかに話を進め
ろ」 me は前出の心的与格である。Cf. 1. 2. 159.

113. come ＝ arrive at, reach　ポンペイは同時に「射精する」という卑猥な意
味も込めて使っている。

114. nor I mean it not 「こっちもその意味で言ったのではない。」nor ... not
は否定の強め。

115. you shall come to it 「そこに話を移します」

　by your honour's leave 「恐れながら」

117. four-score pound a year　年収 80 ポンドは、当時としてはかなりの高額
所得。

　Hallowmas ＝ 11 月 1 日の万聖節（All saints' Day）のこと。

119. All-hallond Eve ＝ eve of All Saints' Day

121. lower chair 「安楽椅子」

　the Bunch of Grapes 「葡萄の間」当時の居酒屋には、個室にそれぞれ名前
がついていた。たとえば、ベン・ジョンソンとその友人が定期的に歓談してい
たのは、フリート・ストリートにあった「悪魔と聖ダンスタン亭」の「アポロ
の間」である。

FROTH   I have so, because it is an open room, and good for
winter.

POMPEY   Why very well then. I hope here be truths.   125

ANGELO   This will last out a night in Russia,
When nights are longest there. I'll take my leave,
And leave you to the hearing of the cause,
Hoping you'll find good cause to whip them all.   *Exit*

ESCALUS   I think no less. Good morrow to your lordship. Now,   130
sir, come on. What was done to Elbow's wife, once more?

POMPEY   Once, Sir? There was nothing done to her once.

ELBOW   I beseech you, sir, ask him what this man did to my
wife.

POMPEY   I beseech your honour, ask me.   135

ESCALUS   Well, sir, what did this gentleman to her?

POMPEY   I beseech you, sir, look in this gentleman's face.
Good Master Froth, look upon his honour; 'tis for a good
purpose. Doth your honour mark his face?

ESCALUS   Ay, sir, very well.   140

POMPEY   Nay, I beseech you mark it well.

ESCALUS   Well, I do so.

POMPEY   Doth your honour see any harm in his face?

ESCALUS   Why, no.

POMPEY   I'll be supposed upon a book, his face is the worst   145
thing about him. Good, then; if his face be the worst thing
about him, how could Master Froth do the constable's wife
any harm? I would know that of your honour.

ESCALUS   He's in the right, constable. What say you to it?

ELBOW   First, an it like you, the house is a respected house;   150
next, this is a respected fellow, and his mistress is a respected
woman.

POMPEY   By this hand, sir, his wife is a more respected person
than any of us all.

ELBOW   Varlet, thou liest! Thou liest wicked varlet! The time is   155

123. open room = public room　個室（private room）と異なり、ここは冬場は常に火が焚かれていた。

126. last out = be longer than

128-29. cause ... cause　「訴訟案件（case）」と「理由（reason）」の両義に掛けている。

129. whip　当時一般的な軽犯罪には公開の鞭打ち刑が適用された。

132. Once, Sir?　Escalus の once more（「もう1回言え」）の once をとらえて、「1回ですって？（1回だってない）」と言ったもの。

133. this man　フロスのこと。

137. look in = look into

138-39. for a good purpose = for something useful, helpful, or important

139. mark = observe, watch

143. harm = wickedness

145. supposed　ここも「宣誓証言する（deposed）」と言うべきところ。

　a book = The Bible

149. He's in the right　「彼は正しい、善良だ」

150. an it like you = if it pleases you　「畏れながら」

150-51. respected ... respected ... respected　「（素行が）疑わしい（suspected）」と言うべきところ。

153. By this hand　「この手に誓って、ほんとうに」　ここでポンペイは手をあげて、正式に誓おうとしている。

155. Varlet = Knave

155-56. The time is yet to come that = there was never such a time that

yet to come that she was ever respected with man, woman, or child.

POMPEY   Sir, she was respected with him before he married with her.

ESCALUS   Which is the wiser here, Justice or Iniquity? Is this   160
true?

ELBOW   O thou caitiff! O thou varlet! O thou wicked Hannibal!
I respected with her, before I was married to her? If ever I was
respected with her, or she with me, let not your worship think
me the poor Duke's officer. Prove this, thou wicked Hannibal,   165
or I'll have mine action of battery on thee.

ESCALUS   If he took you a box o'the ear, you might have your
action of slander too.

ELBOW   Marry, I thank your good worship for it. What is't
your worship's pleasure I shall do with this wicked caitiff?   170

ESCALUS   Truly, officer, because he hath some offences in him
that thou wouldst discover if thou couldst, let him continue
in his courses, till thou know'st what they are.

ELBOW   Marry, I thank your worship for it. Thou seest, thou
wicked varlet now, what's come upon thee. Thou art to   175
continue now, thou varlet, thou art to continue.

ESCALUS   Where were you born, friend?

FROTH   Here in Vienna, Sir.

ESCALUS   Are you of four score pounds a year?

FROTH   Yes, an't please you, sir.   180

ESCALUS   So. [*To Pompey*] What trade are you of, sir?

POMPEY   A tapster, a poor widow's tapster.

ESCALUS   Your mistress' name?

POMPEY   Mistress Overdone.

ESCALUS   Hath she had any more than one husband?   185

POMPEY   Nine, sir: Overdone by the last.

ESCALUS   Nine? Come hither to me, Master Froth. Master
Froth, I would not have you acquainted with tapsters; they

158. respected　ポンペイはわざと suspected の代わりに respected と言って、エルボーの言い間違いをからかっている。

160. Justice or Iniquity　Justice はエルボー、Iniquity はポンペイを指す。ともに中世道徳劇に登場するおなじみの役名。エスカラスは両者が言い間違いを連発するので、「どちらの頭がまともなのだ（Which is the wiser）」と嘆いている。

162. Hannibal　「（カルタゴの名将）ハンニバル」「食人種、野蛮人（cannibal）」と綴りが似ているため、当時はよく混同して使われた。たとえば *Henry IV, Part II* [2. 4] でも、ピストルが Hannibal と言うべきところを Cannibal と誤用している。

163-64. I respected with her, before I was married to her?　「婚前交渉」というこの芝居の中心モティーフが、ここでは喜劇的レヴェルでも展開されている。

165. poor Duke's officer　l. 46 と同じく Duke's poor officer と言うべきところ。

166. have ... action of battery　「暴行で訴える」エルボーは次行の名誉毀損（slander）と取り違えている。

167-68. have ... action of slander　「名誉毀損で訴える」エスカラスもエルボーの言い間違いをからかっている。ちなみに slander もこの芝居の中心モティーフのひとつ。

172. discover = reveal

173. courses = conducts

175-76. to continue ... to continue　エルボーはエスカラスの continue「捨て置く」（l. 172）を、刑罰の一種と勘違いしている。

179. four score pounds a year　エスカラスは年収からフロスの身分を確認している。

185. any more than one husband　女将の名前が「ヤリ過ぎ（overdone）」なので、エスカラスは冗談めかして、亭主の数を聞いている。

186. Overdone by the last　「オーヴァーダンは最後の亭主の名字です」。もちろん、「最後の亭主とヤリ過ぎた（overdone）」という卑猥な意味も効いている。

will draw you, Master Froth, and you will hang them. Get
you gone, and let me hear no more of you. 190

FROTH   I thank your worship. For mine own part, I never
come into any room in a taphouse but I am drawn in.

ESCALUS   Well, no more of it, Master Froth. Farewell. [*Exit Froth*]
Come you hither to me, Master tapster. What's your name,
Master tapster? 195

POMPEY   Pompey.

ESCALUS   What else?

POMPEY   Bum, Sir.

ESCALUS   Troth, and your bum is the greatest thing about you,
so that in the beastliest sense, you are Pompey the Great. 200
Pompey, you are partly a bawd, Pompey, howsoever you
colour it in being a tapster, are you not? Come, tell me true, it
shall be the better for you.

POMPEY   Truly sir, I am a poor fellow that would live.

ESCALUS   How would you live, Pompey? By being a bawd? 205
What do you think of the trade, Pompey? Is it a lawful trade?

POMPEY   If the law would allow it, sir.

ESCALUS   But the law will not allow it, Pompey, nor it shall not
be allowed in Vienna.

POMPEY   Does your worship mean to geld and splay all the 210
youth of the city?

ESCALUS   No, Pompey.

POMPEY   Truly, sir, in my poor opinion they will to't then. If
your worship will take order for the drabs and the knaves,
you need not to fear the bawds. 215

ESCALUS   There is pretty orders beginning I can tell you; it is
but heading and hanging.

POMPEY   If you head and hang all that offend that way but for
ten year together, you'll be glad to give out a commission for
more heads. If this law hold in Vienna ten year, I'll rent the 220
fairest house in it after three pence a bay; If you live to see

189. draw you 「(樽から) 酒を出す」に「(犯罪に) 引き込む」を掛けている。

190. hang = make them to be hanged

192. taphouse = ale house, tavern

　　drawn in 「引っ張り込まれる」だが、「騙される (cheated)」の意味も掛けている。

198. Bum 「お尻、ケツ」

199. the greatest thing about you 詰め物をしたポンペイの半ズボン (breeches) のことか、あるいは彼のお尻が大きいことを指しているのか?

200. beastliest = coarsest, crudest

　　Pompey the Great ジュリアス・シーザーと覇を競ったローマの将軍大ポンペイ (106-48 B.C.) に掛けたジョーク。

202. colour = disguise

204. would live = wants to make a living

210. geld and splay ともに「(動物を) 去勢する」の意味だが、通常 geld はオス、splay はメスに用いる。ポンペイにとっては、人間も動物も性欲や性交という点ではさしたる違いはない。

213. they will to't = they will go to sexual intercourse　it には卑猥な含みがある。

214. take order 「取り締まる」

　　the drabs and the knaves = the prostitutes and the customers

216. is ... beginning = are ... under way

　　pretty orders 「ちょっとした取り締まり」

217. heading = beheading

219-20. give out a commission for more heads = publish a legal order authorizing procreation

220. hold = be valid

221. after three pence a bay 「一区画につき3ペンスで」

　　bay = the space lying under one gable, or included between two party-walls (*OED*)

this come to pass, say Pompey told you so.

ESCALUS   Thank you, good Pompey, and in requital of your prophecy, hark you. I advise you let me not find you before me again upon any complaint whatsoever; no, not for 225 dwelling where you do. If I do, Pompey, I shall beat you to your tent and prove a shrewd Caesar to you; in plain dealing, Pompey, I shall have you whipped. So for this time, Pompey, fare you well.

POMPEY   I thank your worship for your good counsel — [*aside*] 230 but I shall follow it as the flesh and fortune shall better determine.

Whip me? no, no, let carman whip his jade,
The valiant heart's not whipped out of his trade.   *Exit*

ESCALUS   Come hither to me, Master Elbow; come hither, 235 Master Constable. How long have you been in this place of constable?

ELBOW   Seven year and a half, sir.

ESCALUS   I thought by the readiness in the office you had continued in it some time. You say seven years together?   240

ELBOW   And a half, sir.

ESCALUS   Alas, it hath been great pains to you; they do you wrong to put you so oft upon't. Are there not men in your ward sufficient to serve it?

ELBOW   Faith, sir, few of any wit in such matters. As they are 245 chosen, they are glad to choose me for them; I do it for some piece of money, and go through with all.

ESCALUS   Look you bring me in the names of some six or seven, the most sufficient of your parish.

ELBOW   To your worship's house, sir?   250

ESCALUS   To my house. Fare you well.   [*Exit Elbow*]
What's a clock, think you?

JUSTICE   Eleven, sir.

ESCALUS   I pray you home to dinner with me.

222. come to pass　「実現する、起こる」

225. complaint = accusation

226. dwelling where you do = brothel where you live

226-27. I shall beat you to your tent and prove a shrewd Caesar to you　大
ポンペイがファルサリアの戦い（48 B.C.）でシーザーに大敗した際、自らの
テントに退却したというローマ史の故事を踏まえたからかい。　shrewd =
severe

227. in plain dealing = putting it plainly

231. follow it = practice this calling　　**flesh**　「肉欲」

233. carman = driver of a horse and cart

**233-34. let carmen whip his jade, / The valiant heart' not whipped out of his
trade**　この劇に頻出する格言的な表現のひとつ。ここは二行連句になってい
る。

239. readiness　「精通、熟練」

243. put you so oft upon't = elect you to the position so often

244. ward = administrative district（of the city）

　　sufficient = competent enough

245. wit = intelligence

247. go through with all = carry out all the duties

248. Look you　「いいかい」

253. Eleven　当時の標準的な正餐（dinner）の時間。

JUSTICE   I humbly thank you.   255

ESCALUS   It grieves me for the death of Claudio,

But there's no remedy.

JUSTICE   Lord Angelo is severe.

ESCALUS   It is but needful.

Mercy is not itself that oft looks so;

Pardon is still the nurse of second woe.   260

But yet, poor Claudio! There is no remedy.

Come, sir.   *Exeunt*

[ACT II, SCENE II]

Enter Provost [and a] Servant

SERVANT   He's hearing of a cause; he will come straight.

I'll tell him of you.

PROVOST   Pray you do.   [*Exit Servant*]

                                I'll know

His pleasure, maybe he will relent. Alas,

He hath but as offended in a dream.

All sects, all ages smack of this vice, and he   5

To die for't?

Enter Angelo

ANGELO   Now what's the matter, Provost?

PROVOST   Is it your will Claudio shall die tomorrow?

ANGELO   Did not I tell thee yea? Hadst thou not order?

Why dost thou ask again?

PROVOST   Lest I might be too rash.

Under your good correction, I have seen   10

When, after execution, judgement hath

Repented o'er his doom.

ANGELO   Go to, let that be mine.

Do you your office, or give up your place,

259-60. Mercy is not itself that oft looks so; / Pardon is still the nurse of second woe 「慈悲はしばしばほどこせば慈悲ではなくなるし、恩赦は常に次の禍いの温床になる」これもこの劇に頻出することわざ的表現のひとつ。

262. There is no remedy 「どうしようもない」l. 258 行目と同じ表現の繰り返し。エスカラスの性格がよくあらわれている。

〔2. 2〕あらすじ……………………………………………………………………………………………

　監獄長がクローディオの処刑について、アンジェロに再考を促すが一蹴される。そこへルーチオとともにイザベラが登場して、クローディオの命乞いをするが、アンジェロは大義名分を振りかざして、これも容赦なく拒絶する。だがその途中でイザベラに対する邪悪な欲望をかきたてられたアンジェロは、訴えを考慮するから明朝もう一度訪ねるようにと彼女に命じる。

……

1. cause 「訴訟（事件）」

3. His pleasure = his will
relent 「不憫に思う、折れる」

4. He クローディオを指す。

5. sects = classes or ranks（of people）
smack of = have a flavor of, share in

10. Under your good correction = correct me if I was wrong　目上・権力者に対する謙譲の表現。

11. judgement ここでは擬人化して裁判官の意。

12. doom 「判決」
mine = my business

And you shall well be spared.

Provost   I crave your honour's pardon.
What shall be done, sir, with the groaning Juliet?   15
She's very near her hour.

Angelo   Dispose of her
To some more fitter place, and that with speed.

[Enter Servant]

Servant   Here is the sister of the man condemned,
Desires access to you.

Angelo   Hath he a sister?

Provost   Ay, my good lord, a very virtuous maid,   20
And to be shortly of a sisterhood,
If not already.

Angelo   Well, let her be admitted.   *[Exit Servant]*
See you the fornicatress be removed.
Let her have needful, but not lavish means.
There shall be order for't.

Enter Lucio and Isabella

Provost   Save your honour.   25

Angelo   Stay a little while. *[To Isabella]* You're welcome; what's
your will?

Isabella   I am a woeful suitor to your honour,
Please but your honour hear me.

Angelo   Well, what's your suite?

Isabella   There is a vice that most I do abhor,
And most desire should meet the blow of justice;   30
For which I would not plead, but that I must,
For which I must not plead, but that I am
At war 'twixt will and will not.

Angelo   Well, the matter?

Isabella   I have a brother is condemned to die.

14. well be spared = easily be dispensed with

15. groaning 「(陣痛で) 呻いている」

16. hour 「(出産の) 刻限」

　Dispose of = put away

17. more fitter こうした double comparative は、シェイクスピアでは珍しくない。

23. See Cf. 2. 1. 33.

　fornicatress 「淫婦」アンジェロから見たジュリエッタ像。

24. needful = necessary

25. [May God] **Save your honour** 監獄長の退出の挨拶。

26. Stay a little while ここでわざわざ引き止めたのは、監獄長をイザベラとの面会に立ち会わせ、ルーチオと一緒にいわばコーラスの役をさせるためのシェイクスピアの工夫。

　what's your will? = What do you want?

30. blow of justice = punishment

31-32. but that ... but that ... ともに「…ということにならない限り (unless)」の意味。

33. 'twixt will and will not will は助動詞を名詞化して用いたもの。

　matter = point in question

I do beseech you let it be his fault, 35
  And not my brother.
Provost [*Aside*]   Heaven give thee moving graces!
Angelo   Condemn the fault, and not the actor of it?
  Why, every fault's condemned ere it be done.
  Mine were the very cipher of a function,
  To fine the faults, whose fine stands in record, 40
  And let go by the actor.
Isabella   O just but severe law!
  I had a brother, then. Heaven keep your honour.
Lucio [*To Isabella*] Give't not o'er so; to him again, entreat him,
  Kneel down before him, hang upon his gown.
  You are too cold; if you should need a pin, 45
  You could not with more tame a tongue desire it.
  To him, I say.
Isabella   Must he needs die?
Angelo   Maiden, no remedy.
Isabella   Yes, I do think that you might pardon him,
  And neither heaven, nor man grieve at the mercy. 50
Angelo   I will not do't.
Isabella   But can you if you would?
Angelo   Look what I will not, that I cannot do.
Isabella   But might you do't, and do the world no wrong,
  If so your heart were touched with that remorse
  As mine is to him?
Angelo   He's sentenced, 'tis too late. 55
Lucio [*To Isabella*] You are too cold.
Isabella   Too late? Why, no, I that do speak a word
  May call it again. Well, believe this:
  No ceremony that to great ones longs,
  Not the king's crown, nor the deputed sword, 60
  The marshal's truncheon, nor the judge's robe
  Become them with one half so good a grace

35-36. let it be his fault, / And not my brother　当時、広く知られていた 'Hate not the person but the vice' ということわざを踏まえている。

36. moving graces = gift of persuasion

37. actor = doer

38. condemned ere it be done = condemned by the law before it has even been carried out

39. Mine = my function

the very cipher of a function = a very insignificant function　cipher は 「ゼロ」の意。

40. fine ... fine = penalize ... punishment

stand in record = is set down in regal records

41. let go by the actor　「罪を犯した者を見過ごす」

42. I had a brother = I have no more a brother

44. gown　「法服」

45. cold　「あっさりした、素っ気ない」

pin = a trifle thing

46. with more tame a tongue　「より気のない言い方で」

tame = spiritless

49. Yes　前行の no remedy に対して、イザベラは Yes, there is a remedy と反論している。

52. Look what = whatever

53. But might you do't　前行の「する気がない」というアンジェロの応答に対し、イザベラは「もしする気になれば、できるということですか?」と食い下がる。

54. remorse = compassion, pity

57-58. I that do speak a word / May call it again　イザベラは 'A word spoken cannot be called back' ということわざ表現を否定形で使うことで、「手遅れだ ('tis too late)」というアンジェロの態度に反駁(はんばく)している。

59. ceremony = external symbol of state

longs = belongs, pertains

60. deputed sword　「(神や王侯の) 代理の正義の剣」

61. marshal's truncheon　「式部長官の職杖」ちなみに式部長官 (Earl Marshal) は、王室式典を主宰する重要な役職である。

62. grace = gracefulness, elegance の意だが、「神の恩寵」という含みもあり。

As mercy does.
  If he had been as you, and you as he,
  You would have slipped like him, but he like you   65
  Would not have been so stern.
ANGELO   Pray you be gone.
ISABELLA   I would to heaven I had your potency,
  And you were Isabel; should it then be thus?
  No, I would tell what 'twere to be a judge,
  And what a prisoner.   70
LUCIO   [*Aside*]   Ay, touch him, there's the vein.
ANGELO   Your brother is a forfeit of the law,
  And you but waste your words.
ISABELLA   Alas, alas!
  Why all the souls that were, were forfeit once,
  And He that might the vantage best have took   75
  Found out the remedy. How would you be
  If He which is the top of judgement should
  But judge you as you are? O, think on that,
  And mercy then will breathe within your lips
  Like man new made.
ANGELO   Be you content, fair maid.   80
  It is the law, not I, condemn your brother.
  Were he my kinsman, brother, or my son,
  It should be thus with him. He must die tomorrow.
ISABELLA   Tomorrow? O, that's sudden! Spare him, spare him!
  He's not prepared for death. Even for our kitchens   85
  We kill the fowl of season. Shall we serve heaven
  With less respect than we do minister
  To our gross selves? Good, good my lord, bethink you:
  Who is it that hath died for this offence?
  There's many have committed it.
LUCIO   [*Aside*]   Ay, well said.   90
ANGELO   The law hath not been dead, though it hath slept.

65. slipped ＝ fallen into error, sinned

67. I would to heaven ＝ I wish

69. tell 「知る、わかる」

71. touch him ＝ hit him

there's the vein「脈がある、その調子だ」 vein は「（思考、行動などの）方向、流れ」の意。

72. a forfeit of the law ＝ one who has forfeited his life by breaking the law

74-76. Why all the souls ... Found out the remedy ここも聖書を踏まえている。 ⇒後注

75,77. He ＝ God

75. vantage ＝ opportunity（to punish mankind）

79. breathe ＝ to give forth audible sound, to speak（*OED*）

80. Like man new made ＝ regenerate man, one saved and assured of salvation ここもあきらかに聖書を踏まえた表現。

86. of season ＝ in season, in the best state of eating

87. respect ＝ care, attention

minister 「世話をする」

88. gross ＝ physical, bodily（as opposed to spiritual）

bethink you ＝ reflect, consider

Those many had not dared to do that evil
If the first that did the edict infringe
Had answered for his deed. Now 'tis awake,
Takes note of what is done, and like a prophet   95
Looks in a glass that shows what future evils
Either now, or by remissness, new conceived,
And so in progress to be hatched and borne,
Are now to have no successive degrees,
But here they live to end.

ISABELLA   Yet show some pity.   100

ANGELO   I show it most of all when I show justice,
For then I pity those I do not know,
Which a dismissed offence would after gall,
And do him right, that answering one foul wrong
Lives not to act another. Be satisfied.   105
Your brother dies tomorrow. Be content.

ISABELLA   So you must be the first that gives this sentence,
And he, that suffers. O, it is excellent
To have a giant's strength, but it is tyrannous
To use it like a giant.   110

LUCIO   [*Aside*]   That's well said.

ISABELLA   Could great men thunder
As Jove himself does, Jove would never be quiet,
For every pelting petty officer
Would use his heaven for thunder, nothing but thunder.   115
Merciful heaven,
Thou rather with thy sharp and sulphurous bolt
Splits the unwedgeable and gnarlèd oak
Than the soft myrtle. But man, proud man,
Dressed in a little brief authority,   120
Most ignorant of what he's most assured,
His glassy essence, like an angry ape
Plays such fantastic tricks before high heaven

92. evil ＝ sin, crime

94. answered ＝ paid the penalty

96. glass　未来を占うために使う水晶の鏡のこと。

　what future evils　l. 99 の Are に続く。

97. by remissness　「（法を執行する側の）怠慢で」

98. hatched and borne　「殻を割って生まれる」

99. successive degrees ＝ further stages of life

100. here they live to end　「今ここで生を終わらせる」

103. Which ＝ Whom　前行の those を受ける。

　dismissed ＝ forgiven, acquitted

　after ＝ at a later time

　gall ＝ annoy, vex

104. do him right ＝ do justice to him

　that　直前の him を受ける。

108-110. it is excellent ... To use it like a giant　ことわざ的な表現。アンジェロとイザベラは、会話の中で、たびたびこうした応酬をしている。

113. Jove　ローマ神話の最高神。雷を手にした姿で描かれることが多い。

114. pelting ＝ paltry, contemptible

115. use ＝ haunt

　for ＝ in order to obtain

117. Thou　親しみを込めて Heaven ＝ Jove に対して呼びかけている。

118. unwedgeable ＝ incapable of being split with a wedge

　oak　「樫」ブナ科の堅木の常緑樹。神々の王ジュピターの神木。

119. myrtle　「ギンバイカ」芳香性の常緑低木。愛の女神ビーナスの神木であり、暗にクローディオを指している。

120. Dressed in ＝ endowed with

121. what he's most assured ＝ that in which he is certain, confident about　次行の glassy essence と同格。

122. glassy　(1) frail as glass　(2) as though seen or reflected in a mirror

　essence ＝ nature

123. fantastic ＝ grotesque

　tricks ＝ foolish acts

As makes the angels weep, who with our spleens
Would all themselves laugh mortal.   125
LUCIO [*Aside*]   O, to him, to him wench, he will relent,
  He's coming, I perceive't.
PROVOST [*Aside*]   Pray heaven she win him.
ISABELLA   We cannot weigh our brother with ourself.
  Great men may jest with saints; 'tis wit in them,
  But in the less, foul profanation.   130
LUCIO [*Aside*]   Thou'rt i'the right, girl, more o'that.
ISABELLA   That in the captain's but a choleric word
  Which in the soldier is flat blasphemy.
LUCIO [*Aside*]   Art advised o'that? More on't.
ANGELO   Why do you put these sayings upon me?   135
ISABELLA   Because authority, though it err like others,
  Hath yet a kind of medicine in itself
  That skins the vice o'the top. Go to your bosom,
  Knock there, and ask your heart what it doth know
  That's like my brother's fault; if it confess   140
  A natural guiltiness, such as is his,
  Let it not sound a thought upon your tongue
  Against my brother's life.
ANGELO [*Aside*]   She speaks, and 'tis such sense
  That my sense breeds with it. [*To her*] Fare you well.   145
ISABELLA   Gentle my lord, turn back.
ANGELO   I will bethink me. Come again tomorrow.
ISABELLA   Hark how I'll bribe you; Good my lord, turn back.
ANGELO   How! Bribe me?
ISABELLA   I, with such gifts that heaven shall share with you.   150
LUCIO [*Aside*]   You had marred all else.
ISABELLA   Not with fond sicles of the tested gold,
  Or stones whose rate are either rich or poor
  As fancy values them, but with true prayers,
  That shall be up at heaven and enter there   155

124. spleens 「脾臓^{ひぞう}」当時、笑いをコントロールする臓器と考えられていた。

125. themselves laugh mortal 「死ぬほど大笑いする」

127. He's coming = he is going to yield　もちろんルーチオは coming に卑猥な意味も込めている。

128. We cannot weigh our brother with ourself 「自分を基準に他人を測ることはできない」もちろん、クローディオのことも暗に指している。

129-130. 'tis wit in them / But in the less, foul profanation 「彼ら（偉い方々）なら気の利いたことだが、下々の者ならひどい冒瀆だ」イザベラは以下でも格言的な表現を使いながら、アンジェロとクローディオを比較する。

132-133. in the captain's ... in the soldier is flat blasphemy 「指揮官なら腹立ち紛れの言葉だが、一兵卒なら露骨な罰当たりの言動」

134. avised = advised

135. put ... upon me = apply ... to me

sayings 「格言、ことわざ」

138. skins 「（内側は治っていないが）上部だけを覆う」

141. natural guiltiness = innate sin

142. sound a thought = utter an opinion

144-45. sense ... sense　前者は reason、後者は sensuality の意。

145. Fare you well　アンジェロが唐突に会見を切り上げようとしたのは、ここでイザベラへの欲望を自覚したためか？

148. Hark 「聞く」主に命令法で使う文語。

150. such gifts that heaven shall share with you 「神様でもあなたと分け合いたいと思うような贈り物」

151. else = if you had not bribed

152. fond = foolishly valued

sicles 「貨幣、お金」昔のユダヤの貨幣単位 shekel に由来する。

tested = put to proof, pure

153. stones = precious stones, jewels

154. fancy = individual taste

Ere sunrise, prayers from preservèd souls,
From fasting maids whose minds are dedicate
To nothing temporal.

ANGELO   Well, come to me tomorrow.

LUCIO   [*Aside to Isabella*]   Go to, 'tis well. Away.   160

ISABELLA   Heaven keep your honour safe.

ANGELO   [*Aside*]   Amen.
For I am that way going to temptation
Where prayers cross.

ISABELLA   At what hour tomorrow
Shall I attend your lordship?

ANGELO   At any time 'fore noon.

ISABELLA   Save your honour.   [*Exeunt all but Angelo*]   165

ANGELO   From thee, even from thy virtue!
What's this, what's this? is this her fault or mine?
The tempter or the tempted, who sins most, ha?
Not she, nor doth she tempt; but it is I
That, lying by the violet in the sun,   170
Do as the carrion does, not as the flower,
Corrupt with virtuous season. Can it be
That modesty may more betray our sense
Than woman's lightness? Having waste ground enough,
Shall we desire to raze the sanctuary   175
And pitch our evils there? O fie, fie, fie!
What dost thou, or what art thou, Angelo?
Dost thou desire her foully for those things
That make her good? O, let her brother live!
Thieves for their robbery have authority,   180
When judges steal themselves. What, do I love her
That I desire to hear her speak again?
And feast upon her eyes? What is't I dream on?
O cunning enemy, that to catch a saint,
With saints dost bait thy hook! Most dangerous   185

156. preservèd = kept from harm or corruption

157. dedicate = dedicated

160. Go to 「さあさあ」

161. Amen 元々「かくあれかし（Let it be so）」の意。イザベラは直前で your honour を「閣下」の意味で使っているが、アンジェロは「あなたの高潔さ」の意味に取って、こう返答している。

163. prayers cross 「(2人の) 祈りが食い違っている」

166. From thee, even from thy virtue 前行（Save your honour）を受ける。彼女の「純潔（virtue）」こそが、アンジェロの官能を呼び覚まし、堕落へと誘惑するから。

168. ha? An exclamation expressing, according to the intonation, surprise, wonder, joy, suspicion, indignation, etc.（*OED*）

169. Not she, nor doth she tempt アンジェロは前行でイザベラを「誘惑者（the tempter）」と呼ぶが、すぐさま自分が誘惑していることに気がつく。

170. violet a flower associated with fragrancy, modesty and chastity（Oxford版） イザベラが喩えられるにふさわしい花。

172. virtuous season = the time of the year that has a power to promote growth むろんイザベラの virtue も連想させる。

173. betray our sense mislead our desire と deceive our intellect の両義。

174. waste ground 「特定の個人に属さない共有地」つまり「娼婦」を指す。

175. the sanctuary 「聖所、聖域」こちらはイザベラを指す。

176. pitch 「(テント等を) 設営する」

evils = sins, crimes

fie 嫌悪の情を表す感嘆詞。ここではアンジェロの自己嫌悪を表している。

180-81. Thieves for their robbery have authority, / When judges steal themselves 「裁く側が自ら盗みをするなら、窃盗をする泥棒にも理がある」

181. What 苛立ちを表す間投詞。

183. feast upon 「〜を大いに楽しむ」

184. cunning enemy 悪魔あるいはサタン。

saint アンジェロ自身のこと。

185. saints = virtuous women 暗にイザベラを指す。

Is that temptation, that doth goad us on
To sin in loving virtue. Never could the strumpet
With all her double vigour, art and nature,
Once stir my temper, but this virtuous maid
Subdues me quite. Ever till now   190
When men were fond, I smiled and wondered how.   *Exit*

[ACT II, SCENE III]

Enter Duke [disguised as a friar] and Provost

DUKE   Hail to you, Provost — so I think you are.
PROVOST   I am the Provost. What's your will, good friar?
DUKE   Bound by my charity, and my blessed order,
  I come to visit the afflicted spirits
  Here in the prison. Do me the common right   5
  To let me see them, and to make me know
  The nature of their crimes, that I may minister
  To them accordingly.
PROVOST   I would do more than that, if more were needful.

Enter Julietta

  Look, here comes one, a gentlewoman of mine,   10
  Who, falling in the flaws of her own youth,
  Hath blistered her report. She is with child,
  And he that got it, sentenced; a young man
  More fit to do another such offence
  Than die for this.   15
DUKE   When must he die?
PROVOST   As I do think, tomorrow.
  [*To Julietta*]   I have provided for you; stay a while,
  And you shall be conducted.
DUKE   Repent you, fair one, of the sin you carry?   20
JULIETTA   I do, and bear the shame most patiently.

88

186. goad ＝ spur, impel

187. sin in loving virtue ＝ loving virtue of Isabella leads on to sin（＝ lust for her） イザベラに対するアンジェロのアンビバレントな感情が反映した表現。

188. double 「二重の」と「偽りの」の両義。

art and nature ＝ her skill as a courtesan combined with her inherent sexuality

190. Subdues ＝ overcomes

191. fond ＝ foolishly doting, infatuated

〔2. 3〕あらすじ‥‥‥‥‥‥‥‥‥‥‥‥‥‥‥‥‥‥‥‥‥‥‥‥‥‥‥‥‥‥‥‥‥‥‥‥

　公爵は修道士に変装して監獄長を訪ね、収監されているジュリエッタと面会する。公爵は深く罪を悔いている彼女に、明日クローディオが処刑されると告げる。

‥‥

1. so I think you are 公爵は Provost と呼びかけてから、自分が変装していることを思い出し、言い繕っている。

3. order ＝ the religious order to which he belongs

5. Do ＝ grant

common right 「あらゆる聖職者が有する権利」

7-8. minister 「世話をする、役に立つ」

10. a gentlewoman of mine ＝ a lady in my charge

11. falling ＝ sinning

flaws ＝ storms, (figuratively) bursts of passion

12. blistered her report ＝ blemished her reputation

17. As I do think, tomorrow ジュリエッタはクローディオの処刑が明日であることを、l. 38 で初めて公爵から知らされる。つまり、この監獄長の台詞は聞いていない。

18. have provided for 「(出産のための) 手はずは整えた」

19. conducted 「(別室へ) 案内される」

20. the sin you carry お腹の中の子供のことを指す。

DUKE   I'll teach you how you shall arraign your conscience
  And try your penitence, if it be sound
  Or hollowly put on.
JULIETTA   I'll gladly learn.
DUKE   Love you the man that wronged you?   25
JULIETTA   Yes, as I love the woman that wronged him.
DUKE   So then it seems your most offenceful act
  Was mutually committed.
JULIETTA   Mutually.
DUKE   Then was your sin of heavier kind than his.
JULIETTA   I do confess it, and repent it, father.   30
DUKE   'Tis meet so, daughter, but lest you do repent
  As that the sin hath brought you to this shame,
  Which sorrow is always toward ourselves, not heaven,
  Showing we would not spare heaven as we love it,
  But as we stand in fear —   35
JULIETTA   I do repent me, as it is an evil,
  And take the shame with joy.
DUKE   There rest.
  Your partner, as I hear, must die tomorrow,
  And I am going with instruction to him.
  Grace go with you, *Benedicite*.   *Exit*   40
JULIETTA   Must die tomorrow? O injurious love,
  That respites me a life, whose very comfort
  Is still a dying horror!
PROVOST   'Tis pity of him.   *Exeunt*

[ACT II, SCENE IV]
  Enter Angelo

ANGELO   When I would pray and think, I think and pray
  To several subjects. Heaven hath my empty words,
  Whilst my invention, hearing not my tongue,

22. arraign = bring to trial

23. try = test　　**sound** = truthful

24. hollowly put on = insincerely assumed

25. wronged you = caused you moral harm

27. offenceful = sinful

29. heavier = more serious, more wicked　当時、違法な性行為では女の方が罪が重いとされることが多かったようだ。家父長制の二重規範である。また「より重い（heavier）」のは胎児の重さゆえという、言葉遊びも読み取れる。

31. 'Tis meet so = it is fitting that you do so

31-35. but lest you do repent ... But as we stand in fear　以下の公爵の説論は英国教会の教義に基づいている。　⇒後注

32. As that = because

34. spare heaven = forbear to offend heaven

35. stand = are

36. repent me = repent myself

37. There rest = stay at that point, remain in that attitude

39. instruction = spiritual advice

40. *Benedicite* = (God) Bless you!　修道士が使うラテン語のあいさつ。

41. injurious love　「残酷な愛」love はジュリエッタの妊娠を指す。クローディオのみが処刑され、自分が妊娠を理由に刑を免れることが injurious であるとの嘆き。

42-43. whose very comfort / Is still a dying horror　「恐ろしい死の思いがかえっていつもなぐさめであるような（命）」

〔2. 4〕あらすじ……………………………………………………………………

　アンジェロがイザベラへの邪念を独白しているところへ、彼女自身が訪ねてくる。アンジェロは、自分に身を許せばクローディオを釈放するが、拒否すれば拷問の上で処刑すると告げて退場する。イザベラはたとえ兄弟の命を救うためでも貞操を捨てることはできないし、クローディオも姉妹が汚されるよりは潔く死を選ぶはずと語る。

………………………………………………………………………………………

1-7. When I would pray and think ... Of my conception　祈ろうとして祈れず、心の暗部と葛藤するアンジェロのこの独白は、*Hamlet* におけるクローディアスの同様の独白（3. 3. 36-72）を想起させる。

1. think = meditate

2. several = different

3. invention = thinking, imagination

Anchors on Isabel. Heaven in my mouth,
As if I did but only chew his name, 5
And in my heart the strong and swelling evil
Of my conception. The state whereon I studied
Is like a good thing being often read,
Grown seared and tedious; yea, my gravity,
Wherein — let no man hear me — I take pride, 10
Could I with boot change for an idle plume
Which the air beats for vain. O place, O form,
How often dost thou with thy case, thy habit,
Wrench awe from fools and tie the wiser souls
To thy false seeming. Blood, thou art blood. 15
Let's write 'good angel' on the devil's horn,
'Tis not the devil's crest.

Enter Servant.

           How now, who's there?
SERVANT   One Isabel, a sister, desires access to you.
ANGELO   Teach her the way.   *[Exit Servant]*
              O, heavens
Why does my blood thus muster to my heart, 20
Making both it unable for itself
And dispossessing all my other parts
Of necessary fitness?
So play the foolish throngs with one that swoons,
Come all to help him, and so stop the air 25
By which he should revive; and even so
The general subject to a well-wished king
Quit their own part, and in obsequious fondness
Crowd to his presence, where their untaught love
Must needs appear offence.

Enter Isabella

4. Anchors on = fastens on, fixes

   Heaven = God

5. chew = to keep saying or mumbling over（*OED*）

7. conception = idea, thought だが前行の swelling とともに「妊娠」のイメージも喚起する。

   state = statecraft, political writing

9. seared = dried up

   gravity = dignity

11. with boot 「おまけをつけて、熨斗をつけて」

   idle plume 「無駄な（帽子の）羽飾り」おしゃれな若い男のシンボル。l. 9 の gravity との対照。

12. the air beats for vain 「むなしく風になびく」

   place ... form = rank ... ceremony

13. case ... habit = outside ... dress

14. tie = bring into bondage, enthrall

15. Blood ... blood = fleshly nature of man, sexual appetite

16-17. Let's write 'good angel' on the devil's horn, / 'Tis not the devil's crest アンジェロという名前に掛けた言葉遊び。「悪魔の角に「善天使（＝善人アンジェロ）」と書いても、それは悪魔の紋章にはならない（＝性質は変わらない）」当時、悪魔の角はその紋章（crest）であるとされていた。

20. muster 「集結する」当時の医学では、危機に際しては、血液が心臓に一斉に流れ込むと考えられていた。

21. both 次行の And と呼応する。　　**it ... itself** 前行の my heart を受ける。

23. fitness = ability　この行が不規則に短いのは、アンジェロの動揺を表すためか？

26-30. and even so ... Must need appear offence ジェイムズ一世夫妻が1604年3月中旬に、商人たちの様子を見るためお忍びで王立取引所を訪れた時、情報が漏れて民衆が殺到し王の不興を買ったという記録が *The Time Triumphant*（1604）という小冊子に載せられている。エピソードの類似性、そして王自身が群衆嫌いで有名なことも併せて考えれば、この箇所が時事的な言及である可能性は高いだろう。解説4ページも参照。

27. general subject to = common subjects of

   well-wished = beloved

28. Quit ... part = abandon their role

   obsequious fondness = dutiful affection

29. untaught = ignorant

30. Must needs 「〜せざるを得ない」

How now, fair maid? 30

ISABELLA   I am come to know your pleasure.

ANGELO   That you might know it would much better please me
    Than to demand what 'tis. Your brother cannot live.

ISABELLA   Even so. Heaven keep your honour.

ANGELO   Yet may he live a while, and it may be 35
    As long as you or I; yet he must die.

ISABELLA   Under your sentence?

ANGELO   Yea.

ISABELLA   When, I beseech you? That in his reprieve
    Longer or shorter, he may be so fitted 40
    That his soul sicken not.

ANGELO   Ha! Fie, these filthy vices! It were as good
    To pardon him, that hath from nature stolen
    A man already made, as to remit
    Their saucy sweetness that do coin heaven's image 45
    In stamps that are forbid. 'Tis all as easy
    Falsely to take away a life true made,
    As to put metal in restrainèd means
    To make a false one.

ISABELLA   'Tis set down so in heaven, but not in earth. 50

ANGELO   Say you so? Then I shall pose you quickly.
    Which had you rather, that the most just law
    Now took your brother's life, or to redeem him,
    Give up your body to such sweet uncleanness
    As she that he hath stained?

ISABELLA   Sir, believe this, 55
    I had rather give my body than my soul.

ANGELO   I talk not of your soul. Our compelled sins
    Stand more for number than for accompt.

ISABELLA   How say you?

ANGELO   Nay, I'll not warrant that, for I can speak
    Against the thing I say. Answer to this. 60

31-32. pleasure ... it　イザベラは pleasure を「意向」の意味で使っているが、アンジェロはそれを「(性的な)喜び」の意味にずらして、返答している。

33. demand ＝ ask

34. Heaven keep your honour　イザベラはこの台詞で退出しようとするが、アンジェロが yet とさらに言葉を続けたため会話が続く。

39. his reprieve ＝ the time allowed him

40. fitted ＝ prepared

41. sicken　「(魂が)病気になる、絶望に陥る」

43-44. that hath from nature stolen / A man already made ＝ who has killed a man

44. remit ＝ pardon

45. saucy sweetness ＝ lustful self-indulgence

45-46. do coin heaven's image / In stamps that are forbid　「禁じられた刻印を捺して、神の似姿を鋳造する」つまり「私生児を生む」の意。この劇に頻出する貨幣鋳造の比喩のひとつ。Cf. 1. 1. 50

46. easy ＝ insignificant

47. Falsely ＝ illegally, treacherously
　true made ＝ legitimately begotten

48. restrainèd means　「禁じられた手段で」

49. To make a false one　「贋金を作る / 私生児をこしらえる」ここまで貨幣鋳造の比喩が続く。

51. pose ＝ question

52. Which had you rather ＝ Which do you prefer

54. sweet　Cf. l. 45

55. she that he hath stained　ジュリエッタを指す。

58. Stand more for number than for accompt ＝ will be numbered among our sins but we shall not have to pay for them (at the last judgment)
　How say you? ＝ What do you mean?

59. warrant ＝ guarantee as true

59-60. I can speak / Against the thing I say ＝ I can argue a case I don't actually believe in (to test you)　アンジェロはイザベラにあとで問い詰められないように、あらかじめ言い訳を準備している。

I, now the voice of the recorded law,
Pronounce a sentence on your brother's life;
Might there not be a charity in sin
To save this brother's life?

ISABELLA   Please you to do't,
I'll take it as a peril to my soul,   65
It is no sin at all, but charity.

ANGELO   Pleased you to do't, at peril of your soul,
   Were equal poise of sin and charity.

ISABELLA   That I do beg his life, if it be sin
Heaven let me bear it; you granting of my suit,   70
If that be sin, I'll make it my morn prayer
To have it added to the faults of mine,
And nothing of your answer.

ANGELO   Nay, but hear me.
Your sense pursues not mine; either you are ignorant,
Or seem so crafty, and that's not good.   75

ISABELLA   Let be ignorant, and in nothing good
But graciously to know I am no better.

ANGELO   Thus wisdom wishes to appear most bright
When it doth tax itself, as these black masks
Proclaim an enshield beauty ten times louder   80
Than beauty could displayed. But mark me:
To be receivèd plain, I'll speak more gross.
Your brother is to die.

ISABELLA   So.

ANGELO   And his offence is so, as it appears,   85
Accountant to the law upon that pain.

ISABELLA   True.

ANGELO   Admit no other way to save his life —
As I subscribe not that, nor any other —
But, in the loss of question, that you, his sister,   90
Finding yourself desired of such a person

61. the recorded law = the law as already written

63. a charity in sin 「慈悲のこもった罪」アンジェロは「イザベラがクローディオを救うため自分と寝ること」を示唆しているが、イザベラは「アンジェロが法を曲げてクローディオの命を救うこと」と取った。

64-66. Please you to do't, / I'll take it as a peril to my soul, / it is no sin at all, but charity. 「もしそれをして（＝命を救って）いただけるのなら、私の魂にかけて、それは罪ではなく慈悲です。」

67-68. Pleased you to do't, at peril of your soul, / Were equal poise of sin and charity. 「もしお前の魂を危険にさらしても、それをして（＝私と寝て）くれるなら、罪と慈悲はちょうど釣り合うだろう。」アンジェロはイザベラの表現をそのまま繰り返しながら、自分の意図を伝えようとする。

69. it 直前の That I do beg his life を受ける。

73. nothing of your answer = not a sin for which you must answer

74. Your sense pursues not mine = You don't understand my meaning

75. Or seem so crafty = craftily pretend to be (ignorant)

77. graciously = through divine grace

79. tax = accuse

    masks = veils

80. enshield = screened by a shield

82. gross = plainly, clearly

85. appears = is clearly evident

86. Accountant = accountable, responsible

    pain = punishment

89. subscribe 「（しばしば否定文で）同意する、賛成する」

90. in the loss of question 意味が不明瞭なため、「議論の余地はないとして（provided there is no dispute）」あるいは「無駄話として言うが（in idle conversation）」など、さまざまに解釈されている箇所。

Whose credit with the judge, or own great place,
Could fetch your brother from the manacles
Of the all-binding law, and that there were
No earthly mean to save him, but that either   95
You must lay down the treasures of your body
To this supposed, or else to let him suffer;
What would you do?

ISABELLA   As much for my poor brother as myself;
That is, were I under the terms of death,   100
The impression of keen whips I'd wear as rubies,
And strip myself to death as to a bed
That longing have been sick for, ere I'd yield
My body up to shame.

ANGELO   Then must your brother die.   105

ISABELLA   And 'twere the cheaper way.
Better it were a brother died at once
Than that a sister by redeeming him
Should die for ever.

ANGELO   Were not you then as cruel as the sentence   110
That you have slandered so?

ISABELLA   Ignomy in ransom and free pardon
Are of two houses; lawful mercy
Is nothing kin to foul redemption.

ANGELO   You seemed of late to make the law a tyrant,   115
And rather proved the sliding of your brother
A merriment than a vice.

ISABELLA   O pardon me, my lord, it oft falls out
To have what we would have, we speak not what we mean.
I something do excuse the thing I hate   120
For his advantage that I dearly love.

ANGELO   We are all frail.

ISABELLA   Else let my brother die,
If not a fedary but only he

92. credit = influence

94. all-binding　Folio 版では building だが、前行の manacles とのつながりから、現在ではどの版でも binding に校訂されている。

96. the treasures of your body = your chastity

97. this = this person
supposed「仮定上の、想定の」

99.〔I would do〕**As much**

100. terms = sentence

101-103. whips ... rubies ... strip ... death ... bed ... longing　イザベラは自らを殉教者に喩えるが、それは娼婦のイメージとも重なっており、無意識のうちにアンジェロのサディスティックな欲望を刺激することになる。

101. impression = mark
rubies　殉教者が流す血のこと。

103. longing〔I〕**have been sick for**　longing と sick は意味が重複。

106. the cheaper = less expensive, of better value（*OED*)

107. at once = immediately

109. die for ever = suffer eternal damnation

112. Ignomy「恥辱、不名誉」ignominy の古形。

113. of two houses = unrelated families

114. kin to「〜と親類である」　前行の houses を受けた比喩。

116. sliding = moral slip

115-17. You seemed ... A merriment than a vice　アンジェロはクローディオの婚前交渉は merriment だと主張するイザベラが、自分に身を任せることは vice として拒否する性規範の二重性を指摘する。

118. falls out = happens

120. something = somewhat

121. his advantage that I dearly love = the advantage of him whom I dearly love

122. We are all frail　この劇に頻出する格言風の表現だが、*Hamlet* の有名な台詞 'Frailty, thy name is woman'（2. 1. 146）も連想させる。
Else = if that is not so

123. fedary = accomplice

Owe and succeed thy weakness.

ANGELO   Nay, women are frail too.   125

ISABELLA   I, as the glass where they view themselves,
Which are as easy broke as they make forms.
Women? Help heaven! Men their creation mar
In profiting by them. Nay, call us ten times frail,
For we are soft, as our complexions are.   130
And credulous to false prints.

ANGELO   I think it well,
And from this testimony of your own sex —
Since I suppose we are made to be no stronger
Than faults may shake our frames — let me be bold;
I do arrest your words. Be that you are,   135
That is, a woman; if you be more, you're none.
If you be one, as you are well expressed
By all external warrants, show it now
By putting on the destined livery.

ISABELLA   I have no tongue but one; gentle my lord,   140
Let me entreat you speak the former language.

ANGELO   Plainly conceive I love you.

ISABELLA   My brother did love Juliet,
And you tell me that he shall die for it.

ANGELO   He shall not, Isabel, if you give me love.   145

ISABELLA   I know your virtue hath a licence in't,
Which seems a little fouler than it is
To pluck on others.

ANGELO   Believe me on mine honour,
My words express my purpose.

ISABELLA   Ha! Little honour, to be much believed,   150
And most pernicious purpose. Seeming, seeming!
I will proclaim thee, Angelo, look for't.
Sign me a present pardon for my brother,
Or with an outstretched throat I'll tell the world aloud

124. Owe and succeed thy weakness = own and inherit the weakness you refer to

125. women are frail too　アンジェロは前行のイザベラの thy weakness を「あなたのおっしゃる弱さ」ではなく「男性の弱さ」と取り、「女性も弱い」と答えた。

127. make forms = create images (through reflection)

128-29. Men their creation mar / In profiting by them　難解な箇所だが、Oxford 版では以下のようにパラフレーズしている。Men, who were created superior to women, debase themselves by taking advantage of women's weakness.

131. credulous = susceptible　　**false prints**　贋金の鋳造を指すが、同時に insincere persuasion さらには illegitimate pregnancy といったイメージが重なる。　　**I think it well** = I thoroughly agree with you

134. faults = sins　　**shake our frames** = disturb our human bodies

135. arrest = take as security

136. if you be more, you're none = if you insist on remaining a virgin, you are no woman.　ここはもちろん、*Macbeth* の I dare do all that may become a man; / Who dares do more is none（1. 7. 46-47）という有名な台詞を想起させる。

137. expressed = revealed, shown to be

138. warrants = tokens, assurances given

139. destined livery = uniform of frailty, which women are destined to wear

140. I have no tongue but one　イザベラは暗にアンジェロの二枚舌の口説きを非難している。

141. the former language = the more intelligible language he had used earlier

142. conceive = understand（me）

146. license = freedom（allowed by his official state）

148. pluck on others = in order to test others

149. purpose = meaning

151. pernicious = wicked

152. proclaim = denounce publicly　　**thee, Angelo**　イザベラは、ここでこれまでの丁寧な you から、彼女の怒りを示す thee に切り替え、さらに敬称ではなく名前で呼ぶ。　　**look for't** = expect it

153. present = immediate

154. an outstretched throat = mouth wide open so as to make a maximum sound

What man thou art.

ANGELO   Who will believe thee, Isabel?   155
My unsoild name, the austereness of my life,
My vouch against you, and my place i'the state,
Will so your accusation overweigh
That you shall stifle in your own report
And smell of calumny. I have begun,   160
And now I give my sensual race the rein.
Fit thy consent to my sharp appetite;
Lay by all nicety and prolixious blushes
That banish what they sue for. Redeem thy brother
By yielding up thy body to my will,   165
Or else he must not only die the death,
But thy unkindness shall his death draw out
To lingering sufferance. Answer me tomorrow,
Or, by the affection that now guides me most,
I'll prove a tyrant to him. As for you,   170
Say what you can; my false o'erweighs your true.   *Exit*

ISABELLA   To whom should I complain? Did I tell this,
Who would believe me? O perilous mouths,
That bear in them one and the selfsame tongue
Either of condemnation or approof,   175
Bidding the law make curtsy to their will,
Hooking both right and wrong to the appetite,
To follow as it draws. I'll to my brother;
Though he hath fallen by prompture of the blood,
Yet hath he in him such a mind of honour   180
That had he twenty heads to tender down
On twenty bloody blocks, he'd yield them up
Before his sister should her body stoop
To such abhorred pollution.
Then Isabel, live chaste, and brother, die;   185
More than our brother is our chastity.

155. thee アンジェロも、ここで呼び方を丁寧な you から親しげな thee に切り替える。イザベラがすでに手中にあると確信してのことか？

157. vouch = assertion, allegation

158. overweigh = outweigh, crush

159. stifle = be silenced, be choked

  report =（1）narration （2）reputation

161. give ... the rein = allow full scope

  race = natural or inherited disposition（*OED*）

162. Fit thy consent = prepare thyself by consent to

163. Lay by = put aside

  nicety and prolixious blushes = coyness and tedious shyness

164. banish what they sue for = reject what in fact they are eager for

166. die the death = to be put to death　聖書的な表現である。

167. unkindness =（1）harshness towards Angelo （2）lack of sisterly feeling to Claudio

168. lingering sufferance = torture

169. the affection that now guides me most = the mood I am in at the moment

170. you ここでまた丁寧な you に戻る。

171. o'erweighs 天秤ばかりの比喩。天秤は正義の女神のアトリビュートであるところが皮肉。また、貨幣の純度を量る道具でもある。

176. make curtsy to = bow to

177. Hooking = fastening, attaching

178. it = appetite

179. prompture = prompting　シェイクスピアの造語か？

181. tender down = lay down in payment

186. More than our brother is our chastity　これも格言的表現。

I'll tell him yet of Angelo's request,
And fit his mind to death, for his soul's rest.   *Exit*

187. yet = nonetheless
188. fit his mind = prepare him

[ACT III, SCENE I]

Enter Duke [disguised as a friar], Claudio and Provost

DUKE So then you hope of pardon from Lord Angelo?

CLAUDIO The miserable have no other medicine
But only hope.
I've hope to live, and am prepared to die.

DUKE Be absolute for death; either death or life   5
Shall thereby be the sweeter. Reason thus with life:
If I do loose thee, I do loose a thing
That none but fools would keep; a breath thou art
Servile to all the skyey influences
That dost this habitation where thou keep'st   10
Hourly afflict. Merely thou art death's fool,
For him thou labour'st by thy flight to shun,
And yet run'st toward him still. Thou art not noble,
For all the accommodations that thou bear'st,
Are nursed by baseness. Thou'rt by no means valiant,   15
For thou dost fear the soft and tender fork
Of a poor worm. Thy best of rest is sleep,
And that thou oft provok'st, yet grossly fear'st
Thy death, which is no more. Thou art not thyself,
For thou exists on many a thousand grains   20
That issue out of dust. Happy thou art not,
For what thou hast not, still thou striv'st to get,
And what thou hast, forget'st. Thou art not certain,
For thy complexion shifts to strange effects
After the moon. If thou art rich, thou'rt poor,   25
For like an ass, whose back with ingots bows,
Thou bear'st thy heavy riches but a journey,
And death unloads thee. Friend hast thou none,
For thine own bowels which do call thee sire,
The mere effusion of thy proper loins   30

〔3.1〕あらすじ…………………………………………………………………

　修道士に扮した公爵は収監されているクローディオに死への心構えを説く。そこへイザベラが登場し、アンジェロへの嘆願が不首尾に終わったことを知らせる。助命と引き換えに身を許すよう迫るアンジェロをはねつけたイザベラの決断に、最初は賛成したクローディオだが、途中から命に執着して、アンジェロの要求を承諾するよう懇願したため、イザベラは激怒する。物陰から立ち聞きしていた公爵が再登場し、クローディオの命とイザベラの貞潔を共に救う手段として、かつてアンジェロと婚約していたマリアナをイザベラの身代わりに立てる提案をする。

……………………………………………………………………………………

5. absolute = determined

6. Reason thus with life　「命に対して、このように説きなさい」公爵は以下のクローディオへの長い説教で life を擬人化して thou, thee, thy で受けるが、これは同時に聞き手のクローディオへの呼びかけにもなっている。

9. skyey = issuing from the sky

　　influences　「（星が人の運命に与える）影響力」

10. this habitation where you keep'st = this body you dwell

11. Merely = only

13. still = always

14. accommodations = clothing and personal adornment

　　bear'st = carry about, wear

15. Are nursed by baseness = have base or unworthy origins

16-17. fork / Of a poor worm = double tongue of a snake

18. provok'st = call upon, invite

19. which is no more [than sleep]

20. grains　（1）穀物　（2）塵の粒

21. That issue out of dust　(1)土から育った　(2)塵から生じた　Cf. Genesis 3. 19: 'because thou art dust, and to dust shalt thou returne'

23. certain = constant

24. complexion = temperament, disposition

25. After = in obedience to, in accordance with

26. ingots　「金の延べ棒」

27. but a journey　「一回限りの旅（＝人生）」

29. bowels = children　聖書的な慣用表現。

　　sire = father

30. The mere effusion of thy proper loins = the very issue of your own body「腰（loin）」は生殖力の宿る部位とされた。

Do curse the gout, serpigo, and the rheum
For ending thee no sooner. Thou hast nor youth, nor age,
But as it were an after-dinner's sleep
Dreaming on both, for all thy blessed youth
Becomes as agèd, and doth beg the alms   35
Of palsied eld; and when thou art old and rich,
Thou hast neither heat, affection, limb, nor beauty
To make thy riches pleasant. What's yet in this
That bears the name of life? Yet in this life
Lie hid more thousand deaths; yet death we fear,   40
That makes these odds all even.

CLAUDIO   I humbly thank you.
To sue to live, I find I seek to die,
And seeking death, find life. Let it come on.

ISABELLA [*Within*]   What ho! Peace here, grace, and good company.

PROVOST   Who's there? Come in, the wish deserves a welcome.   45

DUKE   Dear sir, ere long I'll visit you again.

CLAUDIO   Most holy sir, I thank you.

ISABELLA   My business is a word or two with Claudio.

PROVOST   And very welcome. Look, signior, here's your sister.

DUKE   Provost, a word with you.   50

PROVOST   As many as you please.

DUKE   Bring me to hear them speak, where I may be concealed.

                              [*Exeunt Duke and Provost*]

CLAUDIO   Now sister, what's the comfort?

ISABELLA   Why,
As all comforts are, most good, most good indeed.   55
Lord Angelo, having affairs to heaven
Intends you for his swift ambassador,
Where you shall be an everlasting lieger.
Therefore your best appointment make with speed;
Tomorrow you set on.

CLAUDIO   Is there no remedy?   60

31. serpigo 「白癬（はくせん）」 creeping or spreading skin disease (*OED*)

　rheum = catarrh

32. ending = killing

　nor ... nor = neither ... no

33. after-dinner's sleep 「午睡、昼寝」当時 dinner といえば、一般的に昼食だった。

34-36. for all thy blessed youth ... Of palsied eld このあたりは難解なためテクストの欠落を想定する編者もいるが、Arden 3 版は because your happy (blessed) youth becomes old (aged) and begs assistance from those yet older, who shake with age (palsied eld) とパラフレーズしている。

37. heat, affection = vigor, passion ほぼ同じ意味で、どちらも sexual connotation がある。

　limb = use of the body

38-40. yet ... Yet ... yet 「それなのに、しかも」

41. makes these odds all even = level these inequalities 以下のようなことわざもある。'Death is the end of every worldly score.'

42. To sue to live, I find I seek to die / And seeking death, find life 新約聖書の有名な教え。　⇒後注

44. Peace here 「ごめんください」

　grace, and good company = May God's grace and the companionship of the angels be yours!

52. SD. *Exeunt Duke and Provost* おそらく、公爵は舞台のどこかに身を隠す演出になるだろう。

54. Why 「そりゃ、もちろん」(間投詞)

56. affairs to = business with

58. lieger 「駐在大使」

59. appointment = equipment, preparation

ISABELLA   None, but such remedy as, to save a head
To cleave a heart in twain.

CLAUDIO   But is there any?

ISABELLA   Yes, brother, you may live.
There is a devilish mercy in the judge,
If you'll implore it, that will free your life,   65
But fetter you till death.

CLAUDIO   Perpetual durance?

ISABELLA   Ay, just, perpetual durance; a restraint,
Through all the world's vastidity you had,
To a determined scope.

CLAUDIO   But in what nature?

ISABELLA   In such a one, as you consenting to't,   70
Would bark your honour from that trunk you bear
And leave you naked.

CLAUDIO   Let me know the point.

ISABELLA   O, I do fear thee, Claudio, and I quake
Lest thou a feverous life shouldst entertain,
And six or seven winters more respect   75
Than a perpetual honour. Dar'st thou die?
The sense of death is most in apprehension,
And the poor beetle that we tread upon
In corporal sufferance finds a pang as great
As when a giant dies.

CLAUDIO   Why give you me this shame?   80
Think you I can a resolution fetch
From flowery tenderness? If I must die,
I will encounter darkness as a bride,
And hug it in mine arms.

ISABELLA   There spake my brother; there my father's grave   85
Did utter forth a voice. Yes, thou must die;
Thou art too noble, to conserve a life
In base appliances. This outward-sainted deputy,

66. Perpetual durance 「終身刑」

68. Through though と校訂している版が多いが、Folio 版の原綴りで意味が通ると判断した。

  vastidity = vastness　おそらくシェイクスピアの造語。

69. determined scope = limited space

  nature = kind

70. you consenting = if you consent

71. bark = strip away (as if stripping bark from the tree)

74. feverous = feverish

  entertain = maintain, cherish

75. respect = regard, value, consider important (*OED*)

77. sense = painful awareness, perception

  apprehension = anticipation

79. corporal sufferance = bodily suffering

  finds = experiences, feels

81. resolution fetch = draw resoluteness or firmness of purposes

82. flowery 「美辞麗句」　full of fine words (*OED*)

83. darkness = death

85. There spake my brother 「それでこそ私の兄のお言葉です」

87. conserve = preserve

88. base appliances 「不名誉な手段」

  outward-sainted = externally holy

Whose settled visage, and deliberate word
Nips youth i'the head, and follies doth enew   90
As falcon doth the fowl, is yet a devil;
His filth within being cast, he would appear
A pond as deep as hell.

CLAUDIO   The prenzie Angelo?

ISABELLA   O, 'tis the cunning livery of hell
The damnedst body to invest and cover   95
In prenzie guards. Dost thou think, Claudio,
If I would yield him my virginity
Thou might'st be freed?

CLAUDIO   O heavens, it cannot be!

ISABELLA   Yes, he would give't thee, from this rank offence,
So to offend him still. This night's the time   100
That I should do what I abhor to name,
Or else thou diest tomorrow.

CLAUDIO   Thou shalt not do't.

ISABELLA   O, were it but my life,
I'd throw it down for your deliverance
As frankly as a pin.

CLAUDIO   Thanks, dear Isabel.   105

ISABELLA   Be ready, Claudio, for your death tomorrow.

CLAUDIO   Yes. Has he affections in him,
That thus can make him bite the law by the nose
When he would force it? Sure it is no sin,
Or of the deadly seven it is the least.   110

ISABELLA   Which is the least?

CLAUDIO   If it were damnable, he being so wise,
Why would he for the momentary trick
Be perdurably fined? O Isabel —

ISABELLA   What says my brother?   115

CLAUDIO   Death is a fearful thing.

ISABELLA   And shamèd life a hateful.

89. settled = grave, composed

　deliberate = precise and careful

90. Nips ... i'the head = to give a decisive check to　元々は鷹が獲物の首筋に鋭い爪で一撃を加えることを指す。

　follies = lewd actions or desires

　enew = drive (a fowl) into the water (*OED*)　前行から鷹狩りの比喩が続く。

92. cast = vomit

93. as deep as hell = very deep　ただしアンジェロが悪魔に喩えられているので、hell も文字通りの意味にとれる。

　prenzie = too precise?　正確な意味は不明。シェイクスピアの造語か？　ちなみに *OED* にも a doubtful word; pro. an error とある。

95. invest = clothe, adorn

96. guards = ornaments, trimmings on a garment

99. give't thee = grant you freedom

　rank = of offensively strong smell

100. So to offend him still = to go on sinning against Angelo in the same way

105. frankly = freely, readily

107. affections = sexual feelings

108. bite ... by the nose = treat with contempt (*OED*)

109. force = enforce

110. the deadly seven　「(キリスト教の) 七つの大罪」具体的には「傲慢・強欲・色欲・憤怒・暴食・嫉妬・怠惰」(pride, covetousness, lust, anger, gluttony, envy, sloth) を指す。

111. Which is the least?　七つの大罪に軽重はないので、イザベラは驚いて (あるいは呆れて) クローディオに問い返している。

113. trick = foolish act

114. perdurably fined = eternally punished

CLAUDIO   Ay, but to die, and go we know not where,
  To lie in cold obstruction, and to rot,
  This sensible warm motion to become   120
  A kneaded clod; and the delighted spirit
  To bathe in fiery floods or to reside
  In thrilling region of thick-ribbed ice,
  To be imprisoned in the viewless winds
  And blown with restless violence round about   125
  The pendant world, or to be worse than worst
  Of those that lawless and incertain thought
  Imagine howling — 'tis too horrible.
  The weariest and most loathèd worldly life
  That age, ache, penury, and imprisonment   130
  Can lay on nature is a paradise
  To what we fear of death.

ISABELLA   Alas, alas!

CLAUDIO   Sweet sister, let me live.
  What sin you do to save a brother's life,
  Nature dispenses with the deed so far   135
  That it becomes a virtue.

ISABELLA   O you beast!
  O faithless coward, O dishonest wretch!
  Wilt thou be made a man out of my vice?
  Is't not a kind of incest to take life
  From thine own sister's shame? What should I think?   140
  Heaven shield my mother played my father fair,
  For such a warpèd slip of wilderness
  Ne'er issued from his blood. Take my defiance,
  Die, perish! Might but my bending down
  Reprieve thee from thy fate, it should proceed.   145
  I'll pray a thousand prayers for thy death,
  No word to save thee.

CLAUDIO   Nay hear me, Isabel —

119. in cold obstruction = with the vital functions stopped, the condition of the body in death

120. sensible warm motion = warm organism capable of sensitive feeling

121. kneaded clod = shapeless lump of earth

delighted = endowed or attended with delight（*OED*）

122. fiery floods　キリスト教で、死後罪人が罰せられる場所とされる lake of fire への言及か？

123. thrilling = piercingly cold, causing shudder

thick-ribbed = piled or compressed into ridges

124. viewless = invisible

126. pendant = hanging unsupported in space　Cf. *Paradise Lost*, II. 1052 にも this pendant world という表現がある。

127-28. that lawless and incertain thought / Imagine howling　この箇所は、欠落があるのか、あるいはシェイクスピアが意図的にクローディオの興奮状態を示そうとしているのか、構文が乱れていて意味が取りにくい。たとえば Folger 版では those **howling** in hell, which uncontrolled **thought** imagines it can hear というパラフレーズが提案されている。

129. worldly life = mortal life

131. lay on nature = impose on human physical constitution

132. To = in comparison to

135. dispenses with = pardons, excuses

137. dishonest = dishonorable

138. made a man = given life again

my vice = my shameful act

141. shield = forbid（*OED*）

played ... fair = was a faithful wife

142. warpèd = perverse, twisted

slip of wilderness = (1) shoot of wild stock　(2) licentious descendant

143. defiance = declaration of aversion or contempt（*OED*）

145. it = thy fate

proceed = take its course

ISABELLA   O, fie, fie, fie!
  Thy sin's not accidental, but a trade.
  Mercy to thee would prove itself a bawd,   150
  'Tis best that thou diest quickly.
CLAUDIO   O hear me, Isabella —

[Enter Duke as a friar]

DUKE   Vouchsafe a word, young sister, but one word.
ISABELLA   What is your will?
DUKE   Might you dispense with your leisure, I would by and   155
  by have some speech with you. The satisfaction I would
  require is likewise your own benefit.
ISABELLA   I have no superfluous leisure, my stay must be stolen
  out of other affaires; but I will attend you a while.
DUKE   *[To Claudio]*   Son, I have overheard what hath past   160
  between you and your sister. Angelo had never the purpose
  to corrupt her; only he hath made an assay of her virtue, to
  practice his judgement with the disposition of natures. She,
  having the truth of honour in her, hath made him that
  gracious denial which he is most glad to receive. I am   165
  confessor to Angelo, and I know this to be true; therefore
  prepare yourself to death. Do not satisfy your resolution
  with hopes that are fallible: tomorrow you must die. Go to
  your knees and make ready.
CLAUDIO   Let me ask my sister pardon. I am so out of love   170
  with life that I will sue to be rid of it.
DUKE   Hold you there. Farewell. *[Exit Claudio]* Provost, a word
  with you.

[Enter Provost]

PROVOST   What's your will, father?
DUKE   That now you are come, you will be gone. Leave me a   175
  while with the maid, my mind promises, with my habit, no

116

148. fie　Cf. 2. 2. 176

149. trade = habit, occupation

150. Mercy to thee would prove itself a bawd　「慈悲をかけることは、あなた
に放蕩を取り持つことになるだろう」

153. Vouchsafe = grant

155. dispense with = give up, spare

155-56. by and by = immediately

157. require = ask

159. attend = listen to, wait for

162. made an assay of = made a trial of

163. practice = exercise

　the disposition of natures = way people think and behave

165. gracious = godly, pious

168. fallible = liable to error

168-69. Go to your knees　「（神に祈るため）ひざまずく」

170-71. out of love with = disgusted with

172. Hold you there = stay in that state of mind

175. [My will is] **That now you are come, you will be gone**　「来てもらった
のは、席を外してほしいからだ」イザベラとのこれからの相談を聞かれたくな
いための指示だろう。公爵が監獄長をまだ全面的には信頼していない様子を示
す。

176. with my habit = along with my clothing

loss shall touch her by my company.

Provost   In good time.   *Exit*

Duke   The hand that hath made you fair hath made you good.
The goodness that is cheap in beauty makes beauty brief in   180
goodness, but grace, being the soul of your complexion, shall
keep the body of it ever fair. The assault that Angelo hath
made to you, fortune hath conveyed to my understanding;
and but that frailty hath examples for his falling, I should
wonder at Angelo. How will you do to content this substitute,   185
and to save your brother?

Isabella   I am now going to resolve him. I had rather my
brother die by the law than my son should be unlawfully
born. But O, how much is the good Duke deceived in Angelo!
If ever he return, and I can speak to him, I will open my lips   190
in vain, or discover his government.

Duke   That shall not be much amiss. Yet, as the matter now
stands, he will avoid your accusation: he made trial of you
only. Therefore fasten your ear on my advisings; to the love I
have in doing good a remedy presents itself. I do make myself   195
believe that you may most uprighteously do a poor wronged
lady a merited benefit, redeem your brother from the angry
law, do no stain to your own gracious person, and much
please the absent Duke, if peradventure he shall ever return
to have hearing of this business.   200

Isabella   Let me hear you speak farther. I have spirit to do
anything that appears not foul in the truth of my spirit.

Duke   Virtue is bold, and goodness never fearful. Have you
not heard speak of Mariana the sister of Frederick, the great
soldier, who miscarried at sea?   205

Isabella   I have heard of the lady, and good words went with
her name.

Duke   She should this Angelo have married; was affianced to
her oath, and the nuptial appointed. Between which time of

177. loss = harm　　**touch** = injure

178. In good time = certainly, very well

180. The goodness that is cheap in beauty = virtue, if it is lightly esteemed by beautiful women

180-81. makes beauty brief in goodness = makes beauty lose its good quality soon.　このあたりは 'beauty and chastity seldom meet' ということわざを踏まえた表現。ハムレットのオフィーリアへの難詰 (3. 1) を想起させる。

181. grace = virtue, piety

　soul = quintessence

　complexion = disposition, character

182. body = main part

　assault = sexual advance

183. fortune hath conveyed to my understanding = I have by chance been informed

184. but that = unless

　examples = precedents, parallel cases

185. substitute = deputy

187. resolve = answer, convince

190-91. I will open my lips in vain 「無駄でも口を開くつもりです」

191. discover = reveal

　government = (1) moral conduct　(2) political rule

192. amiss = wrong, not as it should be

193. avoid = refute, disprove (a legal term)

193-94. made trial of you only 「あなたを試しただけ」

195. presents itself 「姿を現わす、現われる」

195-96. make myself believe = have persuaded myself, am convinced

196. uprighteously = in an upright manner (*OED*)　シェイクスピアの造語か？

197. merited benefit = deserved kindness

201-02. spirit ... spirit = courage ... soul

204. speak = talk, discourse

205. miscarried = perished, died

208. should = was to

208-09. was affianced to her oath = be betrothed by oath　マリアナのエピソードもまた、この劇の「結婚の約束／婚前交渉」をめぐるモティーフの変奏。

209. appointed = arranged

the contract and limit of the solemnity, her brother Frederick 210
was wracked at sea, having in that perished vessel the dowry
of his sister. But mark how heavily this befell to the poor
gentlewoman. There she lost a noble and renowned brother,
in his love toward her ever most kind and natural; with him
the portion and sinew of her fortune, her marriage dowry; 215
with both, her combinate husband, this well-seeming Angelo.

ISABELLA Can this be so? did Angelo so leave her?

DUKE Left her in her tears, and dried not one of them with his
comfort; swallowed his vows whole, pretending in her
discoveries of dishonor; in few, bestowed her on her own 220
lamentation, which she yet wears for his sake, and he, a
marble to her tears, is washed with them but relents not.

ISABELLA What a merit were it in death to take this poor maid
from the world! What corruption in this life, that it will let
this man live! But how out of this can she avail? 225

DUKE It is a rupture that you may easily heal, and the cure of
it not only saves your brother, but keeps you from dishonour
in doing it.

ISABELLA Show me how, good father.

DUKE This fore-named maid hath yet in her the continuance 230
of her first affection. His unjust unkindness, that in all reason
should have quenched her love, hath, like an impediment in
the current, made it more violent and unruly. Go you to
Angelo, answer his requiring with a plausible obedience,
agree with his demands to the point. Only refer yourself to 235
this advantage: first, that your stay with him may not be long;
that the time may have all shadow and silence in it; and the
place answer to convenience. This being granted in course,
and now follows all: we shall advise this wronged maid to
stead up your appointment, go in your place. If the encounter 240
acknowledge itself hereafter, it may compel him to her
recompense; and here, by this is your brother saved, your

210. limit of the solemnity = appointed time of celebration

214. natural = full of brotherly affection

215. portion and sinew = inheritance and mainstay

216. combinate = betrothed, promised, settled by contract（*OED*）

　well-seeming 「外面の良い」

219. swallowed ... whole = retracted

　pretending = alleging falsely, using as a pretext

220. in few = in short

　bestowed ... on 「～に捧げる」と「嫁にやる」の言葉遊び。

221. wears = carries about in her heart

222. marble 「大理石の像」

223. What a merit were it in death to = How praiseworthy death would be

225. avail = benefit herself

226. rupture = breaking off of friendly relations（*OED*）

231. unjust = faithless

　in all reason = quite naturally

234. requiring = request, demand

235. to the point 「細部に至るまで」

235-36. refer yourself to this advantage = entrust yourself to this favorable condition

238. answer to convenience = be convenient to you

　in course = in due course

240. stead up = fulfill, keep

　encounter 「逢びき」

241. acknowledge itself = make itself publicly known

honour untainted, the poor Mariana advantaged, and the corrupt deputy scaled. The maid will I frame and make fit for his attempt; if you think well to carry this as you may, the 245 doubleness of the benefit defends the deceit from reproof. What think you of it?

ISABELLA   The image of it gives me content already, and I trust it will grow to a most prosperous perfection.

DUKE   It lies much in your holding up. Haste you speedily to 250 Angelo; if for this night he entreat you to his bed, give him promise of satisfaction. I will presently to Saint Luke's; there at the moated grange resides this dejected Mariana. At that place call upon me, and dispatch with Angelo, that it may be quickly.   255

ISABELLA   I thank you for this comfort. Fare you well, good father.   *Exit*

[ACT III, SCENE II]

Enter Elbow, Pompey, and Officers

ELBOW   Nay, if there be no remedy for it, but that you will needs buy and sell men and women like beasts, we shall have all the world drink brown and white bastard.

DUKE   O heavens, what stuff is here.

POMPEY   'Twas never merry world since, of two usuries, the 5 merriest was put down and the worser allowed by order of law — a furred gown to keep him warm, and furred with fox and lambskins too, to signify that craft, being richer than innocency, stands for the facing.

ELBOW   Come your way, sir. Bless you, good father friar.   10

DUKE   And you, good brother father. What offence hath this man made you, sir?

ELBOW   Marry, sir, he hath offended the law; and, sir, we take him to be a thief too, sir, for we have found upon him, sir, a

244. scaled = weighed as in scale, estimated

　frame = prepare

245. attempt = attack on her honour（*OED*）

　carry this as you may = manage this affair as skillfully as you can

248. image = idea

249. perfection = completion

250. holding up = sustaining（the trick）

　Haste you = hasten

252. Saint Luke's ウィーン郊外の教区名か？

253. at the moated grange resides this dejected Mariana 「堀（moat）をめ
　ぐらした農家にこの見捨てられたマリアナが住んでいる」 ⇒後注

254. dispatch = settle, conclude（business）

〔3. 2〕あらすじ……………………………………………………………………
　ポンペイがエルボーによって監獄へ連行される。そこへ登場したルーチオは、
ポンペイの保釈金を拒絶したあと、修道士（実は公爵）に向かって、公爵を誹謗
中傷し、公爵が戻ってきたらその発言に責任を取ると公言する。続いてエスカラ
スが登場し、アンジェロの裁きの峻厳さやクローディオへの同情を述べる。
_{しゅんげん}
……………………………………………………………………………………

0. SD. *Enter Elbow, Pompey, and Officers* 公爵はそのまま舞台に残る演出
　になるだろう。

1. if there be no remedy for it, but that you will = if you will

3. drink brown and white bastard （1）procure dark and fair-skinned
　illegitimate children　（2）drink red and white Spanish wine

4. what stuff is hear. 「どうしたことなのだ」 stuff = thing（spoken in
　contempt）

5. 'Twas never merry world since 「昔は楽しかった」当時の成句。

　two usuries = prostitution and money lending

7. a furred gown 当時の典型的な金貸しの衣装。

7-8. furred with fox and lambskins 「子羊の皮に狐の毛皮の縁取りを施した」

8. craft = craftiness（associated with fox）

　richer =（1）wealthier　（2）costlier

9. innocency = innocence（associated with lamb）

　stands for the facing 「上辺を飾る」

10. Come your way, sir ポンペイに向かっての台詞。

11. father 老齢者への呼びかけ。シェイクスピアはエルボーをかなり年配に想
　定しているようだ。

strange picklock, which we have sent to the deputy. 15

DUKE   Fie, sirrah, a bawd, a wicked bawd!
   The evil that thou causest to be done,
   That is thy means to live. Do thou but think
   What 'tis to cram a maw, or cloth a back
   From such a filthy vice; say to thyself, 20
   From their abominable and beastly touches
   I drink, I eat, array myself, and live.
   Canst thou believe thy living is a life,
   So stinkingly depending? Go mend, go mend.

POMPEY   Indeed, it does stink in some sort, sir, but yet, sir, I 25
   would prove —

DUKE   Nay, if the devil have given thee proofs for sin,
   Thou wilt prove his. Take him to prison, officer.
   Correction and instruction must both work
   Ere this rude beast will profit. 30

ELBOW   He must before the deputy, sir, he has given him
   warning. The deputy cannot abide a whoremaster; if he be a
   whoremonger and comes before him, he were as good go a
   mile on his errand.

DUKE   That we were all, as some would seem to be, 35
   From our faults, as faults from seeming free!

ELBOW   His neck will come to your waist, a cord, sir.

Enter Lucio

POMPEY   I spy comfort, I cry bail! Here's a gentleman and a
   friend of mine.

LUCIO   How now, noble Pompey? What, at the wheels of 40
   Caesar? Art thou led in triumph? What, is there none of
   Pygmalion's images newly-made woman to be had now for
   putting the hand in the pocket and extracting clutched? What
   reply, ha? What sayst thou to this tune, matter, and method?
   Is't not drowned i'the last rain, ha? What sayst thou, trot? Is 45

15. picklock 「合い鍵」次行の公爵の反応からして、どうやら性的な含意あり。

16. sirrah = a contemptuous term of address

19. cram a maw = fill a stomach 人間に用いると軽蔑的なニュアンスがある。

21. their ... touches 「客と娼婦の（性的な）交渉」

24. depending = (1) sustained, supported (2) dependent, servile

27. proofs for sin = arguments in defense of sin

28. prove his = turn out to be devil's subject 公爵は prove の意味をずらして、ポンペイをやり込める。

29. Correction = punishment **instruction** = counsel, education **work** = take effect

30. profit = improve

33-34. he were as good go a mile on his errand 「（公爵代理に呼び出されるくらいなら）遠方に使いに遣られるほうがましだ＝なんでもする」ことわざをふまえた表現か？

35-36. That we were all ... from seeming free! 難解な箇所。Arden 3 版では Would that we were all as free from our faults as some people seem to be, and that all faults were free from deliberate concealment〔seeming〕と、パラフレーズしている。どうやら、アンジェロとポンペイを比較しているようだ。

37. His neck will come to your waist, a cord 「ポンペイの首は修道士と同様に、腰帯（＝首吊り縄）を巻かれるだろう」

38. cry = beg for, entreat **bail** 「保釈金、保釈保証人」

40-41. How now, noble Pompey? What, at the wheels of Caesar? Art thou led in triumph? 古代ローマの凱旋行列（triumph）では、捕虜は戦車に繋がれて歩かされた。ルーチオは、シーザーがポンペイウスを破った故事にかけて、ポンペイをからかっている。

42. Pygmalion ギリシア神話に登場するキプロス島の王。自分の彫った女性の像ガラテアと恋に落ち、愛の女神アフロディーテによって、その像に命を吹き込んでもらった。 **newly-made woman** 「新顔の売春婦」

43. clutched = clutching coins to pay for them

44. What sayst thou to this tune, matter, and method? = What do you reply to this mood, subject and style?

45. Is't not drowned i'the last rain, ha? 「この前の雨で、（お前の返事も）流されてしまったのではないのか」ポンペイが黙っているのを揶揄した表現だが、rain に reign を掛けて「前の（エリザベス女王の）治世とともに消えた」という意味にもとれる。また the last rain とは 1602-03 年の冬の洪水への言及という説もあり。 **trot** = bawd (usually applied to an old woman)

the world as it was, man? Which is the way? Is it sad, and few words? Or how? The trick of it?

DUKE   Still thus and thus; still worse.

LUCIO   How doth my dear morsel, thy mistress? Procures she still, ha?   50

POMPEY   Troth, sir, she hath eaten up all her beef, and she is herself in the tub.

LUCIO   Why, 'tis good; it is the right of it; it must be so. Ever your fresh whore and your powdered bawd, an unshunned consequence; it must be so. Art going to prison, Pompey?   55

POMPEY   Yes, faith, sir.

LUCIO   Why, 'tis not amiss, Pompey. Farewell. Go say I sent thee thither. For debt, Pompey, or how?

ELBOW   For being a bawd, for being a bawd.

LUCIO   Well, then, imprison him. If imprisonment be the due   60 of a bawd, why, 'tis his right. Bawd is he doubtless, and of antiquity too, bawd-born. Farwell, good Pompey. Commend me to the prison, Pompey. You will turn good husband now, Pompey, you will keep the house.

POMPEY   I hope, sir, your good worship will be my bail.   65

LUCIO   No indeed will I not, Pompey, it is not the wear. I will pray, Pompey, to increase your bondage; if you take it not patiently, why, your mettle is the more. Adieu, trusty Pompey. Bless you, friar.

DUKE   And you.   70

LUCIO   Does Bridget paint still, Pompey, ha?

ELBOW   Come your ways, sir, come.

POMPEY   You will not bail me then, sir?

LUCIO   Then, Pompey, nor now. What news abroad, friar? What news?   75

ELBOW   Come your ways, sir, come.

LUCIO   Go to kennel, Pompey, go.

[*Exeunt Elbow, Pompey and Officers*]

126

46. Which is the way? How are going to answer me?

46-47. Is it sad, and few words? 「真面目くさって、口数が減ったのか？」
sad = melancholic

47. trick of it = way of the world

48. Still thus and thus; still worse 「どいつもいつもこんな風だ、ひどくなる一方だ」ポンペイとルーチオのやり取りについてのコメント。

49. morsel = a small bite

Procures = provides（women for sexual use）

51. hath eaten up all her beef 「手持ちの牛肉（＝娼婦）がすべてなくなった」

51-52. she is herself in the tub 「自身が（牛肉を塩漬けにする）樽の中にいる」当時の梅毒に対する発汗療法（tub に湯を入れ、下半身を浸けて汗をかく）への言及。

53. the right of it = what is due to it 「当然の報い」

Ever = always

54. powdered ＝（1）preserved with salt （2）undergoing treatment for venereal disease （3）wearing cosmetics

57. Go say ＝ go to say

61-62. of antiquity ＝ long continuance, for many years

64. keep the house ＝ remain indoors（as a prisoner）

65. bail 「保釈保証人」

66. wear ＝ fashion

68. your mettle is the more ＝（1）you will show your courage（'mettle'）more clearly （2）you receive more metal（of your chain）ここも mettle/metal の言葉遊び。

71. Bridget ルーチオの馴染みの娼婦の名か？

74. Then ... nor now 前行のポンペイの「それでは（then）」の意味をずらし、「昔も今も」と洒落ている。

abroad ＝ current in the outside world

77. kennel 牢獄を指す。

What news, friar, of the Duke?

Duke   I know none. Can you tell me of any?

Lucio   Some say he is with the Emperor of Russia; other   80
some, he is in Rome; but where is he, think you?

Duke   I know not where, but wheresoever, I wish him well.

Lucio   It was a mad fantastical trick of him to steal from the
state, and usurp the beggary he was never born to. Lord
Angelo dukes it well in his absence, he puts transgression to't.   85

Duke   He does well in't.

Lucio   A little more lenity to lechery would do no harm in
him. Something too crabbed that way, friar.

Duke   It is too general a vice, and severity must cure it.

Lucio   Yes, in good sooth, the vice is of a great kindred, it is   90
well allied; but it is impossible to extirp it quite, friar, till
eating and drinking be put down. They say this Angelo was
not made by man and woman after this downright way of
creation; is it true, think you?

Duke   How should he be made, then?   95

Lucio   Some report, a sea-maid spawned him. Some, that he
was begot between two stockfishes. But it is certain that when
he makes water, his urine is congealed ice, that I know to be
true. And he is a motion generative, that's infallible.

Duke   You are pleasant, sir, and speak apace.   100

Lucio   Why, what a ruthless thing is this in him, for the
rebellion of a codpiece to take away the life of a man! Would
the Duke that is absent have done this? Ere he would have
hanged a man for the getting a hundred bastards, he would
have paid for the nursing a thousand. He had some feeling of   105
the sport; he knew the service, and that instructed him to
mercy.

Duke   I never heard the absent Duke much detected for
women, he was not inclined that way.

Lucio   O sir, you are deceived.   110

83. fantastical trick = whimsical and foolish act

  steal = steal away

84. usurp the beggary 「乞食の地位を簒奪する」ルーチオは、意図せずに公爵が貧しい修道士に変装していることを言い当てている。

85. dukes it = plays the part of a duke

85. puts ... to't = drives ... to extremities

88. crabbed = harsh, obstinate

90. of a great kindred = having many relatives

91. well allied = have powerful allies and relations

91. extirp 「根絶する」

92. put down = abolished

93. downright = straightforward, normal

96. sea-maid = mermaids

97. stockfishes = dried codfish

99. motion generative = puppet, despite having the organs of generation

100. speak apace = speak rapidly, randomly

101. what a ruthless thing is this in him = how ruthless it is of him (that ...) this は続く for 以下を指す。

102. rebellion of codpiece = illicit sex コッドピースとは当時、男性用ズボンの前あきを隠すためにつけた装飾的な袋のこと。ここでは男性器そのものを指す。

103. Ere = rather than

105. have paid for the nursing 「養育費を肩代わりした」

106. the sport ... the service = sexual action, intercourse

108-09. detected for women = accused of lechery

DUKE   'Tis not possible.

LUCIO   Who, not the Duke? Yes, your beggar of fifty; and his
use was to put a ducat in her clack-dish. The Duke had
crochets in him. He would be drunk too, that let me inform
you.   115

DUKE   You do him wrong, surely.

LUCIO   Sir, I was an inward of his. A shy fellow was the Duke,
and I believe I know the cause of his withdrawing.

DUKE   What, I prithee, might be the cause?

LUCIO   No, pardon. 'Tis a secret must be locked within the   120
teeth and the lips. But this I can let you understand: the
greater file of the subject held the Duke to be wise.

DUKE   Wise? Why, no question but he was.

LUCIO   A very superficial, ignorant, unweighing fellow.

DUKE   Either this is envy in you, folly, or mistaking. The very   125
stream of his life, and the business he hath helmed, must
upon a warranted need give him a better proclamation. Let
him be but testimonied in his own bringings-forth, and he
shall appear to the envious a scholar, a statesman, and a
soldier. Therefore you speak unskillfully, or if your knowl-   130
edge be more, it is much darkened in your malice.

LUCIO   Sir, I know him, and I love him.

DUKE   Love talks with better knowledge, and knowledge with
dear love.

LUCIO   Come, sir, I know what I know.   135

DUKE   I can hardly believe that, since you know not what you
speak. But if ever the Duke return, as our prayers are he may,
let me desire you to make your answer before him. If it be
honest you have spoke, you have courage to maintain it. I am
bound to call upon you, and I pray you your name.   140

LUCIO   Sir, my name is Lucio, well known to the Duke.

DUKE   He shall know you better, sir, if I may live to report you.

LUCIO   I fear you not.

112. your beggar of fifty = fifty-year-old beggar

113. use = custom, habit

clack-dish = wooden dish with a lid carried by beggars and clacked as an appeal for contribution　性的な含意あり。

114. crochets = strange whims

117. inward = familiar acquaintance

shy = cautious

118. withdrawing = departure

120. pardon = excuse me; a polite form of denial

122. greater file of the subject = majority of his subject

124. unweighing = thoughtless

125. envy = malice

126. stream = course, current　　**helmed** = directed, steered　ともに航海の比喩。

127. upon a warranted need = when a warrant is needed

give him a better proclamation = proclaim him to be a better man

128. testimonied = tested by evidence

bringings-forth = achievement

129. envious = malicious

129-30. a scholar, a statesman, and a soldier　公爵は自分のことを、学者、政治家、武人の資質を兼ね備えた、ルネサンス期の理想的な君主であると自認している。

130. unskillfully = foolishly, ignorantly

131. darkened = clouded

133-34. Love talks with better knowledge, and knowledge with dear love = If you truly love him you would know him better, and if you really knew him you would love him more.　これもこの劇に頻出する格言的表現のひとつ。

136-37. you know not what you speak　「君はでたらめを言っている」

138. make your answer = defend

139-40. I am bound to = it is my duty

140. call upon = summon

DUKE   O, you hope the Duke will return no more? Or you
imagine me too unhurtful an opposite? But indeed I can do   145
you little harm. You'll forswear this again?

LUCIO   I'll be hanged first; thou art deceived in me, friar. But
no more of this. Canst thou tell if Claudio die tomorrow or
no?

DUKE   Why should he die, sir?   150

LUCIO   Why? For filling a bottle with a tundish. I would the
Duke we talk of were returned again; this ungenitured agent
will unpeople the province with continency. Sparrows must
not build in his house-eaves, because they are lecherous. The
Duke yet would have dark deeds darkly answered; he would   155
never bring them to light. Would he were returned! Marry,
this Claudio is condemned for untrussing. Farewell, good
friar, I prithee pray for me. The Duke — I say to thee again
— would eat mutton on Fridays. He's now past it, yet — and
I say to thee — he would mouth with a beggar though she   160
smelt brown bread and garlic. Say that I said so. Farewell. *Exit*

DUKE   No might nor greatness in mortality
Can censure 'scape; back-wounding calumny
The whitest virtue strikes. What king so strong,
Can tie the gall up in the slanderous tongue?   165
But who comes here?

Enter Escalus, Provost, Mistress Overdone [and Officers]

ESCALUS   Go, away with her to prison.

MISTRESS OVERDONE   Good my lord, be good to me; your
honour is accounted a merciful man. Good my lord.

ESCALUS   Double and treble admonition, and still forfeit in the   170
same kind? This would make mercy swear and play the
tyrant.

PROVOST   A bawd of eleven years' continuance, may it please
your honour.

145. unhurtful = harmless

　opposite = adversary

146. forswear = deny on oath

　again = on another occasion

147. I'll be hanged first　「(否定するくらいなら) 縛り首になる＝絶対に否定しない」

　thou art deceived in me　「あんた、俺を見損なっているぜ」ここからルーチオは公爵を丁寧な you から、親しげなあるいは見下した thou で呼び始める。

151. filling a bottle with a tundish　「(木製の) 漏斗を突っ込んでビンをいっぱいにする」明らかに卑猥な意味。

152. ungenitured = sexless, without genitals

153-54. Sparrows must ... are lecherous　雀は当時好色な鳥とされていた。

155. dark deeds = sexual act done in the dark

　darkly answered = responded to secretly

157. untrussing = untying the strings that hold up a man's breeches

159. eat mutton on Fridays　当時、教会法により金曜の肉食は禁じられていた。また mutton は娼婦を指す隠語。

　past it = beyond the age for it

160. mouth with = kiss

161. brown bread = coarse rye bread for the poor

162. in mortality = among human beings

163. back-wounding = backbiting, slandering behind a person's back

165. tie the gall up = control or restrain the bitterness

170-71. forfeit in the same kind = liable to punishment for the same offence

171. mercy = merciful person

171-72. swear and play the tyrant　ヘロデ王 (Herod) が登場して暴君を演じる中世の「奇跡劇」への言及か？

MISTRESS OVERDONE   My lord, this is one Lucio's information   175
against me. Mistress Kate Keepdown was with child by him
in the Duke's time, he promised her marriage. His child is a
year and a quarter old come Philip and Jacob. I have kept it
myself, and see how he goes about to abuse me.

ESCALUS   That fellow is a fellow of much license; let him be   180
called before us. Away with her to prison, go to, no more
words.   [*Exeunt Officers with Mistress Overdone*]
Provost, my brother Angelo will not be altered, Claudio must
die tomorrow. Let him be furnished with divines, and have all
charitable preparation. If my brother wrought by my pity, it   185
should not be so with him.

PROVOST   So please you, this friar hath been with him, and
advised him for the entertainment of death.

ESCALUS   Good even, good father.

DUKE   Bliss and goodness on you.   190

ESCALUS   Of whence are you?

DUKE   Not of this country, though my chance is now
To use it for my time. I am a brother
Of gracious order, late come from the See,
In special business from his holiness.   195

ESCALUS   What news abroad i'the world?

DUKE   None, but that there is so great a fever on goodness that
the dissolution of it must cure it. Novelty is only in request,
and as it is as dangerous to be aged in any kind of course as
it is virtuous to be constant in any undertaking. There is   200
scarce truth enough alive to make societies secure, but
security enough to make fellowships accursed. Much upon
this riddle runs the wisdom of the world. This news is old
enough, yet it is every day's news. I pray you, sir, of what
disposition was the Duke?   205

ESCALUS   One that above all other strifes contended especially
to know himself.

175. information = accusation; a legal term

177-78. a year and a quarter old come Philip and Jacob 「次の聖フィリップ
と聖ジェイムズの祭日が来ると1歳と3ヶ月」ちなみに2人の聖者の祭日は5
月1日、すなわち May day である。当時は性的な放縦が許される日だったの
で、ルーチオの子はその日に宿されたという含みがある。

179. goes about to abuse = tries to slander

180. license = licentiousness

181. go to 「わかった（もう言わなくていい）」

183. brother = colleague in office

184. divines = clergymen

185. wrought by my pity = affected by my compassion

187. So please you = If you please 「おそれながら」

188. entertainment = reception, acceptance

192. chance = fortune, lot

193. use = dwell in （*OED*）

194. the See = the Holy See 「教皇庁」

195. his holiness = the Pope

197-98. there is so great a fever ... must cure it = goodness is so ill that
only death can cure it

198. Novelty 「（軽蔑的に）目新しいもの」

199-200. it is as dangerous ... constant in any undertaking 「なんであれ古く
からの慣習にこだわるのが危険だということが、いかなる約束でも守るのが美
徳だということと同じになってしまった」inconstant に校訂して、比較をわ
かりやすくしている版もあるが、ここも Folio 版の綴りを残した。

200-01. There is scarce truth enough alive to make societies secure 「付き合
いを保証するにたるほどの誠実さはほとんど死に絶えた」

202. [there is] security enough [alive] to make fellowships accursed 「友情
を呪うにたるほどの借金の担保は生き残っている」security は前行の secure
との言葉遊びになっている。

202-03. upon this riddle = according this paradox

206. strifes = endeavors, efforts

  contended = strove earnestly

DUKE   What pleasure was he given to?

ESCALUS   Rather rejoicing to see another merry than merry at
anything which professed to make him rejoice. A gentleman   210
of all temperance. But leave we him to his events, with a
prayer they may prove prosperous, and let me desire to know
how you find Claudio prepared. I am made to understand
that you have lent him visitation.

DUKE   He professes to have received no sinister measure from   215
his judge, but most willingly humbles himself to the
determination of justice. Yet had he framed to himself, by the
instruction of his frailty, many deceiving promises of life,
which I by my good leisure have discredited to him, and now
is he resolved to die.   220

ESCALUS   You have paid the heavens your function, and the
prisoner the very debt of your calling. I have laboured for the
poor gentleman, to the extremest shore of my modesty, but
my brother-justice have I found so severe that he hath forced
me to tell him he is indeed justice.   225

DUKE   If his own life answer the straitness of his proceeding, it
shall become him well; wherein if he chance to fail, he hath
sentenced himself.

ESCALUS   I am going to visit the prisoner. Fare you well.

DUKE   Peace be with you.   [*Exeunt Escalus and Provost*]   230
He who the sword of heaven will bear
Should be as holy as severe;
Pattern in himself to know,
Grace to stand, and virtue go;
More nor less to others paying   235
Than by self-offences weighing.
Shame to him whose cruel striking
Kills for faults of his own liking;
Twice treble shame on Angelo,
To weed my vice, and let his grow!   240

210. professed ＝ intended

211. temperance 「中庸、節制」　**his events** ＝ the outcome of his business

211-12. with a prayer ＝ praying　続く may は願望をあらわす。

213. I am made to understand ＝ I am informed

214. lent him visitation ＝ made him a visit

215. sinister measure ＝ unjust punishment

217. framed ＝ devised, contrived

219. by my good leisure ＝ by degrees, slowly

　discredited ＝ deprived of credibility

221-22. paid the heavens ... of your calling ＝ fulfilled your duties as a friar both to God and to the prisoner

223. extremest shore of my modesty ＝ furthest limits of propriety

225. indeed justice ＝ justice itself

226. answer the straitness ＝ correspond the strictness

231-52. He who the sword of heaven will bear ... And perform an old contracting　ここからこの場の最後まで、弱強4歩格（iambic tetrameter）のカプレットになっている。シェイクスピアは、異なる韻律とことわざ的な表現を駆使しながら、ここで、これまでの展開を要約し、同時に劇がこれから結末に向かうことを観客に予告しているようだ。

231. sword　「（正義の）剣」

233. Pattern in himself to know　「身を持って知らせる手本」

234. Grace to stand, and virtue go ＝ (he must have) grace to keep him morally upright, and virtue to provoke him in action

235-36. More nor less to others paying / Than by self-offences weighing ＝ judging others neither more nor less severely than he judges his own offences

237. striking ＝ chastising

238. liking ＝ inclination

240. To weed my vice, and let his grow　意味の取りにくい箇所だが、Oxford 版では to uproot the vice for which I was responsible and at the same time to let his own vice flourish とパラフレーズしている。

O, what may man within him hide,
Though angel on the outward side!
How may likeness made in crimes,
Making practice on the times,
To draw with idle spiders' strings   245
Most ponderous and substantial things!
Craft against vice, I must apply:
With Angelo tonight shall lie
His old betrothèd but despisèd;
So disguise shall by the disguisèd   250
Pay with falsehood false exacting,
And perform an old contracting.   *Exit*

243-44. How may likeness made in crimes, / Making practice on the times
= How may false seeming ('likeness') practice deception on the world

**245-46. draw with idle spiders' strings / Most ponderous and substantial
things!** 「蜘蛛の糸のような些細なもので、重大事を引き寄せる」なお、この
二行連句は前行とうまく意味がつながらないため、多くの編者はここになんら
かの欠落があるのではないかと推測している。

247. Craft = deceit

apply = put on (as though to a wound), use as a remedy

250. disguise = deceitful semblance　アンジェロを指す。

the disguisèd　マリアナのこと。

251. falsehood = deception

exacting = exaction

252. contracting = contract (to marry Mariana)

[ACT IV, SCENE I]

Enter Mariana, and Boy singing

BOY [*Sings*]   Take, O take those lips away,
                   That so sweetly were forsworn,
                   And those eyes, the break of day,
                   Lights that do mislead the morn;
                   But my kisses bring again, bring again,   5
                   Seals of love, but sealed in vain, sealed in vain.

Enter DUKE [disguised as a friar]

MARIANA   Break off thy song, and haste thee quick away.
   Here comes a man of comfort, whose advice
   Hath often stilled my brawling discontent.   [*Exit Boy*]
   I cry you mercy, sir, and well could wish   10
   You had not found me here so musical.
   Let me excuse me, and believe me so,
   My mirth it much displeased, but pleased my woe.
DUKE   'Tis good; though music oft hath such a charm
   To make bad good, and good provoke to harm.   15
   I pray you tell me, hath anybody enquired for me here today?
   Much upon this time have I promised here to meet.
MARIANA   You have not been enquired after; I have sat here all
   day.

Enter Isabella

DUKE   I do constantly believe you; the time is come even now. 20
   I shall crave your forbearance a little, maybe I will call upon
   you anon for some advantage to yourself.
MARIANA   I am always bound to you.   *Exit*
DUKE   Very well met, and well come.
   What is the news from this good deputy?   25
ISABELLA   He hath a garden circummured with brick,

　マリアナが少年の歌を聞いている。そこへ修道士に変装した公爵が現れ、さら
にイザベラが登場する。彼女は公爵にアンジェロとの密会の手はずを報告してか
ら、奥でマリアナと打ち合わせをする。2 人が出てくると、公爵はマリアナに今
夜の企ての正当性を保証する。

…………………………………………………………………………………………………

1-6. Take, O take ... sealed in vain　この歌は英詩の著名なアンソロジー *The
Golden Treasury of English Songs and Lyrics*（1861）に 'Madrigal' とい
う題で収録されたこともあって、シェイクスピア作の有名な抒情詩のひとつに
なっている。

2. were forsworn = falsely promised

4. mislead　「（間違った情報で人を）欺く」

5. bring again = bring back

9. brawling = clamorous, noisy

10. cry you mercy = beg your pardon

11. musical = fond of music

12. so = thus　マリアナは次行の言い訳を信じてくれるように、公爵に頼んで
いる。

13. My mirth it much displeased, but pleased my woe = the music［it］did
not make me happy, but it assuaged my melancholy

14. charm = magical spell

15. provoke to harm = invite to evil, wickedness

17. Much upon = just about

20. constantly = confidently

21. forbearance = withdrawing, absence

22. for some advantage to yourself　「少しはあなた自身のためになるように」

23. I am always bound to you　「いつもお世話になっています」

26. circummured = walled around（*OED*）

Whose western side is with a vineyard backed,
And to that vineyard is a planchèd gate
That makes his opening with this bigger key;
This other doth command a little door,   30
Which from the vineyard to the garden leads.
There have I made my promise,
Upon the heavy middle of the night,
To call upon him.

Duke   But shall you on your knowledge find this way?   35

Isabella   I have ta'en a due and wary note upon't.
With whispering, and most guilty diligence,
In action all of precept, he did show me
The way twice o'er.

Duke   Are there no other tokens
Between you 'greed, concerning her observance?   40

Isabella   No, none but only a repair i'the dark;
And that I have possessed him my most stay
Can be but brief, for I have made him know
I have a servant comes with me along,
That stays upon me, whose persuasion is   45
I come about my brother.

Duke   'Tis well borne up.
I have not yet made known to Mariana
A word of this. What ho, within, come forth!

Enter Mariana

I pray you be acquainted with this maid;
She comes to do you good.

Isabella   I do desire the like.   50

Duke   Do you persuade yourself that I respect you?

Mariana   Good friar, I know you do, and have found it.

Duke   Take then this your companion by the hand,
Who hath a story ready for your ear.

27. is ... backed ＝ has a vineyard adjoining it

28. planchèd ＝ made of planks or boards

29. makes his opening ＝ is opened

33. heavy ＝ （1） sleepy, drowsy　（2） gloomy

35. on your knowledge 「自分の知識を頼りに」

36. I have ta'en a due and wary note upon't 「それについてしっかりと注意深く心に留めました」

38. action ＝ gesture

　precept ＝ detailed direction

39. tokens ＝ prearranged sign or password （*OED*）

40. her observance ＝ what she must do

41. repair ＝ visit

42. possessed ＝ informed

　most ＝ utmost, longest

45. stays upon ＝ waits for

　whose persuasion is ＝ who is persuaded that

46. borne up ＝ sustained, carried out

48. What ho 「（あいさつ・呼び掛けに用いて）おおい、やあ」

50. the like ＝ to do you good

51. Do you persuade yourself ＝ Do you convinced

　respect ＝ have a high regard for

I shall attend your leisure, but make haste,   55
   The vaporous night approaches.
MARIANA   [*To Isabella*]   Will't please you walk aside?
                        [*Exeunt Mariana and Isabella*]
DUKE   O place, and greatness, millions of false eyes
   Are stuck upon thee; volumes of report
   Run with these false and most contrarious quests   60
   Upon thy doings; thousand escapes of wit
   Make thee the father of their idle dream,
   And rack thee in their fancies.

                  Enter Mariana and Isabella

   Welcome, how agreed?
ISABELLA   She'll take the enterprise upon her, father,   65
   If you advise it.
DUKE   It is not my consent,
   But my entreaty too.
ISABELLA   Little have you to say
   When you depart from him but, soft and low,
   'Remember now my brother.'
MARIANA   Fear me not.
DUKE   Nor gentle daughter, fear you not at all.   70
   He is your husband on a pre-contract;
   To bring you thus together 'tis no sin,
   Sith that the justice of your title to him
   Doth flourish the deceit. Come, let us go;
   Our corn's to reap, for yet our tithe's to sow.   *Exeunt*   75

[**ACT IV, SCENE II**]
Enter Provost and Pompey

PROVOST   Come hither, sirrah. Can you cut off a man's head?
POMPEY   If the man be a bachelor, sir, I can; but if he be a

55. attend your leisure = wait until you are unoccupied

56. vaporous = damp（and hence injurious to health）

58. place, and greatness = majestic office

　false = treacherous

59. stuck = fixed

　volumes of report = a mass of rumours

60. contrarious quests = hostile bark of hunting dogs

59-61. このあたりは「猟犬」（volumes of report）が「獲物」（thy doings）を
追うという狩猟の比喩が使われている。

61. escapes = involuntary outbursts of feeling, sallies of wit（*OED*）

62. Make thee the father of their idle dream = attribute to you their own
irresponsible fancies

63. rack = torture, tear apart

65. take = undertake

66. not = not only

69. Fear me not = don't distrust me or doubt me

70. fear you not = don't be afraid

73. Sith that = since

74. flourish = embellish, make fair

75. Our corn's to reap, for yet our tithe's to sow　Arden 3 版 の The crop
[corn] of our plan is still to be harvested [to reap] for we have still [yet]
to distribute [sow] a tenth [tithe] of the seed というパラフレーズがわか
りやすい。　　**tithe**　当時、教会に十分の一税として納められていた穀物。

〔**4. 2**〕……………………………………………………………………………………
　ポンペイは監獄で首切り役人アブホーソンの助手を務めることに同意する。修
道士に扮した公爵は、監獄を訪れ、クローディオが赦免される知らせを待ってい
るが、そこへ届いたアンジェロからの書状には、クローディオを即刻処刑し、首
を届けるようにと記されていた。公爵はクローディオの処刑を延期して、代わり
に死刑囚バーナディンの首を届けるようにと、監獄長を説得する。
……………………………………………………………………………………………………

married man, he's his wife's head, and I can never cut off a
woman's head.

PROVOST   Come, sir, leave me your snatches, and yield me a   5
direct answer. Tomorrow morning are to die Claudio and
Barnardine. Here is in our prison a common executioner,
who in his office lacks a helper. If you will take it on you to
assist him, it shall redeem you from your gyves; if not, you
shall have your full time of imprisonment, and your   10
deliverance with an unpitied whipping, for you have been a
notorious bawd.

POMPEY   Sir, I have been an unlawful bawd time out of mind,
but yet I will be content to be a lawful hangman. I would be
glad to receive some instruction from my fellow partner.   15

PROVOST   What ho, Abhorson! Where's Abhorson there?

Enter Abhorson

ABHORSON   Do you call, sir?

PROVOST   Sirrah, here's a fellow will help you tomorrow in
your execution. If you think it meet, compound with him by
the year, and let him abide here with you; if not, use him for   20
the present, and dismiss him. He cannot plead his estimation
with you, he hath been a bawd.

ABHORSON   A bawd, sir? Fie upon him, he will discredit our
mystery.

PROVOST   Go to, sir, you weigh equally, a feather will turn the   25
scale.   *Exit*

POMPEY   Pray sir, by your good favour — for surely, sir, a good
favour you have, but that you have a hanging look — do you
call, sir, your occupation a mystery?

ABHORSON   Ay, sir, a mystery.   30

POMPEY   Painting, sir, I have heard say, is a mystery; and your
whores, sir, being members of my occupation, using painting,
do prove my occupation, a mystery. But what mystery there

3. he's his wife's head　聖書の以下の表現を踏まえた戯れ言。Ephesians 5: 23 'For the husband is the wives head, eve[n] as Christ is the head of the Church.'

5. snatches = quibbles

7. common = public

8. lacks = needs

9. gyves = shackles, fetters

11. deliverance = release（from prison）

13. time out of mind　「大昔から」

16. Abhorson　「ゾッとするほど嫌う（abhor）」と「娼婦の子＝私生児（whoreson）」をあわせた名前。

18. Sirrah「おい、こら」（身分の低い者に使う）

19. compound = contract

19-20. by the year　「1年契約で」

20. abide = stay

　use = employ

21. plead his estimation = make claim for his worthiness

24. mystery　「（熟練を要する）職業」原義は「奥義、秘訣」。

25-26. you weigh equally, a feather will turn the scale　「重さは同じだ、羽1枚の重さで秤が傾く」つまり「五十歩百歩だ」の意味。

27-28. by your good favour　「失礼ですが」に good favour「立派なお顔」を掛けた洒落。

28. hanging look =（1）gloomy look　（2）look of a hangman

31-32. Painting ... using painting　ポンペイは画家の描く「絵（painting）」を娼婦の「化粧（painting）」にかけて、洒落ている。

33. prove = show ... to be

should be in hanging, if I should be hanged, I cannot imagine.

ABHORSON   Sir, it is a mystery.   35

POMPEY   Proof.

ABHORSON   Every true man's apparel fits your thief —

POMPEY   If it be too little for your thief, your true man thinks
it big enough. If it be too big for your thief, your thief thinks
it little enough. So every true man's apparel fits your thief.   40

Enter Provost

PROVOST   Are you agreed?

POMPEY   Sir, I will serve him, for I do find your hangman is a
more penitent trade than your bawd; he doth oftener ask
forgiveness.

PROVOST   You, sirrah, provide your block and your axe   45
tomorrow, four o'clock.

ABHORSON   Come on, bawd, I will instruct thee in my trade.
Follow.

POMPEY   I do desire to learn, sir, and I hope, if you have
occasion to use me for your own turn, you shall find me yare.   50
For truly, sir, for your kindness, I owe you a good turn.

PROVOST   Call hither Barnardine and Claudio.

Exeunt Abhorson and Pompey

The one has my pity, not a jot the other,
Being a murderer, though he were my brother.

Enter Claudio

Look, here's the warrant, Claudio, for thy death.   55
'Tis now dead midnight, and by eight tomorrow
Thou must be made immortal. Where's Barnardine?

CLAUDIO   As fast locked up in sleep as guiltless labour
When it lies starkly in the travailer's bones.
He will not wake.

PROVOST   Who can do good on him?   60

34. if I should be hanged = if I were to be hanged

38-40. If it be too little ... fits your thief 「その服が盗人にとって小さすぎて
も、正直者はそれを十分大きいと思う。大きすぎるにしても、盗人は少々小さ
いと思う。だから、正直者の服はみな盗人にぴったりだ」この３行もアブホー
ソンのセリフに当てている版も多いが、ここでは Folio 版にしたがってポンペ
イに当てた。ただいずれにせよ、この箇所は hangman が mystery であるこ
との proof にはなっていない。おそらく、当時 hangman が、処刑された囚
人の衣服を与えられるという特典を有していた事実と関係があると思われる
が、これまでの諸版では納得のいく説明は提示されていない。

39. your = used with no definite meaning: often expressed contempt
(*OED*) ちなみに、42-43 行目の your hangman, your bawd も同じ用法。

43-44. ask forgiveness hangman は罪人を処刑する前に、その許しを乞う習
慣があった。

46. four o'clock 監獄長は 56 行目では処刑は by eight と言っている。シェイ
クスピアにときおり見かける不注意か？

50. for your own turn = when you are executed

yare = ready, prepared

51. a good turn = a kind service ここは「情けは人の為ならず（one good
turn deserves another）」ということわざを踏まえている。

56. dead = profoundly quiet

57. made immortal = turned into immortal spirit（by the execution）

59. starkly = stiffly

travailer's bones = labourer's body

60. do good on = prevail on, produce an effect on

Well, go, prepare yourself —

[*Knocking within*]   But hark, what noise?

Heaven give your spirits comfort!   [*Exit Claudio*]

[*Knocking within*]   By and by!

I hope it is some pardon, or reprieve

For the most gentle Claudio.

Enter Duke [disguised as a friar]

Welcome, father.

DUKE   The best, and wholesom'st spirits of the night   65

Envelop you, good Provost! Who called here of late?

PROVOST   None since the curfew rung.

DUKE   Not Isabel?

PROVOST   No.

DUKE   They will then ere't be long.   70

PROVOST   What comfort is for Claudio?

DUKE   There's some in hope.

PROVOST   It is a bitter deputy.

DUKE   Not so, not so; his life is paralleled

Even with the stroke and line of his great justice.   75

He doth with holy abstinence subdue

That in himself which he spurs on his power

To qualify in others. Were he mealed with that

Which he corrects, then were he tyrannous,

But this being so, he's just.

[*Knocking within*]   Now are they come. [*Exit Provost*] 80

This is a gentle Provost; seldom when

The steelèd gaoler is the friend of men.

[Knocking within]

How now? what noise? That spirit's possessed with haste,

That wounds the unsisting postern with these strokes.

[Enter Provost]

62. By and by = just a minute　戸口を叩いている者への返事。

66. Envelop = surround, wrap

67. curfew　「晩鐘」中世の都市では、夜の一定の時刻（8時か9時）に鐘が鳴らされ、それを合図に市民は火を消すことになっていた。

70. ere't be long = before long

73. bitter = severe, cruel

74. paralleled = matched, brought into conformity (with)

75. the stroke and line = straight course　ただ stroke には「（首切り役人の）斧の一撃」、line には「首締め縄」という言葉遊びも読み取れる。

77. spurs on = urges

78. qualify = control, regulate

　mealed = spotted, stained (*OED*)

80. this being so = his life being so virtuous

81. seldom when = (it is) seldom that

82. steelèd = hardened

83. spirit　「人、人物」

84. unsisting　類例がないため、*OED* でも of doubtful meaning としている単語。そのため、例えば unresisting, insisting, unassisting 等さまざまな校訂が提案されているが、どれも決定的とは言えないので、ここは Folio 版の綴りをそのまま残した。

　postern = small back door

PROVOST   There he must stay until the officer   85
  Arise to let him in; he is called up.

DUKE   Have you no countermand for Claudio yet,
  But he must die tomorrow?

PROVOST   None, sir, none.

DUKE   As near the dawning, Provost, as it is,
  You shall hear more ere morning.

PROVOST   Happily   90
  You something know, yet I believe there comes
  No countermand; no such example have we.
  Besides, upon the very siege of justice,
  Lord Angelo hath to the public ear
  Professed the contrary.

Enter a Messenger

DUKE   This is his lordship's man.   95

PROVOST   And here comes Claudio's pardon.

MESSENGER   My Lord hath sent you this note, and by me this
  further charge, that you swerve not from the smallest article
  of it, neither in time, matter, or other circumstance. Good
  morrow; for, as I take it, it is almost day.   100

PROVOST   I shall obey him.   [*Exit Messenger*]

DUKE   [*Aside*]   This is his pardon purchased by such sin,
  For which the pardoner himself is in.
  Hence hath offence his quick celerity,
  When it is borne in high authority.   105
  When vice makes mercy, mercy's so extended
  That for the fault's love is the offender friended.
  Now, sir, what news?

PROVOST   I told you: Lord Angelo, belike thinking me remiss
  in mine office, awakens me with this unwonted putting-on,   110
  methinks strangely, for he hath not used it before.

DUKE   Pray you let's hear.

85. he 戸を叩いている者を指す。

officer = guard

86. he officer を受ける。

92. example = parallel case in the past

93. siege of justice = seat of judgment

95. his lordship's man = Angelo's servant

95-96. This is ... Claudio's pardon ll. 91-92 で監獄長が取り消し命令はこない と断言していることから、l. 95 を監獄長に、l. 96 を公爵の台詞に割り当てる 版が多いが、ここも Folio 版のままで特に支障ないと判断した。

98. swerve = deviate

99-100. Good morrow 時間の経過を観客に自然に意識させるシェイクスピア の巧みな技。

103. is in = is involved in

104. his = its

quick celerity = swift speed

105. borne in = supported by

106. extended = widened in scope

107. the fault's love = love of the fault

friended = befriended（by those in authority who love the sin he has committed）

109. belike = I suppose

remiss = negligent

110. putting-on = spur, urging

111. methinks 「（…と私には）思われる」

PROVOST [*Reads the letter*] 'Whatsoever you may hear to the contrary, let Claudio be executed by four of the clock, and in the afternoon Bernardine. For my better satisfaction, let me 115 have Claudio's head sent me by five. Let this be duly performed, with a thought that more depends on it than we must yet deliver. Thus fail not to do your office, as you will answer it at your peril.' What say you to this, sir?

DUKE What is that Barnardine who is to be executed in the 120 afternoon?

PROVOST A Bohemian borne, but here nursed up and bred, one that is a prisoner nine years old.

DUKE How came it, that the absent Duke had not either delivered him to his liberty or executed him? I have heard it 125 was ever his manner to do so.

PROVOST His friends still wrought reprieves for him, and indeed his fact, till now in the government of Lord Angelo, came not to an undoubtful proof.

DUKE It is now apparent? 130

PROVOST Most manifest, and not denied by himself.

DUKE Hath he borne himself penitently in prison? How seems he to be touched?

PROVOST A man that apprehends death no more dreadfully but as a drunken sleep, careless, reckless, and fearless of 135 what's past, present, or to come; insensible of mortality, and desperately mortal.

DUKE He wants advice.

PROVOST He will hear none. He hath evermore had the liberty of the prison; give him leave to escape hence, he would not. 140 Drunk many times a day, if not many days entirely drunk. We have very oft awaked him, as if to carry him to execution, and showed him a seeming warrant for it; it hath not moved him at all.

DUKE More of him anon. There is written in your brow, 145

115. better satisfaction = greater assurance

117-18. more depends on it than we must yet deliver 「余がまだ言えない重大な結果を伴う」

    deliver = make known

119. at your peril 「危険を覚悟で、自分の責任で」当時の命令文書の決まり文句。

122. Bohemian 当時ボヘミアは、ウィーンを首都とする神聖ローマ帝国の一部だった。

    here = in Vienna

123. nine years old = for nine years

127. still wrought = continually brought about

128. his fact = his crime

129. undoubtful = certain

132. borne himself = behave

133. touched = moved, affected

134. apprehends = anticipates, imagines

134-35. no more ... but = no more ... than

136. mortality = death

137. desperately mortal = irretrievably doomed to die

138. wants = lacks

139-40. the liberty of = permission to go anywhere within

143. a seeming warrant = that which looks like a warrant

145. anon = soon, in a little while

Provost, honesty and constancy. If I read it not truly, my ancient skill beguiles me; but in the boldness of my cunning I will lay myself in hazard. Claudio, whom here you have warrant to execute, is no greater forfeit to the law than Angelo who hath sentenced him. To make you understand 150 this in a manifested effect, I crave but four days' respite, for the which you are to do me both a present and a dangerous courtesy.

Provost   Pray, sir, in what?

Duke   In the delaying death.   155

Provost   Alack, how may I do it? Having the hour limited, and an express command, under penalty to deliver his head in the view of Angelo? I may make my case as Claudio's to cross this in the smallest.

Duke   By the vow of mine order, I warrant you. If my 160 instructions may be your guide, let this Barnardine be this morning executed, and his head borne to Angelo.

Provost   Angelo hath seen them both, and will discover the favour.

Duke   O, death's a great disguiser, and you may add to it. 165 Shave the head, and tie the beard, and say it was the desire of the penitent to be so bared before his death; you know the course is common. If anything fall to you upon this more than thanks and good fortune, by the saint whom I profess I will plead against it with my life.   170

Provost   Pardon me, good father, it is against my oath.

Duke   Were you sworn to the Duke or to the deputy?

Provost   To him, and to his substitutes.

Duke   You will think you have made no offence if the Duke avouch the justice of your dealing?   175

Provost   But what likelihood is in that?

Duke   Not a resemblance but a certainty. Yet since I see you fearful, that neither my coat, integrity, nor persuasion can

146-47. my ancient skill beguiles me = my experienced judgement deceives me

147. in the boldness of my cunning = confident of my skill

148. lay myself in hazard = dare to bet　さいころ遊びの比喩。

149. forfeit = criminal

151. manifested effect = clear demonstration

152. present = immediate

153. courtesy = kindness, politeness

156. limited = fixed, appointed

157. express command　「明示された命令」

158. make my case as Claudio's = make my situation the same as Claudio's

159. in the smallest = in the slightest degree

160. warrant you = guarantee your safety

163-64. discover the favour = recognize the face

166. tie the beard　この表現については様々な校訂が提案されているが、そのまま「（人相をわかりにくくするため）長い髭を結ぶ」と取るのが自然か？

167. bared = shaved

168. course = practice

　fall to = befall, happen

169. profess = avow

171. Pardon me = I'm sorry　丁寧な断り方である。

175. avouch = confirm, vouch for

176. likelihood = probability

177. resemblance = likelihood

178. coat = friar's robe

with ease attempt you, I will go further than I meant, to
pluck all fears out of you. Look you, sir, here is the hand and   180
seal of the Duke. You know the character I doubt not, and
the signet is not strange to you.

PROVOST   I know them both.

DUKE   The contents of this is the return of the Duke. You shall
anon over-read it at your pleasure, where you shall find   185
within these two days, he will be here. This is a thing that
Angelo knows not, for he this very day receives letters of
strange tenor, perchance of the Duke's death, perchance
entering into some monastery, but by chance nothing of
what is writ. Look, the unfolding star calls up the shepherd.   190
Put not yourself into amazement how these things should be;
all difficulties are but easy when they are known. Call your
executioner, and off with Barnardine's head. I will give him a
present shrift, and advise him for a better place. Yet you are
amazed, but this shall absolutely resolve you. Come away, it   195
is almost clear dawn.   [*Exeunt*]

[ACT IV, SCENE III]

Enter Pompey

POMPEY   I am as well-acquainted here as I was in our house of
profession. One would think it were Mistress Overdone's
own house, for here be many of her old customers. First,
here's young Master Rash, he's in for a commodity of brown
paper and old ginger, nine score and seventeen pounds, of   5
which he made five marks ready money. Marry, then ginger
was not much in request, for the old women were all dead.
Then is there here one Master Caper, at the suit of Master
Three-pile the mercer, for some four suits of peach-coloured
satin, which now peaches him a beggar. Then have we here,   10
young Dizzy and young Master Deep-vow, and Master

179. attempt = tempt, win

180-81. here is the hand and seal　公爵はここでおそらく監獄長に、蠟（ろう）で封印（seal）された公爵直筆（hand）の手紙を示す。

181. character =（an individual's）handwriting

182. signet　「（指輪に彫った）認印」公爵が見せた手紙の封印に押してある。

188. tenor　「趣旨」

189. by chance = as it falls out, incidentally　前行の perchance との言葉遊び。

190. writ = written here　　**the unfolding star calls up the shepherd**　「明けの明星が（羊の群れを野に放てと）羊飼いを起こしている」シェイクスピアは牧歌の伝統を踏まえた表現を使って、巧みに時の経過を示している。

192. all difficulties are ... are known　'Everything is easy after it has been done'ということわざを踏まえた表現。

194. shrift = confession（made to a priest）

195. this　公爵が示した手紙　　**resolve you** = answer your doubts

196. clear = bright

〔4. 3〕あらすじ・・・
　ポンペイが死刑囚バーナディンを迎えに行くが、彼は泥酔しており処刑を拒否する。修道士に扮した公爵は監獄長に諮（はか）って、ちょうど熱病で死んだラゴージンという囚人の首を代わりにアンジェロに届け、クローディオは秘密の監房に入れることにする。さらに公爵は、そこへ登場したイザベラに、アンジェロの命によってクローディオはすでに処刑されたと偽り、明日になれば公爵が帰国するので、アンジェロの悪行について直訴するようにと指示する。
・・・

1-2. house of profession = brothel

4. Rash　「（金遣いが）荒い（男）」　　**in** = in prison

4-6. for a commodity ... five marks ready money　Rash の破産の詳細については⇒後注参照。

4-5. brown paper = coarse wrapping-paper, of little value

5. old ginger = stale ginger that has lost its savour

6. marks　当時の通貨単位（1 mark = 13s. 4d.）　　**ready money**　「現金（で）」

8. Caper　「飛び跳ねて踊る（男）」caper = leap, jump in dancing
　at the suit of　「起訴されて」9 行目の suits「スーツ」との言葉遊び。

9. Three-pile = three-piled「毛足が長い、最高級の服を着た（男）」
　mercer「（高級織物の）呉服屋」

10. peaches him = impeaches him as（9 行目の peach-coloured との言葉遊び）

11. Dizzy「泥酔した、無分別な（男）」　　**Deep-vow**「やたらに誓う（男）」

Copper-spur, and Master Starve-lackey the rapier and dagger man, and young Drop-heir that killed lusty Pudding, and Master Forthright the tilter, and brave Master Shoe-tie the great traveller, and wild Half-can that stabbed Pots, and I 15 think forty more, all great doers in our trade, and are now 'for the Lord's sake.'

Enter Abhorson

ABHORSON   Sirrah, bring Barnardine hither.

POMPEY   Master Barnardine, you must rise and be hanged, Master Barnardine! 20

ABHORSON   What ho, Barnardine!

BARNADINE   [*Within*]   A pox o'your throats! Who makes that noise there? What are you?

POMPEY   Your friends, sir, the hangman. You must be so good, sir, to rise and be put to death. 25

BARNADINE   [*Within*]   Away, you rogue, away, I am sleepy.

ABHORSON   Tell him he must awake, and that quickly, too.

POMPEY   Pray, Master Barnardine, awake till you are executed, and sleep afterwards.

ABHORSON   Go in to him, and fetch him out. 30

POMPEY   He is coming, sir, he is coming, I hear his straw rustle.

Enter Barnadine

ABHORSON   Is the axe upon the block, sirrah?

POMPEY   Very ready, sir.

BARNADINE   How now, Abhorson, what's the news with you?

ABHORSON   Truly, sir, I would desire you to clap into your 35 prayers, for look you, the warrant's come.

BARNADINE   You rogue, I have been drinking all night, I am not fitted for it.

POMPEY   O, the better, sir, for he that drinks all night, and is hanged betimes in the morning, may sleep the sounder all the 40

12. Copper-spur 「(模造品の) 銅製の拍車をつけている (男)」

Starve-lackey「従者を飢えさせる、けちん坊な (男)」

12-13. the rapier and dagger man 「細身の剣と短剣 (＝今流行りの武器) で決闘する男」それまでの一般的な決闘の装備は剣と盾 (sword and buckler) だった。

13. Drop-heir 「遺産をなくす (男)」heir ＝ hair の言葉遊びで「(梅毒で) 毛が抜けた」の意もある。

Pudding 「太っちょの (男)」pudding はソーセージのこと。

14. Forthright「猪突猛進する (男)」

tilter ＝ jouster

Shoe-tie 「靴ひも (男)」おしゃれな靴ひもはフランス直輸入のファッションなので、続けて the great traveler という表現が来る。

15. Half-can ... Pots それぞれ「(飲酒用の) 小ジョッキ (男)」と「大ジョッキ (男)」。

16. forty 漠然とした多数を指す。

17. 'for the Lord's sake' 囚人が牢屋の格子の窓のところで、通行人に喜捨を求めるときの決まり文句。すなわち「牢屋暮らし」の意。

19. be hanged 「くたばっちまえ」という罵りの言葉だが、ここでは文字通りの意味に使われているところが滑稽。

22. A pox o'your throats! 「喉が梅毒に取りつかれろ (＝うるさい) ！」

25. rise ＝ (1) get up (2) mount the scaffold

31. straw ＝ bed straw

35. clap into ＝ enter briskly into

40. betimes ＝ early

next day.

Enter Duke [disguised as a friar]

ABHORSON   Look you, sir, here comes your ghostly father. Do
we jest now, think you?

DUKE   Sir, induced by my charity, and hearing how hastily you
are to depart, I am come to advise you, comfort you, and   45
pray with you.

BARNADINE   Friar, not I. I have been drinking hard all night,
and I will have more time to prepare me, or they shall beat
out my brains with billets. I will not consent to die this day,
that's certain.   50

DUKE   O, sir, you must, and therefore I beseech you
Look forward on the journey you shall go.

BARNADINE   I swear I will not die today for any man's persuasion.

DUKE   But hear you —

BARNADINE   Not a word. If you have anything to say to me,   55
come to my ward, for thence will not I today.   *Exit*

DUKE   Unfit to live or die; O gravel heart!
After him, fellows, bring him to the block.

[Exeunt Abhorson and Pompey]

Enter Provost

PROVOST   Now, sir, how do you find the prisoner?

DUKE   A creature unprepared, unmeet for death,   60
And to transport him in the mind he is
Were damnable.

PROVOST   Here in the prison, father,
There died this morning of a cruel fever
One Ragozine, a most notorious pirate,
A man of Claudio's years, his beard and head   65
Just of his colour. What if we do omit
This reprobate till he were well inclined,

42. ghostly ＝ spiritual

42-43. Do we jest now, think you? ＝ Do you think we are jesting now?

48. prepare me ＝ prepare myself

　shall beat ＝ will have to beat

49. billets 「こん棒」

52. Look forward on ＝ look forward to　on は古形。

56. ward ＝ cell in a prison

57. gravel ＝ stony, hard

58. After him, fellows, bring him to the block こうした命令は公爵にはふさわしくないとして、監獄長に割り当てている版もあるが、ここも Folio 版を生かして支障ないと判断した。

60. unprepared ＝ not ready spiritually

61. transport him ＝ send him from this world to the next

62. damnable ＝ subject to divine condemnation（*OED*)

64. Ragozine 海賊という設定からして、当時栄えていたアドリア海に面した都市共和国 Ragusa（今はクロアチア共和国のドゥブロヴニク）にちなんだ名か？

66. omit ＝ leave disregarded

67. This reprobate Barnadine のことを指す。

　well inclined ＝ in a suitable frame of mind

And satisfy the deputy with the visage
Of Ragozine, more like to Claudio?

DUKE   O, 'tis an accident that heaven provides.   70
Dispatch it presently, the hour draws on
Prefixed by Angelo. See this be done,
And sent according to command, whiles I
Persuade this rude wretch willingly to die.

PROVOST   This shall be done, good father, presently.   75
But Barnardine must die this afternoon,
And how shall we continue Claudio,
To save me from the danger that might come
If he were known alive?

DUKE   Let this be done:
Put them in secret holds, both Barnardine and Claudio.   80
Ere twice the sun hath made his journal greeting
To yonder generation, you shall find
Your safety manifested.

PROVOST   I am your free dependant.

DUKE   Quick, dispatch, and send the head to Angelo.

Exit [Provost]

Now will I write letters to Angelo —   85
The Provost he shall bear them — whose contents
Shall witness to him I am near at home,
And that by great injunctions I am bound
To enter publicly. Him I'll desire
To meet me at the consecrated fount,   90
A league below the city, and from thence,
By cold gradation and weale-balanced form,
We shall proceed with Angelo.

Enter Provost

PROVOST   Here is the head, I'll carry it myself.

DUKE   Convenient is it. Make a swift return,   95

郵便はがき

113-8790

東京都文京区湯島2-1-1

大修館書店 販売部 行

‖‖|‖‖|‖‖‖|‖‖‖‖…|‖|‖|‖|‖|‖|‖|‖|‖|‖|‖|‖|‖|‖|‖

■ご住所

	都道府県		市区郡

■年齢

歳

■性別

男

女

■ご職業 （数字に○を付けてください）

1　会社員　　2　公務員　　3　自営業

4　小学校教員　　5　中学校教員　　6　高校教員　　7　大学教員

8　その他の教員（　　　　　　　　　　　　）

9　小学生・中学生　　10　高校生　　11　大学生　　12　大学院生

13　その他（　　　　　　　　　　　　）

14269　尺には尺を

愛読者カード

* **本書をお買い上げいただきまして誠にありがとうございました。**

(1) 本書をお求めになった動機は何ですか?

① 書店で見て (店名:)

② 新聞広告を見て (紙名:)

③ 雑誌広告を見て (誌名:)

④ 雑誌·新聞の記事を見て   ⑤ 知人にすすめられて

⑥ その他 (   )

(2) 本書をお読みになった感想をお書きください。

(3) 当社にご要望などがありましたらご自由にお書きください。

◎ ご記入いただいた感想等は、匿名で書籍のPR等に使用させていただくことがございます。

70. accident = chance

72. Prefixed = appointed

73. And 〔that Ragozine's head be〕 **sent**

74. this rude wretch バーナディンを指す。

77. continue = retain, keep alive

80. holds = prison cells

81. journal = daily

82. yonder generation = those persons 〔generation〕 outside these walls 〔yonder〕

83. I am your free dependant 「御意のままに」

88. by great injunctions = by authoritative orders

90. consecrated font = sacred fountain dedicated to the saint or other religious figure

91. below 「〜の南に」

92. cold gradation = advancing step by step

weale-balanced = adjusted with due regard to the public welfare　ちなみに Oxford 版や New Cambridge 版は well-balanced と校訂しているが、本版では Folio 版の weale をそのまま生かした。

93. We Plural of royalty

For I would commune with you of such things
That want no ear but yours.

PROVOST   I'll make all speed.   *Exit [Provost]*

ISABELLA   [*Within*]   Peace ho, be here.

DUKE   The tongue of Isabel. She's come to know   100
   If yet her brothers pardon be come hither.
   But I will keep her ignorant of her good,
   To make her heavenly comforts of despair
   When it is least expected.

Enter Isabella

ISABELLA   Ho, by your leave!   105

DUKE   Good morning to you, fair and gracious daughter.

ISABELLA   The better given me by so holy a man.
   Hath yet the deputy sent my brother's pardon?

DUKE   He hath released him, Isabel, from the world.
   His head is off, and sent to Angelo.   110

ISABELLA   Nay, but it is not so!

DUKE   It is no other.
   Show your wisdom, daughter, in your close patience.

ISABELLA   O, I will to him, and pluck out his eyes!

DUKE   You shall not be admitted to his sight.

ISABELLA   Unhappy Claudio, wretched Isabel,   115
   Injurious world, most damnèd Angelo!

DUKE   This nor hurts him, nor profits you a jot.
   Forbear it therefore, give your cause to heaven.
   Mark what I say, which you shall find
   By every syllable a faithful verity.   120
   The Duke comes home tomorrow — nay, dry your eyes.
   One of our convent, and his confessor,
   Gives me this instance: already he hath carried
   Notice to Escalus and Angelo,
   Who do prepare to meet him at the gates,   125

96. commune = talk, consult

99. Peace ho, be here. Cf. 1. 4. 6.

101. yet = already l. 108 も同様。

102-04. But I will keep ... is least expected 公爵のこの計略については、いかにも取ってつけたように聞こえるため、たとえばジョンソン博士のように'A better reason might have been given'と指摘する批評家も多い。だがおそらく、シェイクスピアは合理性よりは、悲劇と喜劇が目まぐるしく切り替わるこの劇の特徴を強調するため、あえてこのようなプロットに仕立てたのではないだろうか？

103. of = from

106. gracious = virtuous

107. better [morning, for being] **given**

112. close = reticent, quiet

117. This イザベラの取り乱した様子を指す。

  nor hurts = neither hurts

118. give ... cause 「（訴訟を）申し立てる」

120. a faithful verity = truth you can rely on

122. convent 「修道会」

123. instance = proof

124. Notice 「通知、予告」

There to give up their power. If you can pace your wisdom
In that good path that I would wish it go,
And you shall have your bosom on this wretch,
Grace of the Duke, revenges to your heart,
And general honour.

ISABELLA   I am directed by you.   130

DUKE   This letter then to Friar Peter give;
'Tis that he sent me of the Duke's return.
Say, by this token I desire his company
At Mariana's house tonight. Her cause and yours
I'll perfect him withal, and he shall bring you   135
Before the Duke, and to the head of Angelo
Accuse him home and home. For my poor self,
I am combinèd by a sacred vow,
And shall be absent. Wend you with this letter.
Command these fretting waters from your eyes   140
With a light heart; trust not my holy order
If I pervert your course. Who's here?

Enter Lucio

LUCIO   Good even, friar, where's the Provost?

DUKE   Not within, sir.

LUCIO   O pretty Isabella, I am pale at mine heart to see thine   145
eyes so red; thou must be patient. I am fain to dine and sup
with water and bran; I dare not for my head fill my belly, one
fruitful meal would set me to't. But they say the Duke will be
here tomorrow. By my troth, Isabel, I loved thy brother; if the
old fantastical Duke of dark corners had been at home, he   150
had lived.   [*Exit Isabella*]

DUKE   Sir, the Duke is marvelous little beholding to your
reports, but the best is, he lives not in them.

LUCIO   Friar, thou know'st not the Duke so well as I do. He's a
better woodman than thou tak'st him for.   155

126. pace = train to walk（originally from the training of horses）

128. bosom = desire

this wretch「この卑劣漢」アンジェロを指す。

129. Grace「愛顧」

to your heart = as ample as you heart could wish

132. 'Tis that = This is that which　that は this letter を受ける。

135. perfect = inform completely

withal = with　文や句の終わりで用いられるときの形。

136. to the head = to his face, a directly personal way

137. home and home = thoroughly

138. combinèd = bound（by oath）

139. Wend「進む、行く」（文語）

140. Command ... from = order ... to leave

fretting = vexing, corroding

142. pervert your course = lead you in a wrong direction

145. pale at mine heart = fearful, frightened

146. fain = compelled

147. with water and bran「水とぬか」、すなわち粗食の意。

for my head = for fear of, in exchange for

148. fruitful = abundant

set me to't = prompt me to commit lechery

150. old　親しみを込めた呼称で「年老いた」という意味はない。

fantastical = whimsical

dark corners　ルーチオは性的合意を込めている。

150-51. he had lived = he［Claudio］would have lived.

152. beholding = obliged

153. he lives not in them = his life is not as you report it

155. woodman = hunter（of women）, womanizer

DUKE Well, you'll answer this one day. Fare ye well.

LUCIO Nay, tarry, I'll go along with thee. I can tell thee pretty tales of the Duke.

DUKE You have told me too many of him already, sir, if they be true. If not true, none were enough.   160

LUCIO I was once before him for getting a wench with child.

DUKE Did you such a thing?

LUCIO Yes, marry did I; but I was fain to forswear it. They would else have married me to the rotten medlar.

DUKE Sir, your company is fairer than honest. Rest you well.   165

LUCIO By my troth, I'll go with thee to the lane's end. If bawdy talk offend you, we'll have very little of it. Nay, friar, I am a kind of burr, I shall stick.   *Exeunt*

[ACT IV, SCENE IV]

Enter Angelo and Escalus

ESCALUS Every letter he hath writ, hath disvouched other.

ANGELO In most uneven and distracted manner. His actions show much like to madness; pray heaven his wisdom be not tainted. And why meet him at the gates and redeliver our authorities there?   5

ESCALUS I guess not.

ANGELO And why should we proclaim it in an hour before his entering, that if any crave redress of injustice, they should exhibit their petitions in the street?

ESCALUS He shows his reason for that: to have a dispatch of   10 complaints and to deliver us from devices hereafter, which shall then have no power to stand against us.

ANGELO Well, I beseech you let it be proclaimed betimes i'the morn. I'll call you at your house. Give notice to such men of sort and suit as are to meet him.   15

ESCALUS I shall, sir. Fare you well.

156. answer = answer for, pay the penalty for

160. none were enough 「なにも聞かなくても、もう十分だ」

161. before him = a defendant before his court

163. marry　Cf. 1. 2. 60

　fain =喜んで…する

164. medlar　「カリン」その果実は腐りかけ（rotten）が美味とされる。形状が女性器を連想させるところから、当時は、売春婦に対する蔑称としても使われた。類音の meddler「おせっかい屋」にも掛けている。

165. fairer than honest　「楽しいが品がない」

　[God] **Rest you well**　別れのあいさつ。

166. to the lane's end　「どこまでも」

168. burr　「（クリなどの実の）いが」'To stick like a burr'ということわざもある。

〔4. 4〕あらすじ……………………………………………………………………

　アンジェロとエスカラスは公爵からの手紙でその帰還を知る。一人になったアンジェロは、イザベラをレイプしたことへの後ろめたさ、そして約束を反故にしてクローディオを処刑したことへの罪の意識に苦悩する。

………………………………………………………………………………………

1. disvouched = contradicted, disavouched,

2. uneven = irregular

4. tainted = infected（with mental disease）

4-5. redeliver our authorities = give back the power conferred on us

9. exhibit = present, offer officially

10. dispatch = prompt settlement

11. devices　「陰謀、策略」

12. stand against = oppose

14. call you = call on you

14-15. of sort and suit　「（高い）位にあり、従者を従えた」suit は suite の異形。

16. I shall　「必ずやいたします」長上の命に対する返答に用いられる shall。

ANGELO   Good night.   Exit[Escalus]
   This deed unshapes me quite, makes me unpregnant
   And dull to all proceedings. A deflowered maid,
   And by an eminent body that enforced   20
   The law against it! But that her tender shame
   Will not proclaim against her maiden loss,
   How might she tongue me! Yet reason dares her no,
   For my authority bears of a credent bulk
   That no particular scandal once can touch   25
   But it confounds the breather. He should have lived,
   Save that his riotous youth with dangerous sense
   Might in the times to come have ta'en revenge
   By so receiving a dishonoured life
   With ransom of such shame. Would yet he had lived!   30
   Alack, when once our grace we have forgot,
   Nothing goes right; we would, and we would not.   Exit

[ACT IV, SCENE V]
Enter Duke [in his own robes] and Friar Peter

DUKE   These letters at fit time deliver me.
   The Provost knows our purpose and our plot.
   The matter being a foot, keep your instruction,
   And hold you ever to our special drift,
   Though sometimes you do blench from this to that   5
   As cause doth minister. Go call at Flavius' house,
   And tell him where I stay. Give the like notice
   To Valencius, Rowland, and to Crassus,
   And bid them bring the trumpets to the gate.
   But send me Flavius first.
FRAIR PETER   It shall be speeded well.   [Exit]   10

Enter Varrius

172

18. unshapes ＝ destroys

18-19. unpregnant / And dull to all proceedings「起こっていることに無反応な」

20. body ＝ person

  enforced ＝ compelled others to obey

21. But that ＝ unless

22. maiden loss ＝ loss of virginity

23. tongue ＝ chide, reproach

  reason dares her no ＝ reason tells her she dare not do it

24. a credent bulk「絶大な信用」

25. particular ＝ personal

26. breather ＝ person who speaks it

27. riotous youth ＝ youthful wildness

  sense ＝ passion

29. By ＝ because of

31. grace ＝ virtue

32. we would, and we would not　聖書的な表現である。　⇒後注

⇒後注

〔4. 5〕あらすじ……………………………………………………………………………

　変装を解いた公爵は、修道士ピーターに手紙を渡して準備に抜かりがないよう指示し、ヴァリアスを迎える。

…………………………………………………………………………………………

1. me ＝心性的与格（ethical dative）。Cf. 1. 2. 159.

3. a foot ＝ in operation

4. drift ＝ aim or intention

5. blench ＝ swerve, deviate

6. As cause doth minister ＝ According as the affair prompts you

9. trumpets ＝ trumpeters

10. speeded ＝ hastened

10. SD. *Enter Varrius*　ヴァリアスに台詞がないのは、公爵を舞台上で迎え、先導して舞台から退出させるためだけに必要な役だから？

DUKE I thank thee, Varrius, thou hast made good haste.
  Come, we will walk. There's other of our friends
  Will greet us here anon, my gentle Varrius.   *Exeunt*

[**ACT IV, SCENE VI**]

Enter Isabella and Mariana

ISABELLA To speak so indirectly I am loath.
  I would say the truth, but to accuse him so
  That is your part. Yet I am advised to do it,
  He says, to veil full purpose.
MARIANA   Be ruled by him.
ISABELLA Besides he tells me, that if peradventure   5
  He speak against me on the adverse side,
  I should not think it strange, for 'tis a physic
  That's bitter to sweet end.
MARIANA   I would Friar Peter —

                    Enter Friar Peter

ISABELLA O peace, the friar is come.
FRIAR PETER Come, I have found you out a stand most fit,   10
  Where you may have such vantage on the Duke
  He shall not pass you. Twice have the trumpets sounded.
  The generous, and gravest citizens
  Have hent the gates, and very near upon
  The Duke is entering, therefore hence, away!   *Exeunt* 15

174

12. walk ＝ walk about

〔**4. 6**〕あらすじ‥‥‥‥‥‥‥‥‥‥‥‥‥‥‥‥‥‥‥‥‥‥‥‥‥‥‥‥‥‥‥‥‥
　イザベラとマリアナが、公爵に直訴する際のお互いの役割について議論しているところへ、修道士ピーターがあらわれ、公爵がまもなく到着すると告げる。
‥‥‥

1. indirectly ＝ dishonestly

2. so ＝ directly

4-6. He ... him ... he ... He　すべて「（修道士に扮した）変装した公爵」を指すと考えるのが自然。修道士ピーターを指すという解釈もあるが、かえって煩雑だろう。

4. veil full purpose ＝ conceal our full plan

5. peradventure ＝ perhaps

7. physic ＝ medicine

8. bitter to sweet end ＝ unpleasant to swallow but having a good effect
　たとえば、'Men take bitter portions for sweet health' など同様の趣旨のことわざは多くある。

10. stand ＝ place to stand

11. vantage ＝ advantage of position

13. generous, and gravest ＝ most high-born and most respected

14. hent ＝ reached, arrived at（*OED*）　　**near upon** ＝ soon

[Vᴄᴛ V, Sᴄᴇɴᴇ I]

Enter Duke [in his own robes], Varrius, Lords, Angelo, Escalus,
Lucio, [Provost, Officers,] Citizens, at several doors

Dᴜᴋᴇ My very worthy cousin, fairly met.
  Our old, and faithful friend, we are glad to see you.
Aɴɢᴇʟᴏ ᴀɴᴅ Esᴄᴀʟᴜs Happy return be to your royal grace.
Dᴜᴋᴇ Many and hearty thankings to you both.
  We have made enquiry of you, and we hear   5
  Such goodness of your justice that our soul
  Cannot but yield you forth to public thanks
  Forerunning more requital.
Aɴɢᴇʟᴏ You make my bonds still greater.
Dᴜᴋᴇ O, your desert speaks loud, and I should wrong it   10
  To lock it in the wards of covert bosom,
  When it deserves with characters of brass
  A forted residence 'gainst the tooth of time
  And razure of oblivion. Give me your hand,
  And let the subject see, to make them know   15
  That outward courtesies would fain proclaim
  Favours that keep within. Come, Escalus,
  You must walk by us on our other hand,
  And good supporters are you.

Enter Friar Peter and Isabella

Fʀɪᴀʀ Pᴇᴛᴇʀ Now is your time. Speak loud, and kneel before him. 20
Isᴀʙᴇʟʟᴀ Justice, O royal Duke, vail your regard
  Upon a wronged — I would fain have said a maid.
  O worthy Prince, dishonour not your eye
  By throwing it on any other object
  Till you have heard me in my true complaint,   25
  And given me justice, justice, justice, justice!
Dᴜᴋᴇ Relate your wrongs. In what, by whom? Be brief.

〔**5. 1**〕あらすじ……………………………………………………………………………………………

　イザベラは入城しようとする公爵の前にひざまずいてアンジェロの罪を訴えるが、公爵は彼女を狂人扱いする。引き続きマリアナが登場し、アンジェロを夫であると主張するが、これもアンジェロに否定される。アンジェロに裁きを任せて、一旦退場した公爵が修道士に扮して現れると、ルーチオが悪口雑言を吐きながら頭巾をもぎ取る。その結果、修道士が実は公爵だったことが明らかになり、すべてを知られていると悟ったアンジェロは、自らの罪を認めて死を願う。公爵はマリアナと結婚ののち、アンジェロを処刑するように命じる。アンジェロの妻となって戻ってきたマリアナは、イザベラとともに彼の助命を嘆願するが、公爵はそれに耳を貸さない。だがそこに登場した囚人が覆面をはがされ、クローディオが無事であることが明らかになると、公爵はアンジェロを許す。またルーチオに対しては、君主への誹謗は許すが、放蕩の報いとして彼が子供を産ませた売春婦との結婚を命じ、自らはイザベラに求婚する。

……………………………………………………………………………………………………

1. worthy cousin = fellow nobleman　アンジェロを指す。

2. faithful friend　エスカラスを指す。

3. your royal grace　王侯への尊称。

6. our soul = we

7. yield you forth to = make you receive

8. Forerunning more requital　「後で与えるより大きな褒美に先駆けて」

9. bonds = obligations, duties owed

11. wards of covert bosom = secret recesses of my heart

12. characters of brass = bronze letters (found on a tomb or monument)

13. forted = fortified　おそらくシェイクスピアの造語。

14. razure = effacement, erasure

15. the subject　ウィーン市民を指す。

16. would fain　「喜んで、進んで」

17. keep within = remain concealed

19. supporters　「介添人」　同時に紋章学の「大紋章の盾を左右から支えるもの」という含みもある。たとえばイギリスの国章の supporters はライオンとユニコーンである。

21. vail your regard = lower your glance

22. I would fain have said a maid　「生娘と言いたかったのですが（そうは言えない）」

25. complaint = accusation

Here is Lord Angelo shall give you justice;
Reveal yourself to him.

ISABELLA   O worthy Duke,
You bid me seek redemption of the devil.   30
Hear me yourself, for that which I must speak
Must either punish me, not being believed,
Or wring redress from you. Hear me, O hear me, here!

ANGELO   My Lord, her wits I fear me are not firm.
She hath been a suitor to me for her brother   35
Cut off by course of justice —

ISABELLA   By course of justice!

ANGELO   And she will speak most bitterly and strange.

ISABELLA   Most strange, but yet most truly will I speak.
That Angelo's forsworn, is it not strange?
That Angelo's a murderer, is't not strange?   40
That Angelo is an adulterous thief,
An hypocrite, a virgin-violator,
Is it not strange and strange?

DUKE   Nay, it is ten times strange.

ISABELLA   It is not truer he is Angelo,
Than this is all as true as it is strange.   45
Nay, it is ten times true, for truth is truth
To the end of reckoning.

DUKE   Away with her. Poor soul,
She speaks this in the infirmity of sense.

ISABELLA   O prince, I conjure thee, as thou believ'st
There is another comfort than this world,   50
That thou neglect me not with that opinion
That I am touched with madness. Make not impossible
That which but seems unlike. 'Tis not impossible
But one the wicked'st caitiff on the ground
May seem as shy, as grave, as just, as absolute   55
As Angelo. Even so may Angelo,

30. redemption「救い」(「キリストによる罪の贖^{あがな}い」も含意)

32. not being believed = if I am not believed

33. here! hear に校訂しているものも多いが、ここも Folio 版にしたがって、イザベラは「この場で（here）」の判決を望んでいると取った。

36. Cut off = executed

　by course of = according to the customary procedure of

37. strange = strangely

39-41. That Angelo's ... That Angelo's ... That Angelo is 「首句反復（anaphora）」という修辞技法。先頭の言葉を繰り返すことによって、それを強調する。

41. adulterous thief アンジェロはすでにマリアナと結婚しているので adulterous であり、イザベラの処女を奪ったので thief でもある。

44-45. It is not truer ... as it is strange 「彼がアンジェロであることより、これがすべて奇妙でも真実であることのほうが、より真実だ」つまりイザベラは、自分の主張がそれほど確かなことだと強調している。

47. To the end of reckoning 「何回数えても」

48. in the infirmity of sense = from her diseased mind

49. conjure = implore

50. There is another comfort than this world 「この世の彼方にもうひとつの慰め（＝天国）がある」

52-53. Make not impossible / That which but seems unlike 「ありそうもないように思えるというだけで、ありえないと決めつけないでください」

54. But = that

　one〔who is〕**the wicked'st caitiff on the ground** 「この世で最も邪悪な悪党」

55. shy = reserved

　absolute = perfect

In all his dressings, caracts, titles, forms,
Be an arch-villain. Believe it, royal prince.
If he be less, he's nothing; but he's more,
Had I more name for badness.

DUKE   By mine honesty   60
If she be mad, as I believe no other,
Her madness hath the oddest frame of sense,
Such a dependency of thing on thing,
As e'er I heard in madness.

ISABELLA   O gracious Duke,
Harp not on that, nor do not banish reason   65
For inequality, but let your reason serve
To make the truth appear where it seems hid,
And hide the false seems true.

DUKE   Many that are not mad
Have sure more lack of reason. What would you say?

ISABELLA   I am the sister of one Claudio,   70
Condemned upon the act of fornication
To lose his head, condemned by Angelo.
I, in probation of a sisterhood,
Was sent to by my brother; one Lucio
As then the messenger —

LUCIO   That's I, an't like your grace.   75
I came to her from Claudio, and desired her
To try her gracious fortune with Lord Angelo
For her poor brother's pardon.

ISABELLA   That's he indeed.

DUKE   [*To Lucio*]   You were not bid to speak.

LUCIO   No, my good Lord,
Nor wished to hold my peace.

DUKE   I wish you now then.   80
Pray you take note of it, and when you have
A business for yourself, pray heaven you then

57. dressings = robes of office

　caracts = badges of rank

　forms = ceremonies

58. arch-villain 「大悪党」

59. If he be less, he's nothing = he is no less than an arch-villain

60. Had I more name for badness = if I had a greater word for evil

62. frame of sense 「論理の一貫性、首尾一貫した意味」

63. dependency of thing on thing = logical connection between one thing and another

65. Harp ... on that = insist ... my (presumed) madness

66. For inequality = (1) アンジェロと私の地位が隔たっているので　(2) 私の話が辻褄があわないので

68. hide = put out of sight

　the false [that] **seems**

73. probation 「（宗教団体が希望者に課す）聖職見習い期間」

75. As then = being at that time

　an't like your grace = if you please

77. gracious = happy, prosperous

80. Nor wished = nor was I commanded

　hold my peace = stay silent

Be perfect.

LUCIO   I warrant your honour.

DUKE   The warrant's for yourself, take heed to't.

ISABELLA   This gentleman told somewhat of my tale.   85

LUCIO   Right.

DUKE   It may be right, but you are i'the wrong
To speak before your time. Proceed.

ISABELLA   I went
To this pernicious caitiff deputy —

DUKE   That's somewhat madly spoken.

ISABELLA   Pardon it.   90
The phrase is to the matter.

DUKE   Mended again. The matter; proceed.

ISABELLA   In brief, to set the needless process by —
How I persuaded, how I prayed and kneeled,
How he refelled me, and how I replied,   95
For this was of much length — the vile conclusion
I now begin with grief and shame to utter.
He would not but by gift of my chaste body
To his concupiscible intemperate lust
Release my brother; and after much debatement,   100
My sisterly remorse confutes mine honour
And I did yield to him. But the next morn betimes,
His purpose surfeiting, he sends a warrant
For my poor brother's head.

DUKE   This is most likely!

ISABELLA   O that it were as like as it is true.   105

DUKE   By heaven, fond wretch, thou know'st not what thou
    speak'st,
Or else thou art suborned against his honour
In hateful practice. First, his integrity
Stands without blemish; next, it imports no reason
That with such vehemency he should pursue   110

83. perfect ＝ fully prepared

83. warrant 「保証する、受け合う」

84. warrant 「召喚状」この言葉遊びは結末へ向けての伏線にもなっている。

85. somewhat ＝ something

88. Proceed 「（話を）続けて」イザベラに向かっての台詞。

89. pernicious caitiff deputy 「邪悪で卑劣な公爵代理」本人の前で激しく罵っているので、次行で公爵は madly spoken と受ける。

91. to the matter 「適切な、要を得た」

92. Mended again 「気違いじみたもの言いだ」(madly spoken) と言われて、イザベラが、再度、自分は狂気ではなく、言っていることは「適切です」(to the matter) と公爵に言い返したことを指す。　Cf. ll. 60-68.

93. set the needless process by 「不要な話は省いて」

95. refelled ＝ refused, rejected

96. of much length ＝ very long

98. but ＝ except

99. concupiscible intemperate 「好色で度を越した」

100. debatement ＝ argument, debate

101. remorse ＝ pity, compassion
　confutes 「（…を）論駁する、論破する」

102. betimes ＝ early

103. surfeiting ＝ grown sick because of his over-indulgence in sexuality

105. O that it were as like as it is true 「真実だと（公爵が）信じてくれるほど、ありそうなことだったらいいのに」

106. fond ＝ foolish

107. suborned 「（わいろなどで）偽証させられた」

108. practice 「計画、陰謀」

109. imports no reason ＝ means nothing reasonable, makes no sense

110. pursue ＝ follow（in order to punish）

Faults proper to himself. If he had so offended,
He would have weighed thy brother by himself,
And not have cut him off. Someone hath set you on.
Confess the truth, and say by whose advice
Thou cam'st here to complain.

ISABELLA   And is this all?   115
Then, O you blessèd ministers above,
Keep me in patience, and with ripened time
Unfold the evil which is here wrapped up
In countenance! Heaven shield your grace from woe,
As I, thus wronged, hence unbelievèd go.   120

DUKE   I know you'd fain be gone. An officer!
To prison with her! Shall we thus permit
A blasting and a scandalous breath to fall
On him so near us? This needs must be a practice.
Who knew of your intent and coming hither?   125

ISABELLA   One that I would were here, Friar Lodowick.

DUKE   A ghostly father, belike. Who knows that Lodowick?

LUCIO   My lord, I know him, 'tis a meddling friar.
I do not like the man; had he been lay, my lord,
For certain words he spake against your grace   130
In your retirement, I had swinged him soundly.

DUKE   Words against me? This' a good friar belike.
And to set on this wretched woman here
Against our substitute! Let this friar be found.

LUCIO   But yesternight, my lord, she and that friar   135
I saw them at the prison; a saucy friar,
A very scurvy fellow.

FRIAR PETER   Blessed be your royal grace!
I have stood by, my lord, and I have heard
Your royal ear abused. First, hath this woman
Most wrongfully accused your substitute,   140
Who is as free from touch or soil with her

184

111. Faults proper to himself　「自分自身も犯している（姦淫の）罪」

112. weighed ... by himself　「自分を基準に裁く」

116. ministers above　「天使たち」

117. with ripened time　「機が熟したら」

118. Unfold = bring to light, open up

　wrapped up = concealed

119. In countenance =（1）by patronage or authority　（2）through outward show

120. wronged　「ぬれぎぬを着せられて、不当に取り扱われて」

123. blasting ... scandalous breath　「讒言、誹謗中傷」

124. needs = necessarily

126. Friar Lodowick　公爵が修道士に扮しているときの名前。ここで初めて言及されるのは、おそらく修道士ピーター（Friar Peter）と区別する必要が生じたため。

127. ghostly =（1）spiritual　（2）shadowy

128. meddling = interfering

129. lay = secular, layman

131. swinged ... soundly「したたかに鞭打つ、懲らしめる」

132. This' = this is　シェイクスピアでは時に見かける短縮形。

136. saucy = insolent, rude

137. scurvy = worthless, contemptible

139. abused = deceived, imposed upon

141. touch or soil = sexual contact or stain

As she from one ungot.

DUKE   We did believe no less.

Know you that Friar Lodowick that she speaks of?

FRIAR PETER   I know him for a man divine and holy,

Not scurvy, nor a temporary meddler,   145

As he's reported by this gentleman,

And on my trust a man that never yet

Did, as he vouches, misreport your grace.

LUCIO   My lord, most villainously, believe it.

FRIAR PETER   Well, he in time may come to clear himself,   150

But at this instant he is sick, my lord,

Of a strange fever. Upon his mere request,

Being come to knowledge, that there was complaint

Intended 'gainst Lord Angelo, came I hither,

To speak as from his mouth what he doth know   155

Is true and false, and what he with his oath

And all probation will make up full clear

Whensoever he's convented. First, for this woman,

To justify this worthy nobleman

So vulgarly and personally accused,   160

Her shall you hear disprovèd to her eyes,

Till she herself confess it.

DUKE   Good friar, let's hear it.

Do you not smile at this, Lord Angelo?

O heaven, the vanity of wretched fools.

Give us some seats. Come, cousin Angelo,   165

In this I'll be impartial: be you judge

Of your own cause.

Enter Mariana [veiled]

Is this the witness, friar?

First, let her show your face, and after speak.

MARIANA   Pardon my Lord, I will not show my face

142. As she from one ungot 「彼女がまだ生まれていない男に触れたことがないのと同様に」

145. temporary meddler 「俗事にいらぬ世話を焼くやつ」

147. on my trust = as I am trusted, on my word

148. he ルーチオのこと。

　misreport = slander

152. strange = exceptionally severe（*OED*）

　his mere request = a request from him alone

153. Being come to knowledge = he having learned

155. his mouth = the mouth of Friar Lodowick

157. probation = proof

　make up full clear = establish clearly as the complete truth

158. convented 「（法廷に）召喚された」convene の古形。

160. vulgarly =（1）publicly　（2）grossly

161. disprovèd 「論破されて、誤りであることを示されて」

　to her eyes 「彼女に面と向かって」

164. vanity = futility

166. impartial = not taking part

167. cause 「訴訟事件」

167. SD. *Enter Mariana*　現行の大半の版では、マリアナが登場する以前に、「イザベラ退出」等のト書きがある。しかし本版では、Folio 版にならって、この指示は補足しなかった。イザベラが、一旦、舞台上の目立たない位置に退く等の演出で、対応できると判断したためである。

Until my husband bid me. 170

DUKE   What, are you married?

MARIANA   No, my lord.

DUKE   Are you a maid?

MARIANA   No, my lord.

DUKE   A widow, then? 175

MARIANA   Neither, my lord.

DUKE   Why, you are nothing then: neither maid, widow, nor wife?

LUCIO   My lord, she may be a punk, for many of them, are neither maid, widow, nor wife.

DUKE   Silence that fellow. I would he had some cause to prattle   180 for himself.

LUCIO   Well, my lord.

MARIANA   My lord, I do confess I ne'er was married,
And I confess besides I am no maid.
I have known my husband, yet my husband   185
Knows not that ever he knew me.

LUCIO   He was drunk then, my lord, it can be no better.

DUKE   For the benefit of silence, would thou wert so too.

LUCIO   Well, my lord.

DUKE   This is no witness for Lord Angelo. 190

MARIANA   Now I come to't, my lord.
She that accuses him of fornication
In self-same manner, doth accuse my husband,
And charges him, my lord, with such a time
When I'll depose I had him in mine arms   195
With all the effect of love.

ANGELO   Charges she mo than me?

MARIANA   Not that I know.

DUKE   No? You say your husband.

MARIANA   Why just, my lord, and that is Angelo,   200
Who thinks he knows that he ne'er knew my body,

171. What 疑問詞の前につける間投詞。ここでは驚きを表す。

177. neither maid, widow, nor wife? 当時おなじみの謎掛け。答えはルーチオの言う通り「娼婦」。

178. punk = whore, prostitute

180. cause 「訴訟」ここでも公爵はルーチオへの裁判があることを暗示している。

185-86. known ... knew = had sexual intercourse with　なお、この場では know が「(性的) に知る」という意味でしばしば使われている。

188. For the benefit of silence 「静かにしていてもらうために」

so = drunk

190. witness for = evidence on behalf of

191. I come to't = I am about to speak of it

194-95. charges ... depose = accuses ... testify（under oath）　マリアナは裁判用語を用いて訴えている。

194. with such a time = at the very time

196. all the effect of love = full sexual union

197. mo = more, other than

198. that I know = as far as I know

200. just = exactly, just so

201-02. knew ... knows　Cf. ll. 185-86

But knows, he thinks, that he knows Isabel's.

ANGELO This is a strange abuse. Let's see thy face.

MARIANA [*Unveiling*] My husband bids me, now I will unmask.

    This is that face, thou cruel Angelo, 205

    Which once thou swor'st was worth the looking on;

    This is the hand, which with a vowed contract

    Was fast belocked in thine; this is the body

    That took away the match from Isabel,

    And did supply thee at thy garden-house 210

    In her imagined person.

DUKE Know you this woman?

LUCIO Carnally, she says.

DUKE Sirrah, no more!

LUCIO Enough, my lord.

ANGELO My Lord, I must confess I know this woman, 215

    And five years since there was some speech of marriage

    Betwixt myself and her, which was broke off,

    Partly for that her promisèd proportions

    Came short of composition, but in chief

    For that her reputation was disvalued 220

    In levity. Since which time of five years

    I never spake with her, saw her, nor heard from her,

    Upon my faith and honour.

MARIANA [*Kneels*] Noble prince,

    As there comes light from heaven, and words from breath,

    As there is sense in truth, and truth in virtue, 225

    I am affianced this man's wife as strongly

    As words could make up vows; and, my good lord,

    But Tuesday night last gone, in's garden-house,

    He knew me as a wife. As this is true,

    Let me in safety raise me from my knees, 230

    Or else for ever be confixèd here

    A marble monument.

203. abuse = imposture, deceit

207. contract 「(結婚の) 約定」

208. belocked = intensive form of 'locked'

209. match 「逢い引きの約束」

210. supply = satisfy

　garden-house エリザベス朝の富裕な家庭では、庭にあずまや (garden-house) を建てたが、これは手の込んだつくりになっており、部屋数も多く、歩廊もついていた。また、この劇でのように逢い引きに利用される悪名高い場所でもあった。

214. [I have said] **Enough**

216. speech = mention

218, 220. for that = because

218. proportions 「持参金、婚資」

219. composition = what had been agreed upon, agreement

220. disvalued = diminished in value, disparaged

221. levity 「軽佻浮薄、尻軽」

　of five years = during five years

224. As = as surely as

225. sense = reason

226. affianced = betrothed

　strongly = firmly

230. in safety = without risking punishment

231. confixèd = fixed firmly

232. marble monument 「大理石の像」大理石は永遠性の象徴。

ANGELO   I did but smile till now.
   Now, good my lord, give me the scope of justice.
   My patience here is touched; I do perceive
   These poor informal women are no more   235
   But instruments of some more mightier member
   That sets them on. Let me have way, my lord,
   To find this practice out.
DUKE   Ay, with my heart,
   And punish them to your height of pleasure.
   Thou foolish friar, and thou pernicious woman,   240
   Compact with her that's gone, think'st thou thy oaths,
   Though they would swear down each particular saint,
   Were testimonies against his worth and credit
   That's sealed in approbation? You, Lord Escalus,
   Sit with my cousin, lend him your kind pains   245
   To find out this abuse, whence 'tis derived.
   There is another friar that set them on;
   Let him be sent for.
FRIAR PETER   Would he were here, my lord, for he indeed
   Hath set the women on to this complaint.   250
   Your Provost knows the place where he abides,
   And he may fetch him.
DUKE   Go, do it instantly.   [*Exit Provost*]
   And you, my noble and well-warranted cousin,
   Whom it concerns to hear this matter forth,
   Do with your injuries as seems you best   255
   In any chastisement. I for a while
   Will leave you, but stir not you till you have
   Well determined upon these slanderers.
ESCALUS   My lord, we'll do it thoroughly.   *Exit* [DUKE]
   Signior Lucio, did not you say you knew that Friar Lodowick   260
   to be a dishonest person?
LUCIO   *Cucullus non facit Monachum.* Honest in nothing but in

233. scope = full extent

234. My patience ... is touched 「堪忍袋の緒が切れた」

235. informal = disordered in mind（*OED*）

236. more mightier member = more powerful person in the community

237. have way = have freedom of action

239. to your height of pleasure 「君の望むように厳しく、徹底的に」

241. Compact = in league, joined together

242. swear down each particular saint 「聖者をすべて一人ずつ地上に呼びおろして証人にする」

244. sealed in approbation 「権威を保証する公印が押された」

246. abuse = deception

253. well-warranted = approved by good authority

254. it concerns = it is important to（whom）

　forth = thoroughly, to the end

255. Do with = deal with

　injuries =（1）wrongs　（2）calumnies

258. determined = reached a judgment

262. *Cucullus non facit Monachum* = The cowl does not make the monk 「（僧服の）頭巾が僧を作るわけではない」当時一般的だったことわざ表現。シェイクスピアは *Twelfth Night*（1. 5. 52-53）でも使っている。

his clothes, and one that hath spoke most villainous speeches
of the Duke.

ESCALUS We shall entreat you to abide here till he come, and   265
enforce them against him. We shall find this friar a notable
fellow.

LUCIO As any in Vienna, on my word.

ESCALUS Call that same Isabel here once again, I would speak
with her.   [*Exit an Officer*]   270
Pray you, my lord, give me leave to question, you shall see
how I'll handle her.

LUCIO Not better than he, by her own report.

ESCALUS Say you?

LUCIO Marry, sir, I think if you handled her privately she   275
would sooner confess, perchance publicly she'll be ashamed.

Enter Duke [disguised as a friar], Provost, Isabella

ESCALUS I will go darkly to work with her.

LUCIO That's the way, for women are light at midnight.

ESCALUS Come on, mistress, here's a gentlewoman denies all
that you have said.   280

LUCIO My lord, here comes the rascal I spoke of, here with
the Provost.

ESCALUS In very good time. Speak not you to him, till we call
upon you.

LUCIO Mum.   285

ESCALUS Come, sir, did you set these women on to slander
Lord Angelo? They have confessed you did.

DUKE 'Tis false.

ESCALUS How? Know you where you are?

DUKE Respect to your great place, and let the devil   290
Be sometime honoured for his burning throne.
Where is the Duke? 'Tis he should hear me speak.

ESCALUS The Duke's in us, and we will hear you speak.

266. enforce ＝ urge strongly, emphasize

notable ＝ notorious, egregious

269. that same ＝ that　same は that を強調する。

272-73. handle her. / Not better than he, by her own report　handle「扱う」を
ルーチオはわざと「手で触れる」と取り、No better than he「アンジェロの
ほうが上手」とエスカラスをからかう。

274. Say you? ＝ What is it that you say?

275. Marry　Cf. 1. 2. 60

277. darkly ＝ secretly

278. women are light at midnight　「女は真夜中だと尻軽だ」　ルーチオは前行
の darkly「密かに」を「暗がりで」の意味にずらして、またエスカラスをか
らかっている。

283. In very good time ＝ at the right moment

285. Mum ＝ I'll keep quiet

289. How? ＝ What?

Know you where you are?　エスカラスは、法廷での嘘は偽証罪に問われると
脅している。

290. 〔Let me pay〕 **Respect**

290-91. let the devil / Be sometime honoured for his burning throne　devil
は暗にアンジェロを指す。burning は堕天する以前は最上級の熾天使（してんし）であっ
たとされるルシファーからの連想か？

293. The Duke's in us ＝ The Duke's authority is vested in us

Look you speak justly.

DUKE   Boldly, at least. But O, poor souls,   295
  Come you to seek the lamb here of the fox?
  Good night to your redress! Is the Duke gone?
  Then is your cause gone too. The Duke's unjust
  Thus to retort your manifest appeal,
  And put your trial in the villain's mouth   300
  Which here you come to accuse.

LUCIO   This is the rascal, this is he I spoke of.

ESCALUS   Why, thou unreverend and unhallowed friar!
  Is't not enough thou hast suborned these women,
  To accuse this worthy man, but in foul mouth,   305
  And in the witness of his proper ear,
  To call him villain, and then to glance from him
  To the Duke himself, to tax him with injustice?
  Take him hence. To the rack with him! We'll touze you
  Joint by joint, but we will know his purpose.   310
  What! Unjust?

DUKE   Be not so hot. The Duke
  Dare no more stretch this finger of mine than he
  Dare rack his own. His subject am I not,
  Nor here provincial. My business in this state
  Made me looker-on here in Vienna,   315
  Where I have seen corruption boil and bubble
  Till it o'errun the stew; laws for all faults,
  But faults so countenanced that the strong statutes
  Stand like the forfeits in a barber's shop,
  As much in mock as mark.   320

ESCALUS   Slander to the state! Away with him to prison.

ANGELO   What can you vouch against him, Signior Lucio?
  Is this the man you did tell us of?

LUCIO   'Tis he, my lord. Come hither, goodman baldpate. Do
  you know me?   325

294. Look = see that

295. poor souls　イザベラとマリアナに向かっての台詞。

296. to seek the lamb ... of the fox　「狐から子羊を探す」当時の慣用的な表現で「無駄足を踏む」という意味だが、通常は wolf のところ、シェイクスピアは fox を使っている点が珍しい。

297. Good night = farewell

298. cause =（1）訴訟　（2）大義

299. retort = reject, turn back

303. unreverend and unhallowed　「不遜で邪悪な」

306. in the witness of his proper ear　「彼自身の聞こえるところで」

307-08. glance from him / To the Duke himself　「（矢、非難などが）彼をかすめて、公爵ご自身に向かう」

309. rack = instrument of torture designed to stretch its victim's joint
touze = pull apart

309-10. We'll touze you ... but we will know his purpose　l. 309 の you と l. 310 の his の不一致から、前半は公爵への台詞、but 以下は周りの者に向けた台詞と考えられる。

314. provincial　「（教会の）管区、教区に属する」

317. stew =（1）vessel for boiling, cauldron　（2）brothel

318. countenanced = encouraged, supported

319. forfeits in a barber's shop　「床屋の罰則」Arden 2 版の説明には 'It was customary for barber-surgeons to hang up jocular lists of graded penalties（blood-letting, extraction of teeth, etc.）for bad manners on their customers' part' とある。ちなみに当時、髪を切ることは身体を切ることと同じであると考えられていたため、床屋は外科医や歯科医の仕事も兼ねた。また体内から血液の一部を抜き取る「瀉血（blood-letting）」という治療も、しばしば行っていた。

320. As much in mock as mark　「注目されると同様に嘲られる」

322. vouch against = allege against

324. goodman baldpate　「ハゲ頭のおっさん」どちらもからかいの表現。「ハゲ」は修道士が剃髪しているから。

Duke I remember you, sir, by the sound of your voice. I met you at the prison, in the absence of the Duke.

Lucio O, did you so? And do you remember what you said of the Duke?

Duke Most notedly, sir. 330

Lucio Do you so, sir? And was the Duke a fleshmonger, a fool, and a coward, as you then reported him to be?

Duke You must, sir, change persons with me, ere you make that my report. You indeed spoke so of him, and much more, much worse. 335

Lucio O thou damnable fellow, did I not pluck thee by the nose for thy speeches?

Duke I protest I love the Duke as I love myself.

Angelo Hark how the villain would close now, after his treasonable abuses. 340

Escalus Such a fellow is not to be talked withal. Away with him to prison. Where is the Provost? Away with him to prison! Lay bolts enough upon him; let him speak no more. Away with those giglets too, and with the other confederate companion. 345

[The Provost lays hand on the Duke]

Duke Stay, sir, stay a while.

Angelo What, resists he? Help him, Lucio.

Lucio Come, sir, come, sir, come sir! Foh, sir! Why, you bald-pated lying rascal, you must be hooded, must you? show your knave's visage, with a pox to you. Show your sheep-biting 350 face, and be hanged an hour. Will't not off?

[He pulls off the Friar's hood and discovers the Duke]

Duke Thou art the first knave that e'er mad'st a duke.
First, Provost, let me bail these gentle three.
[To Lucio] Sneak not away, sir, for the friar and you

326. I remember you, sir, by the sound of your voice 公爵は身元を隠すた
め、おそらく頭巾をいつも目深に被っていたので、ルーチオを声で聞き分け
た。

330. notedly = notably

331. fleshmonger = fornicator

333. change = exchange

333-34. make that my report = attribute those remarks to me

336-37. pluck ... by the nose 「鼻をつまむ、軽蔑的に扱う」

339. close = （1）come to terms （2）conclude

340. abuses = insulting speeches

343. bolts 「（鉄の）足枷」

344. giglets = wanton women

344-45. confederate companion 「共犯の一味」修道士ピーターを指す。

347. him 監獄長を指す。

348. Foh 「ふん、へっ」嫌悪・軽蔑を表す間投詞。

350. with a pox to you 「この野郎、こん畜生」怒りやいらだちの表現。

sheep-biting 「（羊を噛む牧羊犬のように）こそこそと卑劣な」おそらく
sheep-biter = a woman hunter, whoremonger（*OED*）の含みもあるだろ
う。

351. an hour = for a little while

352. first knave that e'er mad'st a duke 公爵に叙することができるのは、通
常王侯のみだから。

353. bail 「保釈させる」

three イザベラ、マリアナ、僧ピーターを指す。

354. the friar 「さっきの僧」すなわち公爵を指す。

Must have a word anon. Lay hold on him.   355

Lucio   This may prove worse than hanging.

Duke [*To Escalus*]   What you have spoke, I pardon; sit you down.

We'll borrow place of him. [*To Angelo*] Sir, by your leave.

Hast thou or word, or wit, or impudence

That yet can do thee office? If thou hast   360

Rely upon it till my tale be heard,

And hold no longer out.

Angelo   O, my dread lord,

I should be guiltier than my guiltiness,

To think I can be undiscernible,

When I perceive your grace, like power divine,   365

Hath looked upon my passes. Then, good prince,

No longer session hold upon my shame,

But let my trial be mine own confession.

Immediate sentence, then, and sequent death

Is all the grace I beg.

Duke   Come hither, Mariana.   370

[*To Angelo*]   Say, wast thou e'er contracted to this woman?

Angelo   I was, my lord.

Duke   Go take her hence, and marry her instantly.

Do you the office, friar, which consummate,

Return him here again. Go with him, Provost.   375

             Exeunt [*Angelo, Mariana, Friar Peter, Provost*]

Escalus   My lord, I am more amazed at his dishonour

Than at the strangeness of it.

Duke   Come hither, Isabel.

Your friar is now your prince. As I was then

Advertising and holy to your business,

Not changing heart with habit, I am still   380

Attorneyed at your service.

Isabella   O give me pardon

That I, your vassal, have employed and pained

358. by your leave　「すみませんが」丁寧表現だが、ここではアイロニカルな含み。

359. thou　ここから公爵はアンジェロに対する呼び方を、丁寧な you から、目下の者への thou に切り替える。

  or ... or ... or ＝ either ... or ... or

360. office ＝ service

362. hold no longer out ＝ give up resistance and admit the truth

363. guiltier than my guiltiness　「私の（犯した）罪以上に、罪深い」

364. undiscernible ＝ undiscovered

366. passes ＝ courses of action, what I have done

367. session　「（裁判所の）開廷」

369. sequent ＝ consequent, subsequent

374. [being] consummate　「（結婚を）完了したら」シェイクスピアでは -ate で終わる動詞の過去形、過去分詞形は無変化の場合がある。

377. strangeness ＝ strange manner in which it revealed itself

379. Advertising ＝ attentive, heedful

  holy ＝ dedicated, devoted（*OED*）

380. habit ＝ dress, clothing

381. Attorneyed ＝ employed as an agent

382. vassal　「しもべ、臣下」

  pained「手を煩わせる」

Your unknown sovereignty.

DUKE You are pardoned, Isabel.
And now, dear maid, be you as free to us.
Your brother's death, I know, sits at your heart,   385
And you may marvel why I obscured myself,
Labouring to save his life, and would not rather
Make rash remonstrance of my hidden power
Than let him so be lost. O most kind maid,
It was the swift celerity of his death,   390
Which I did think with slower foot came on,
That brained my purpose; but peace be with him.
That life is better life, past fearing death,
Than that which lives to fear. Make it your comfort,
So happy is your brother.

ISABELLA I do, my Lord.   395

Enter Angelo, Maria, Friar Peter and Provost

DUKE For this new-married man approaching here,
Whose salt imagination yet hath wronged
Your well-defended honour, you must pardon
For Mariana's sake. But as he adjudged your brother,
Being criminal in double violation   400
Of sacred chastity and of promise-breach,
Thereon dependent for your brother's life,
The very mercy of the law cries out
Most audible, even from his proper tongue:
'An Angelo for Claudio, death for death;   405
Haste still pays haste, and leisure answers leisure;
Like doth quit like, and measure still for measure.'
Then, Angelo, thy fault's thus manifested,
Which, though thou wouldst deny, denies thee vantage.
We do condemn thee to the very block   410
Where Claudio stooped to death, and with like haste.

383. unknown = unrecognized

384. free 「寛容に」クローディオを救えなかったことに対して。

385. sits at your heart = affect you deeply

388. rash remonstrance = hasty manifestation, urgent demonstration

392. brained = dashed, defeated 「脳を打ち砕く」の意から比喩的に転用したもの。

393-94. That life is better life, past fearing death, / Than that which lives to fear いかにもこの劇らしいことわざ的な表現。

395. So happy is your brother = that your brother has that happiness (of not fearing death)

397. yet = in spite of, nevertheless Cf. l. 434

salt = lecherous 元々は「（獣が）発情した」の意味で、*Othello* でも 2. 1. 238 と 3. 3. 407 でこの意味に使われている。

399. adjudged = condemned

401. sacred chastity イザベラは修道女なので sacred がつく。

401-02. promise-breach ... life 難解な箇所だが、New Cambridge 版では、breach of promise (to save Claudio's life), which promise was dependent on violating your chastity とパラフレーズしている。

403. The very mercy of the law = even the most merciful aspect of the law

404. even from his proper tongue 「まさに彼（＝法）自身の口から」

405-07. An Angelo for Claudio ... measure still for measure この箇所には 'Death for death', 'Like will to like', 'Measure for measure' といった有名な慣用句が使われているだけでなく、全体としてもことわざを模した対句的な構成になっている。特に 'measure ... for measure' というこの劇の題名の由来となる聖書の句については、⇒後注を参照のこと。

407. quit = require

409. denies thee vantage = denies you the right to claim superior treatment

Away with him.

MARIANA   O my most gracious lord,
    I hope you will not mock me with a husband.

DUKE   It is your husband mocked you with a husband.   415
    Consenting to the safeguard of your honour,
    I thought your marriage fit; else imputation,
    For that he knew you, might reproach your life,
    And choke your good to come. For his possessions,
    Although by confiscation they are ours,   420
    We do instate and widow you with all,
    To buy you a better husband.

MARIANA   O my dear lord,
    I crave no other, nor no better man.

DUKE   Never crave him, we are definitive.

MARIANA   Gentle my liege — [*Kneeling*]

DUKE   You do but loose your labour.   425
    Away with him to death. [*To Lucio*] Now, sir, to you.

MARIANA   O my good Lord! Sweet Isabel, take my part,
    Lend me your knees, and all my life to come
    I'll lend you all my life to do you service.

DUKE   Against all sense you do importune her.   430
    Should she kneel down, in mercy of this fact,
    Her brother's ghost his pavèd bed would break
    And take her hence in horror.

MARIANA   Isabel,
    Sweet Isabel, do yet but kneel by me.
    Hold up your hands, say nothing; I'll speak all.   435
    They say best men are moulded out of faults,
    And for the most become much more the better
    For being a little bad. So may my husband.
    O Isabel, will you not lend a knee?

DUKE   He dies for Claudio's death.

ISABELLA   [*Kneeling*]   Most bounteous sir,   440

414. mock = delude, tantalize

416. Consenting = agreeing　次行の marriage に掛かる。

　safeguard = protection

417. imputation = censure, slander

418. For that = because

　knew　Cf. ll. 185-86

419. choke your good to come = destroy your future benefit

　For = As for

421. instate and widow you = endow and grant to you as a widow's portion

424. definitive = resolute

425. loose your labour = waste your efforts

428. Lend me your knees「私のためにひざまずいて（公爵に頼んでください）」

　all my life to come　「今後一生のあいだ」

430. Against all sense = completely unreasonably

　importune = implore, beg

431. in mercy of　「～を許して」

432. pavèd bed = grave covered with stone slab

433. hence = away from here

434. yet　Cf. l. 397

　but = only

436. They say　ことわざを示唆する定形表現だが、対応するものは特定されていない。

　moulded = created, formed

437. for the most = for the most part

440. bounteous = generous

Look if it please you, on this man condemned
As if my brother lived. I partly think
A due sincerity governed his deeds,
Till he did look on me; since it is so,
Let him not die. My brother had but justice, 445
In that he did the thing for which he died.
For Angelo,
His act did not o'ertake his bad intent,
And must be buried but as an intent
That perished by the way. Thoughts are no subjects, 450
Intents but merely thoughts.
MARIANA   Merely, my lord.
DUKE   Your suit's unprofitable. Stand up I say.
   I have bethought me of another fault.
   Provost, how came it Claudio was beheaded
   At an unusual hour?
PROVOST   It was commanded so. 455
DUKE   Had you a special warrant for the deed?
PROVOST   No, my good lord, it was by private message.
DUKE   For which I do discharge you of your office,
   Give up your keys.
PROVOST   Pardon me, noble lord.
   I thought it was a fault, but knew it not, 460
   Yet did repent me after more advice.
   For testimony whereof, one in the prison
   That should by private order else have died
   I have reserved alive.
DUKE   What's he? 465
PROVOST   His name is Barnardine.
DUKE   I would thou hadst done so by Claudio.
   Go fetch him hither, let me look upon him.   [*Exit Provost*]
ESCALUS   I am sorry one so learned and so wise
   As you, Lord Angelo, have still appeared, 470

442. partly 「ある程度は、幾分かは」

443. due = fitting, proper

445. had but justice = was only dealt with justly

449. buried = hidden away, forgotten

450. perished by the way = was never fulfilled

Thoughts are no subjects = (1) thoughts have no real independent existence (2) thoughts are not subject to our control

453. bethought me = remembered

455. It was commanded so 監獄長は、実は「クローディオを処刑した」とは言っていない。シェイクスピアの細かいテクニック。

459. keys〔to the jail-cells〕 監獄長としての職務のシンボル。

460. knew it not = was not certain of it

461. repent me = feel penitence

advice = consideration, reflection

462. For testimony whereof 「悔恨のしるしとして」

465. What's he? = Who is he?

467. by = in the case of, toward

470. still = always

Should slip so grossly, both in the heat of blood
And lack of tempered judgement afterward.

ANGELO   I am sorry that such sorrow I procure,
And so deep sticks it in my penitent heart
That I crave death more willingly than mercy.   475
'Tis my deserving, and I do entreat it.

    Enter Barnardine, Provost, Claudio [muffled] and Julietta.

DUKE   Which is that Barnardine?
PROVOST   This, my Lord.
DUKE   There was a friar told me of this man.
Sirrah, thou art said to have a stubborn soul
That apprehends no further than this world,   480
And squar'st thy life according. Thou'rt condemned;
But, for those earthly faults, I quit them all,
And pray thee take this mercy to provide
For better times to come. Friar, advise him;
I leave him to your hand. What muffled fellow's that?   485
PROVOST   This is another prisoner that I saved,
Who should have died when Claudio lost his head,
As like almost to Claudio as himself.

        [He unmuffles Claudio]

DUKE   If he be like your brother, for his sake
Is he pardoned, and for your lovely sake   490
Give me your hand, and say you will be mine,
He is my brother too — but fitter time for that.
By this Lord Angelo perceives he's safe;
Methinks I see a quickening in his eye.
Well, Angelo, your evil quits you well.   495
Look that you love your wife, her worth worth yours.
I find an apt remission in myself,
And yet here's one in place I cannot pardon.

471. slip = err, sin

  grossly = flagrantly, extremely

  blood = sexual appetite

472. tempered = temperate, balanced

473. procure = cause, bring about

476. SD. [*muffled*] = wrapped up so as to conceal identity

480. apprehends = understands, anticipates

481. squar'st = regulates, arranges

  according = accordingly

482. quit = remit, forgive

484. better times to come 「来世」

488. As like almost to Claudio as himself 「クローディオとほとんど瓜二つ」

488. SD. *He unmuffles Claudio* このあとにイザベラの驚きや喜びのせりふはない。だが、たとえば「2人が無言で抱き合う」といった所作が入る演出もありうるだろう。

489. for his sake = for your brother's sake

490. for your lovely sake = on your account

491. Give me your hand = if you give me your hand (and consent to marry me) ここでもイザベラは無言である。これを同意のしるしと取るかは、解釈が分かれるところ。

493. this クローディオが生きていたことを指す。

494. quickening = revival, return of liveliness

495. quits = requites, rewards

  you 公爵はここからまた、アンジェロに対する呼称を thou から、丁寧な you に戻している。罪を許すというサインだろう。

496. Look that 「～であるように気をつける」

  her worth worth yours = her worth is fully equal to your worth

497. apt remission = willing forgiveness

498. in place = present

[*To Lucio*]   You, sirrah, that knew me for a fool, a coward,
One all of luxury, an ass, a madman,   500
Wherein have I so deserved of you
That you extoll me thus?

LUCIO   Faith, my lord, I spoke it but according to the trick. If
you will hang me for it, you may, but I had rather it would
please you, I might be whipped.   505

DUKE   Whipped first, sir, and hanged after.
Proclaim it, Provost, round about the city:
If any woman wronged by this lewd fellow —
As I have heard him swear himself there's one
Whom he begot with child — let her appear,   510
And he shall marry her. The nuptial finished,
Let him be whipped and hanged.

LUCIO   I beseech your highness, do not marry me to a whore.
Your highness said even now, I made you a duke; good my
lord, do not recompense me in making me a cuckold.   515

DUKE   Upon mine honour, thou shalt marry her.
Thy slanders I forgive, and therewithal
Remit thy other forfeits. Take him to prison,
And see our pleasure herein executed.

LUCIO   Marrying a punk, my Lord, is pressing to death,   520
whipping, and hanging.

DUKE   Slandering a prince deserves it.
She, Claudio, that you wronged, look you restore.
Joy to you, Mariana. Love her, Angelo:
I have confessed her, and I know her virtue.   525
Thanks, good friend, Escalus, for thy much goodness;
There's more behind that is more gratulate.
Thanks, Provost, for thy care and secrecy;
We shall employ thee in a worthier place.
Forgive him, Angelo, that brought you home   530
The head of Ragozine for Claudio's;

500. all of luxury = full of lechery, lust

501. deserved of 「〜から報いられるだけの功績がある」

502. extoll 「称<small>たた</small>える」もちろん皮肉。

503. according to the trick = (1) 冗談で (2) 習い性で

508. wronged = disgraced

514. even now = just now

　I made you a duke　Cf. l. 352

517. therewithal = in addition

518. Remit thy other forfeits = cancel your other penalties

519. see 「取り計らう」

　our pleasure = my will

520. punk = prostitute

　pressing to death　罪人に白状させるため、胸に重しを置いてだんだん重くする拷問。石抱きの刑。

523. look = see that

　restore = reinstate her dignity

525. confessed her = heard her confession

526. much = great

527. behind = yet to come（in the way of reward）

　gratulate = gratifying

528. secrecy = keeping of secrets

The offence pardons itself. Dear Isabel,
I have a motion much imports your good,
Whereto if you'll a willing ear incline,
What's mine is yours, and what is yours is mine.   535
So bring us to our palace, where we'll show
What's yet behind, that meet you all should know.   *Exeunt*

532. The offence pardons itself 「その罪は帳消しだ」

533. motion = proposal, suggestion
　　imports = concerns

534. Whereto = to which

535. What's mine is ... yours is mine これもことわざ的な表現。

536. bring = accompany

537. yet behind = still to come
　　meet = appropriate, fitting

後 注

1. 1. 7-9. Then no more remains ... And let them work　18 世紀以降、多くの編者は 8 行目（But that to your sufficiency, as your worth is able）の音節が余分でリズムも乱れていること、またそれに続く 9 行目（And let them work）の them が何を指すか不明であることなどから、sufficiency のあとに何らかの脱落があるのではと推測してきた。たとえば、Oxford 版では韻律を直し、意味を明瞭にするため、以下のような補足の可能性を提示している。

　But that to your sufficiency [you add

　a power as ample] as your worth is able ...

1. 1. 32-35. Heaven doth with us ... As if we had them not　このあたりの表現については、多くの編者が聖書の「マタイ伝」との関係を指摘している。Cf. Matthew 5: 15-16 'Nether do men light a candle, and put it under a bushel, but on a candle stick, and it gives light unto all that are in the house. Let your light so shine before men, that they may se your good works, and glorifie your Father which is in heaven.' マタイ伝「また人は灯火をともして升の下におかず、灯台の上におく。斯て灯火は家にある凡ての物を照らすなり。斯のごとく汝らの光を人の前に輝かせ。これ人の汝らが善き行為を見て、天にいます汝らの父を崇めん為なり。」また 'A candle lights others and consumes itself' のようなことわざとの関連もあるだろう。なお、この箇所だけでなく、聖書表現とことわざ表現からの影響が至るところに見られるのが、この劇の大きな特徴である。

1. 2. 116-17. The words of heaven ... yet still 'tis just　この箇所は聖書の「ロマ書」の神のモーゼへの言葉を連想させる。Cf. Roman 9: 15 and 18 'For he [God] saith to Moses, I will have mercie on him, to whome I will showe mercie ... Therefore he hathe mercie on whom he wil, and whom he will, he hardeneth.' ロマ書［神］「モーセに言い給う『われ憐れまんとする者をあはれみ、慈悲を施さんとする者に慈悲を施すべし』と。…されば神はその憐れまんと欲する者を憐れみ、その頑固にせんと欲する者を頑固にし給うなり。」

1. 3. 54. more to bread than stone　この bread / stone の対比も、聖書によく見られる表現である。Cf. Luke 11: 11 'If a sonne shall aske breade of any of you that is a father, wil be give him a stone?' ルカ伝「汝等のうち父たるもの、たれか其の子、パンを求めんに石を与えんや。」あるいは Matthew 4: 3-4 'If thou be the sonne of God, commande that these stones be made bread.' マタイ伝「なんぢ若し神の子ならば、命じて此等の石をパンと為らしめよ。」なお、公爵はこの時点ですでに「石よりパンを好むとも思えない」アンジェロの人間

性を懸念している。

2. 1. 76-77. accused in fornication, adultery and all uncleaness　ここは聖書の「ガラテア書」の以下の表現に単語レヴェルで酷似しており、おそらく影響関係があるだろう。Galatians 5: 19 'The workes of the flesh are manifest, which are adulteries, fornication, uncleanes, wantonnes.' ガラテア書「それ肉の行為（おこない）はあらわなり。即ち淫行・汚穢（けがれ）・好色。」

2. 2. 74-76. Why all the souls ... Found out the remedy　この箇所は聖書の中核にある思想に基づいている。l. 74 はアダムの犯した原罪への言及。そのため、すべての魂はひとたび失われた（forfeited once）。また ll. 75-76 は、神が人類を罰せず、代わりに彼のひとり子イエスの死によって人類の魂を救済（remedy）した、という意味。以下の「ヨハネ黙示録」の一節を参照せよ。John 3: 16 'For God so loved the worlde, that he hathe given his onely begotten Sone, that whosoever believeth in him, shuld not perish but have everlasting life.' ヨハネ伝「それ神はその独子（ひとりご）を賜うほどに世を愛し給へり、すべて彼を信じるものの亡びずして永遠（とこしへ）の命を得ためなり。」

2. 3. 31-35. but lest you do repent ... But as we stand in fear　公爵はジュリエッタに、罪に対する神罰を恐れるがゆえにではなく、罪それ自体そして神への愛ゆえに改悛するように諭しているが、これは英国教会の教義に基づいている。国教会では、前者を attrition、後者を contrition として区別し、前者はいまだ自己本位の悲しみであり、真の contrition に至る前の不完全な悔悟であるとしている。

3. 1. 42. To sue to live, I find I seek to die / And seeking death, find life　新約聖書の中でたびたび説かれるパラドックス。Cf. Matthew 10: 39 'He that will save his life, shall lose it and he that loseth his life for my sake, shall save it.' マタイ伝「生命（いのち）を得る者は、これを失い、我がために生命を失ふ者は、これを得べし。」あるいは Matthew 16: 25 'For whosoever wil save his lyfe, shall loss it: and whoever shal lose his life for my sake, shall finde it.' マタイ伝「己が生命を救わんと思う者は、これを失い、我がために、己が生命をうしなふ者は、之を得べし。」

3. 1. 253. at the moated grange resides this dejected Mariana　この劇の有名な一節。アルフレッド・テニスンはこの表現をもとに、初期の名詩「マリアナ」（1830）で帰らぬ恋人を待ち暮らす乙女の嘆きを詠っている。さらにラファエロ前派の画家ジョン・エヴァレット・ミレイもこうした孤独なマリアナの姿を情感を込めて描いている。（図6）ビクトリア

図6

215

朝においてはマリアナは、芸術家たちのインスピレーション源だった。

4. 3. 4-6. for a commodity ... five marks ready money　このあたりは、以下の研究社版の説明に詳しい。「金貸し業者は 1571 年の法律で 10% 以上の利息を取ることを禁じられて以来、債務者に品物を売り、それをより安い値段で買い戻し、実質的にその差額だけの利息を取るという抜け道を考え出した。その時の品物を commodity といい、brown paper や ginger が使われた。…Rash の場合、彼は 197 ポンドで brown paper と ginger を買って、£3. 6s. 8d.（＝five marks）の金を借りようとしたわけだが、売り戻すはずのこれらの商品に実際上の買い手がつかなくて、全部を背負い込んだので破産してしまった。」

4. 4. 32. we would, and we would not　ここには聖書の「ロマ書」からのエコーが感じられる。Cf. Romans 7: 19 'For I do not the good thing, which I wolde, but the evil, which I wolde not, that do I.' ロマ書「わが欲する所の善は之をなさず、反つて欲せぬ所の悪は之をなすなり。」

4. 4. 405-07. An Angelo for Claudio ... measure still for measure　この劇の題名にもなっている 'measure for measure' という表現は、もともとは旧約聖書の「目には目を、歯には歯を」という考え方に由来する。Cf. Leviticus 24: 19-21 'Also if a man cause anie blemish in his neighbour: as he hathe done, so shall it be done to him; breache for breache, eie for eie, toothe for toothe.' レビ記「またもし人が隣人に傷を負わせるなら、その人は自分がしたように自分にされなければならない。すなわち、骨折には骨折、目には目、歯には歯をもって。」（『旧約聖書』（日本聖書協会、1975 年）より）

　だが、イザベラのアンジェロに対する許しが示唆するように、シェイクスピアはこの句を新約聖書の視点から、否定的に捉え直している。Cf. Matthew 5: 38-39, 7: 1-2 'Ye have heard that it hathe bene said, An eye for an eye, and a tooth for a tooth. But I say onto you, Resist not evil: but whosoever shal smite thee on thy right cheke, turne to him the other also .... Judge not, that ye be not judged. For with what judgement ye judge, you shal be judged, and with what measure ye mette, it shall be measured to you again.' マタイ伝「「目には目を、歯には歯を」と云へることあるを汝ら聞けり。されど我は汝らに告ぐ、悪き者に抵抗ふな。人もし汝の右の頬を打たば、左をも向けよ。…なんぢら人を審くな、審かれざらん為なり。己がさばく審判にて己もさばかれ、己がはかる量にて己も量らるべし。」

［編注者紹介］

佐々木和貴（ささき　かずき）

1955年生まれ。

北海道大学文学部卒業、同大学院博士課程中退。

現在　秋田大学名誉教授。

［共編著］『イギリス王政復古演劇案内』、『演劇都市はパンドラの匣を開けるか』

［共著］『コメディ・オブ・マナーズの系譜』、『名誉革命とイギリス文学：新しい言説空間の誕生』、『食卓談義のイギリス文学』、『国家身体はアンドロイドの夢を見るか』、『新歴史主義からの逃走』、など

［論文］「感傷喜劇のなかの大英帝国：『西インド諸島人』試論」『十八世紀イギリス文学研究』第6号、「『救われしヴェニス』小論：あるブロードサイド・バラッドの始まりと終わり」『十七世紀英文学研究』XVI、など多数

〈大修館シェイクスピア双書 第2集〉

尺には尺を

©Kazuki Sasaki, 2023　　　　　　　　　　NDC 932／xii, 216p／20cm

初版第1刷──2023年8月20日

編注者────佐々木和貴

発行者────鈴木一行

発行所────株式会社 大修館書店
　　　　　　〒113-8541 東京都文京区湯島2-1-1
　　　　　　電話 03-3868-2651（販売部）　03-3868-2293（編集部）
　　　　　　振替 00190-7-40504
　　　　　　［出版情報］https://www.taishukan.co.jp

装丁・本文デザイン────井之上聖子

印刷所────広研印刷

製本所────ブロケード

ISBN 978-4-469-14269-3　Printed in Japan

大修館 シェイクスピア双書（全12巻）
THE TAISHUKAN SHAKESPEARE

お気に召すまま	*As You Like It*	柴田稔彦 編注
ハムレット	*Hamlet, Prince of Denmark*	高橋康也・ 河合祥一郎 編注
ジュリアス・シーザー	*Julius Caesar*	大場建治 編注
リア王	*King Lear*	Peter Milward 編注
マクベス	*Macbeth*	今西雅章 編注
ヴェニスの商人	*The Marchant of Venice*	喜志哲雄 編注
夏の夜の夢	*A Midsummer-night's Dream*	石井正之助 編注
オセロー	*Othello*	笹山　隆 編注
リチャード三世	*King Richard the Third*	山田昭広 編注
ロミオとジュリエット	*Romeo and Juliet*	岩崎宗治 編注
テンペスト	*The Tempest*	藤田　実 編注
十二夜	*Twelfth Night; or, What You Will*	安西徹雄 編注

大修館 シェイクスピア双書 第2集（全8巻）
THE TAISHUKAN SHAKESPEARE 2nd Series

シェイクスピア，それが問題だ！

シェイクスピアを読み解くための百問百答

井出 新 著

「勉強は得意だった？」「年収と資産は？」「好きな食べものは？」「犬派？猫派？」といった人物像から、「当時、演劇はどんな娯楽だった？」「観劇代はいくら？」「熊いじめって何？」「寝取られ亭主になぜ角が生える？」「無韻詩とは？」など作品理解に役立つ当時の風習や英文の読み方まで、シェイクスピアにまつわるあらゆる Q に答える 1 冊。

四六判・144 ページ・近刊

ゴーストを訪ねるロンドンの旅

平井杏子 著

世界でもっとも幽霊人口の多い国、イギリス。ウェストミンスター寺院やバッキンガム宮殿、大英博物館、ロンドン塔など、ロンドンの有名な観光地を巡りながら、そこに出現すると噂される幽霊のエピソードとその背景を紹介する。英国史に名を残す人々の幽霊を通してイギリスの歴史と文化を知る、カラー写真満載の 1 冊。

A5 判・224 ページ　定価 2,530 円（税込）

ガーデニングとイギリス人

「園芸大国」はいかにしてつくられたか

飯田 操 著

修道院の思索の庭から、権勢誇示のため贅を尽くした整形庭園へ、そして不屈のイングランド精神を主張する風景庭園から、「古き良きイングランド」の象徴であるコテージ・ガーデンまで、何世紀もかけて、岩だらけの島を花いっぱいのエデンの園に変えてきた、「ガーデナー」の国民と庭園とのつきあいの歴史をたどる。

四六判・360 ページ　定価 3,630 円（税込）

ビアトリクス・ポターを訪ねる
イギリス湖水地方の旅
ピーターラビットの故郷をめぐって

北野佐久子 著

ピーターラビットなど、今も世界中で変わらぬ人気を博している絵本を描いた作家ビアトリクス・ポター。彼女が暮らし、作品の舞台として描いた湖水地方を巡りながら、自然保護・菌類研究・牧羊と様々なことにチャレンジしたビアトリクスの人生を辿る。

A5 判・218 ページ　定価 2,530 円（税込）

聖書でたどる英語の歴史

寺澤 盾 著

英米人の生活・文化と深く関わってきた英訳聖書。各時代の聖書の記述を比較しながら、過去 1500 年の間に英語に起こったさまざまな変化をたどる。時代の変化を"体感"しながら学ぶ英語史。

A5 判・262 ページ　定価 2,420 円（税込）

挿絵画家の時代
ヴィクトリア朝の出版文化

清水一嘉 著

挿絵画家ジョージ・クルックシャンクと小説家ディケンズの活躍を軸として、「挿絵の時代」と呼ばれる、19 世紀イギリス出版界に生きた挿絵画家、小説家、木版職人、出版社、貸本屋たちの愛憎劇に満ちた人間模様を描く。挿絵版画約 100 点。カラー口絵つき。

四六判・310 ページ　定価 2,640 円（税込）

2023 年 6 月現在　定価は消費税 10% 込み